Dorothy Little is seventeen, and has a guardian whom she has never met. Travelling back from Paris to London she meets a man whom she thinks unusually attractive. Getting to know him, she finds their relationship is becoming close. And although it is not a case of love at first sight, she somehow manages to overcome the complications which seem to stand in the way of her chance of lasting happiness. In this romantic story, Ruby M. Ayres shows how a lonely, inexperienced person can still make the most of her opportunities, age presenting no barriers when love is genuine and sincere.

Of all the best-selling romantic novelists, Ruby M. Ayres has the greatest insight into human devices and desires. She mirrors the heart of woman.

Also by Ruby M. Ayres and available in Sphere Books

MY OLD LOVE CAME

Little and Good

RUBY M. AYRES

SPHERE BOOKS LIMITED

First published in Great Britain by Hodder & Stoughton Limited, London E.C.4
Revised edition © Estate of Ruby M. Ayres 1968
First Sphere Books edition, 1968

AFRICA
Kenya, Uganda, Tanzania, Zambia, Malawi: Thomas Nelson & Sons Ltd., Kenya
South Africa, Rhodesia: Thomas Nelson & Sons (Africa) (Pty) Ltd., Johannesburg
Ghana, Nigeria, Sierra Leone: Thomas Nelson & Sons Ltd., Nigeria
Liberia: Wadih M. Captan
Angola, Mozambique: Electroliber Limitada, Angola
Zambia: Kingstons (North) Ltd.
AUSTRALIA: Thomas Nelson (Australia) Ltd.
AUSTRIA: Danubia-Auslieferung
BAHAMAS: Calypso Distributors Ltd.
BELGIUM: Agence et Messageries de la Presse, S.A.
CANADA: Thomas Nelson & Sons (Canada) Ltd.
CARIBBEAN: Roland I. Khan (Trinidad)
DENMARK: Sven Gade, Scandinavian Book Wholesale
FRANCE: Librairie Etrangère, Hachette
GERMANY: Distropa Buchvertrieb
GIBRALTAR: Estogans Agencies Ltd.
GREECE: Hellenic Distribution Agency Ltd.
HOLLAND: Van Ditmar
HONG KONG: Western Publications Distribution Agency (HK) Ltd.
ISRAEL: Steimatzky's Agency Ltd.
IRAN: I.A.D.A.
IRAQ: Dar Alaruba Universal Distribution Co.
KUWAIT & GULF STATES: Farajalla Press Agency
LEBANON: The Levant Distributors Co.
MALAYSIA, SINGAPORE & BRUNEI: Marican & Sons (Malaysia) (Sdn) Berhad
MALTA: Progress Press Co. Ltd.
NEW ZEALAND: Hodder & Stoughton Ltd.
PORTUGAL: Electroliber Limitada
SOUTH AMERICA
Colombia: Libreria Central
Chile: Libreria Studio
Mexico & Central America: Libreria Britanica
Peru: Librerias ABC
Venezuela: Distribuidora Santiago
SPAIN: Comercial Atheneum
SWEDEN: Importbokhandeln
SWITZERLAND: Friedr. Daeniker
THAILAND: The Pramuansarn Publishing House
TURKEY: Librairie Hachette
WEST INDIES
Barbados: Wayfarer Bookstore

TRADE MARK

Set in Linotype Times

Text Printed in Great Britain by Hazell Watson & Viney Ltd., Aylesbury, Bucks

CHAPTER ONE

She was so small that, although she was not by any means the youngest in the class, at school she stood last in the line when the girls were drilling: a slim, perfectly formed little creature with very straight thick brown hair cut squarely round her head in the style of a medieval page, and serious eyes of deep blue, framed with curling dark lashes.

In her navy serge uniform frock and flat-heeled shoes she could easily have been mistaken for eight instead of her actual fourteen years, but, as the headmistress remarked, it was a case of an old head on young shoulders, because Dorothy Little was clever, and although she stood last in the drill ranks she was invariably first in her class.

"Weenie" she had been nicknamed by the other girls as soon as she appeared at school, partly because her surname happened to be Little, and partly because she was so very small.

Ray Stevens, the Head Girl, who was rather a supercilious young woman, also dubbed her "Little and Good", because she never by any chance got into trouble with the mistresses or joined in the minor insurrections which occasionally went on in the dormitories and playgrounds. Ray also made the mistake of considering that Dorothy, was rather characterless: "all smooth-sailing, like a duck-pond," so she declared, until one never to be forgotten occasion when the girls were taking a constitutional in "crocodile" fashion and Dorothy broke rank (an unpardonable sin) to rush to the rescue of an unfortunate mongrel dog which was being chased by a gang of boys.

It had just been caught by a snub-nosed tough-looking boy when she dashed in, slapped the astounded youth smartly across the face and tore the dog from his arms.

"*Brute!*" she panted, and hugging the mongrel to her breast returned to her companions.

The under-mistress who was in charge hurried up to her.

"How dare you!" she said, not very effectively, for she too had a decided weakness for all animals. "Put the dog down at once—you can't possibly take it with you."

But Dorothy only hugged the poor creature more tightly to her bosom.

"They're going to drown it, Miss Spears!" she pleaded. "And why should it be drowned—it's got a right to live."

It said a good deal for the pleading eyes of Little and Good that Miss Spears compromised by delivering the dog at a friend's house where it was assured of a happy home for the rest of its life, and that, beyond a slight reprimand from the Head, nothing more was said, but as Ray protested:

"If it had been anyone else—my hat! The whole show would have gone up in flames." Though following the episode she was less condescending in her manner to the younger girl, and even treated her with a certain amount of friendliness.

But Dorothy was very much the odd one out amongst her school-fellows; she was naturally reserved, and perhaps too clever for extreme popularity, besides which she was, as Ray again described her, "nobody's child".

She had been born in India—an apparently unwanted baby who had cost the life of her mother—and when, within a few months, her father, an Army man, had been killed in a border skirmish, the baby had been sent home and given into the care of an expensive and highly efficient nurse, who, until her death, had the entire charge of her.

The child had heard vague allusions to a "Guardian", but as she had never seen him he remained a more or less mythical character. But there was a grey-haired lawyer with spectacles who now and then paid her half an hour's visit to assure himself of her well-being, and he and "Nuggie", the nurse, constituted her whole world until following the latter's death she was sent to boarding-school.

The grey-haired lawyer, whose name was Rachett, had impressed upon her that she must be a good girl and make people proud of her, and then, to his great embarrassment, she had asked a rather pathetic question.

"What people, please?"

Mr. Rachett had hummed and hawed before he could find a suitable reply, and then he said:

"Well, myself—and your guardian."

Dorothy had regarded him steadily with her serious eyes.

"I've never seen my guardian," she said in her clear voice, whereupon Mr. Rachett explained that he was somewhere

6

abroad—he believed in India, but that as at any moment he might return he would naturally hope to find that she was the kind of ward of whom he could be proud.

But Dorothy was not inclined to let the matter rest.

"Why is he in India?" she asked, and her interest in the mythical person was increased when Mr. Rachett answered patiently:

"Because he is a soldier, and he is helping to train the Indian Army."

She was enormously impressed, and when after her arrival at school she was questioned by the other girls as to her parentage and the usual family details she informed them proudly and with great confidence that she had a guardian who was in India.

"Is he an old man?" asked one of her friends.

Dorothy had not the slightest idea as to the age of the mythical person, but she answered unhesitatingly:

"No, he's quite young!" Which, although it was entirely a shot in the dark, was not very far from the truth. But later on it became a more difficult problem, for at half term, for instance, when fathers and mothers appeared on the scene in large cars (it was a very high-class school, and expensive) and other girls were either taken out for the afternoon or were presented with enviable gifts, the obvious question was asked:

"Why doesn't your guardian come, too?"

"He's in India."

"He can't *always* be in India," Peggy Soames protested. "He must come home *sometimes! Doesn't* he come home sometimes?" she insisted, and as by that time Dorothy was entirely out of her depth she merely replied that she did not know.

There was an immediate chorus of: "Don't know! You must know!" And then, as she remained silent, somebody asked: "Doesn't he like you?" And perhaps feeling that in the question there was a faint reflection on her own somewhat difficult position in the school she answered, with rising colour:

"Of *course* he likes me!"

But that did not end the inquisition.

"Do you like *him?*" was the next attack, and then she rose to the heights with the fervent reply:

7

"Yes, I love him!"

Afterwards she felt very guilty about the subterfuge, for how is it possible to love a person you have never seen? But at least she had silenced her tormentors, and for the future they left the subject alone, having decided amongst themselves that this elusive guardian was probably a fat old man with a red face who wore a pith helmet and bullied people.

"My father was in India for years," Ray Stevens informed the company. "And he says that everyone out there either get frightfully fat or frightfully thin, and that they all eat curry and swear dreadfully."

Nobody answered the challenge because nobody was in the position to do so, therefore it was tacitly agreed that Dorothy's guardian was one of the fat kind, and that he was probably enormously rich—and that some day he would die and leave her all his money.

Life on the whole was very uneventful for her until she was sixteen, and by that time she had absorbed most of the knowledge which that particular school had to offer, and found it comparatively easy to walk away with most of the prizes.

Occasionally one of the girls would invite her home for the holidays, but such an invitation was seldom repeated, because they found that amongst an ordinary family of boys and girls she was shy and "different"—that she hated all blood sports and was not very good at games—only asking to be left alone with a book for company, and therefore she was unanimously voted dull.

She spent one Christmas with Mr. Rachett and his wife, and it was a holiday she enjoyed, for Mrs. Rachett was an invalid—partly by choice—and she thoroughly approved of a guest who needed so little attention or entertaining, and it was in the Rachetts' house that Dorothy first saw her guardian —or rather, his portrait. Mr. Rachett had given her permission to take what books she liked from his library, and she enjoyed climbing the ladder-steps which stood against the high shelves, and peering into the stiff-looking legal volumes which were really far beyond her intelligence.

It was while she was perched on those steps, almost on a level with the heavily embossed Victorian ceiling, that she saw the portrait on the opposite wall. It was of quite a young man in uniform, and his eyes seemed to be looking straight at her, so that involuntarily she smiled as though greeting a friend.

He was dark, and she liked dark men best, and he wore his hair brushed straight back from his forehead and clipped in a military fashion, and he had brown eyes with a sparkle in them, and one corner of his mouth was slightly higher than the other, as if he was politely checking a smile which was at somebody's expense.

She felt sure that he must be tall—but then, as she was so small herself, most men seemed like giants and she imagined that he would have a very deep voice—rather like the voice of Canon Johnson, who was a friend of the headmistress, and who once came to present the prizes at the end of term.

His voice had seemed to come right from his boots with the sort of booming sound which is made by the sea as it swirls round a hollow cave before bursting into foam, so that he had made even the mechanical words: "First prize for French— Dorothy Little," sound as if he was investing someone with a knighthood, or ordering out the guard.

She was still perched on the top of the ladder, staring at the man in uniform, when the door opened and Mr. Rachett walked in.

He did not appear to notice her, but as he walked quickly across to the writing-table and began to select a key from a big bunch which he was carrying, she felt that it must be a very private occasion and that she ought to draw his attention to the fact that he was not alone, so she said in her clear high voice:

"I'm here, Mr. Rachett."

Mr. Rachett started violently and looked up towards the ceiling.

"Bless my soul!" he ejaculated. "And what are you doing up there, Dorothy?"

Dorothy smiled.

"You said I might," she reminded him, and with a reluctant sigh she began to climb down from the library steps.

And then again she looked at the portrait.

"Who is he?" she asked.

Mr. Rachett followed the direction of her gaze and a slight frown bent his shaggy eyebrows.

9

"That," he said rather pompously, "is the portrait of a man named Wilfred Clifton."

Dorothy crossed the room and stood below the heavy gilt frame, staring upwards.

"Is he dead?" she asked.

"Dead!" Mr. Rachett echoed. "Certainly not."

"Then why was he painted like that?" she insisted, for some-how or other she had got it into her head that all portraits in heavy gilt frames must be of the departed—her only experience being of art galleries.

"Why?" Mr. Rachett echoed. "I really don't know why—probably it was his father's wish."

She half-turned round to look at him.

"Then—is his father dead?" she asked.

Mr. Rachett said: "He is. He died—five years ago, when you were—how old, Dorothy?"

"I'm nearly seventeen now," she told him.

He peered at her over his spectacles with disbelieving eyes. Seventeen! He had a niece of that age, but she was a grown-up, modern young woman—not a child like this girl!

"Nearly seventeen! Dear me!" he thoughtfully. "Then you were thirteen when General Clifton died."

"Thirteen is unlucky," she said.

There was a moment's silence before she asked, pointing to the portrait above her head:

"Then where is he now?"

Mr. Rachett coughed before he answered.

"Abroad somewhere—in India, I believe."

The words were so familiar in their deliberate vagueness that her quick brain leapt to the right conclusion.

"He is my guardian," she said.

Mr. Rachett looked as if he was going to say "No", but instead, he said almost snappily, as if he disapproved of his own admission:

"Yes, he is your guardian."

"He looks very young," she suggested.

"That portrait was painted some years back," Mr. Rachett said, and he rattled the bunch of keys, but she had not yet finished her inquiries.

"Why have you got his portrait?" she asked.

"Because," Mr. Rachett explained in a martyred voice,

"when his father—Colonel Clifton—died, the house and its contents were sold and Wilfred asked me to take the portrait until he had a home of his own." It was not strictly the truth, for Wilfred's actual words had been:

"You take it. I don't want the darned thing! I hate portraits, anyway." And so Mr. Rachett, conscious that because of the artist's growing fame the portrait might some day be of value, had agreed.

There was the slightest pause before he asked with faint sarcasm whether there were any more questions.

Dorothy said: "Yes, if you don't mind! Isn't he very young to be anyone's guardian?" for in spite of her confident assertion to the girls at school she too had imagined this man as elderly and stout.

Mr. Rachett threw his bunch of keys on to the writing table with an air of desperation.

"Originally his father, Colonel Clifton, was your guardian," he explained. "He and your father were lifelong friends and that is the explanation, but when Colonel Clifton died—as I told you—five years ago, he willed the responsibility to his son Wilfred. Is that quite clear?"

She nodded, and then, her blue eyes turned disconcertingly to the old man's face: "*Am* I a responsibility?" she asked.

"Guardianship is always a responsibility," he answered, not unkindly.

She said, after the barest hesitation:

"But he's never troubled to come and see me, has he?" And then in quick apology: "But of course if he is in the Army ——" She paused, and Mr. Rachett said briefly:

"He is no longer in the Army—and now, do you mind if I ask you to run away, my dear? I have a good deal of important work which needs attention."

She obeyed immediately, but at the door she turned for one last look at the portrait of Wilfred Clifton and she fancied that the eyes still followed her almost as if they regretted her going. It was a very attractive portrait.

And she thought: "It's a pity you're not in the Army any longer; you look so handsome in your uniform." But to her he was never again just a Mythical Person, but someone young and virile and handsome, with one corner of his mouth a

11

little higher than the other, as if he were politely checking a smile at somebody else's expense.

It was Miss Woods, the Head of the School, who next took a hand in Dorothy's future. She wrote to Mr. Rachett:

"We shall be sorry to lose Dorothy—she is a pupil of whom we are all justly proud—but I feel it is time that she was among older girls——"

and she suggested an even more expensive finishing establishment in Paris, which she declared she could most highly recommend.

As a matter of fact, there was an ulterior motive in Miss Wood's rather narrow mind, for on one or two occasions Dorothy had apologetically corrected a mistake made by one of the younger mistresses, which had resulted in suppressed giggling from the class.

But Mr. Rachett eagerly jumped at such a promising solution of the problem of Dorothy's future and after a somewhat lengthy correspondence with Madame Suggia of Paris, the girl was despatched to the expensive establishment, with the usual admonition: "I hope you will do well, and be a credit to us."

And it was in Paris that Dorothy at last began to grow up. In actual stature she increased very little, but she loved Paris, and when the year which Madame Suggia considered a sufficient time in which to "finish" any girl, came to an end, she shed bitter tears at the thought of returning to England.

"But don't you want to go home?" Cecilie Jepson inquired in amazement.

Cecilie was her great friend—the first she had ever had—and although the two girls were totally unlike, there was a very real bond of affection between them.

Dorothy answered bitterly:

"Home! ... I haven't got a home."

Cecilie said comfortingly: "Never mind, you can come and stay with me as often as you like—I'd love to have you." But as there were still three more months of her year left, the prospect seemed rather distant.

Mr. Rachett had written:

"You will of course come direct to my house where you will

be made most welcome until I have had an opportunity to discuss the future with your guardian."

She made a little grimace over the last words, for somehow she no longer had any faith in the once Mythical Person, and she felt that she was condemned for life to make her home with the Rachetts. Not that she really minded—still, after Paris it was bound to be terribly monotonous, though both Mr. Rachett and his wife were always kind.

She would have been less resigned could she have known about the battle of arms which had taken place between husband and wife.

Mrs. Rachett had for once roused herself from her invalid couch in order to make a vigorous protest. "She really can't come *here*," she said firmly. "Yes, I admit that she was a quiet enough girl when we last saw her, but after a year in Paris——"

"But, my dear," Mr. Rachett protested, "what is to become of her? I am legally responsible for her welfare, remember."

"She should have been made a ward in Chancery," his wife declared firmly. "We all know that Wilfred Clifton is never in the least likely to take any useful interest in her future, and the whole position is absurd and impossible. I cannot *believe* that Dorothy is entirely without relations as you say. *Nobody* is entirely without relations—unfortunately!"

Mr. Rachett frowned.

"Dorothy must be the great exception which proves the rule," he said rather shortly, "because as far as I know she has no relatives whatever. There may, of course, be some distant connections, but even so, one can hardly expect them to adopt a perfect stranger."

"She has money," his wife reminded him. "You told me that when she is twenty-one she will be rich, and therefore—surely. ..." But although she used every argument she could think of, her husband was adamant.

Dorothy must come to them—at any rate for the present —and then, as he saw his wife reach a trembling hand for her smelling salts, he added quickly: "No doubt she will marry —and that of course will be the best solution for us all."

So Dorothy was escorted to the Gare du Nord by Madame Suggia and Cecilie Jepson, and amidst shrill last minute

13

instructions from the elder woman, the train moved slowly out of the station. She wished she was going by air.

"You will be met at Dover," Madame screamed after her. "Take care of your ticket ... you will be met at Dover——"

There were tears on Dorothy's cheeks as she turned away from the window and dropped forlornly into her corner seat.

Good-bye! ... It was such an unutterably sad word! She took off the smart little hat which she had bought for the journey and looked at it sympathetically, wondering if it, too, was feeling depressed at the thought of London and of the Rachetts' solemn house.

She sighed and looked out of the window, thinking how short a time ago it seemed since she had first arrived in Paris; a whole year, and yet no time at all!

If only Cecilie had been able to come with her! Things would not have been so bad with Cecilie for company.

Someone dragged open the sliding door which led into the corridor and she turned her head quickly. A tall man was standing there looking at her a little doubtfully. An overcoat was slung carelessly over one shoulder and at his heels was an attendant laden with suit-cases.

Dorothy suddenly smiled, and when the man asked apologetically in French:

"You permit me, Mademoiselle?" she answered quietly: "I'm English."

He laughed. "So am I—May I share your compartment?"

"Please," she said shyly.

"The front part of the train is packed," he told her. "You're lucky to have escaped the crowd."

He threw down the coat, stowed the suit-cases on the rack, tipped the porter and then, with a sigh of relief, took the corner seat furthest from her.

And then he seemed to forget that she was there, but her eyes, alive with excited interest, never left his face.

A tall man—she had always known he must be tall!—very dark hair brushed straight back—brown skin (of course, because he had been in India for so long) and one corner of his mouth slightly higher than the other as if he were politely checking a smile at somebody's expense. Yes, it must be him.

She sat perfectly still, her hands clasped in her lap, watching and wondering. He had taken a cigarette-case from his pocket—and then as if he suddenly remembered her existence he looked across at her.

"Do you mind if I smoke?"

"Please go ahead."

He smiled. "May I offer you one?"

She shook her head.

"No, thank you." She sensed that he thought she was an odd little creature—evidently a schoolgirl—and having lit the cigarette he took up a paper and became engrossed in it.

They might never have exchanged another word had not the train suddenly swerved violently across some points, sending one of his suit-cases crashing down at her feet.

He started up then.

"Are you hurt? I'm frightfully sorry——"

"It didn't touch me," she assured him, and then, somewhat to her surprise, instead of returning to the corner seat he sat down opposite her.

"You're going to England, of course?"

"Yes—I've been in Paris for a year," she answered, and somehow she felt that she really ought to know, seeing that she was sure he was—at least nominally—her guardian.

"Paris is fun," he said casually.

"Yes," she agreed ruefully.

His dark eyes searched her face.

"Sorry to go home?" he asked.

"Yes," she said, "I haven't got a home—not really. I'm going to friends."

"In that tone of voice?" he asked.

"They're very kind," she apologized, wondering how well he knew the Rachetts—if at all!

"If it comes to that," Wilfred Clifton said humorously, "I haven't a home either—but I suppose it's different for a man."

There was a little silence before she asked:

"Have you been staying in Paris?"

"Only for a few days. I am on my way home from Cannes."

Her eyes glowed.

"Cannes is great, isn't it?" she asked.

He shrugged his big shoulders.

"Oh, so-so, I suppose! But then, I know it so well."

"But I suppose you live in London?" she said.

15

He laughed. "I don't 'live' anywhere. I'm a rolling stone. Most of my life has been spent in India."

She very nearly said "I know", but checked the words in time.

"But you're going to London now," she said.

He nodded. "Yes, but not for long—it's a business trip."

"Aren't business trips fun?" she inquired.

A smile crossed his handsome face.

"To be quite truthful, it's almost my first experience," he told her. "And I am hoping that with luck, it will be the last. I dislike responsibility in any shape or form."

Dorothy's long lashes flickered sensitively and she turned her eyes to the window and the flat grey landscape beyond, for something told her that she was the responsibility which he was finding so irksome.

She asked herself: "Shall I tell him?" and then she glanced up at the luggage on the rack above her head, trying to read the name on the suit-cases—not that she really needed any confirmation as to his identity.

There were a great many labels—chiefly of foreign places. She could pick out the names: Rome, Budapest, Prague, Berlin —wonderful to have travelled so much, she thought enviously.

An attendant came to the door to inquire about lunch.

"For two," he asked.

She dived into her bag to produce the required money for her own ticket.

"Do they have a good lunch on the train?" she asked.

Clifton laughed. "All train food seems very much the same to me."

"That's because you've travelled so much," she told him. "But you see, I've never been anywhere except to Paris."

"The place where good Americans go when they die," he submitted humorously.

"I know who said that," she told him eagerly. "It was Thomas Appleton."

He laughed.

"Did he? I didn't know." And then he added "You are fond of reading?"

"Oh, yes—I've read so many books."

"Don't you ever play games?"

She shook her head.

"I'm not very good at games—you see——" she stopped,

16

adding after a moment: "I haven't any brothers or sisters—perhaps that's why."

"But at school——" he hazarded.

She looked at him steadily.

"I liked reading best."

"Were you at school in Paris?" he asked.

"Yes, but I'm finished now and I'm not going back."

"Finished!" he said in amusement.

"I'm nineteen," she answered defensively.

"I'm sorry," he apologized gravely, "I imagined you were younger."

"That's because I'm so little," she said.

"'Little and good'," he suggested.

Her slow smile showed the dimple in her cheek.

"That's what they called me at school," she said. "In England, I mean; not that I was really good," she apologized.

"You funny child," he said impulsively, and then hurriedly: "I'm sorry——"

"I'm not offended," she assured him, and then, as the voice of the attendant sounded along the corridor: "That's lunch," she said.

Clifton rose.

"May I share your table?" he asked, for in a strange way he found this girl interesting—different somehow, from others whom he knew.

"If you don't mind," she answered, and she wondered again what he would say if he knew that he was being so polite to an unwanted responsibility!

But the dining-car was full, so that they were unable to find seats at the same table, and Dorothy had finished her lunch while Wilfred was still talking to his *vis-à-vis*, and she returned to her compartment alone.

And then she knelt up on the seat and examined the exciting-looking labels attached to his suit-cases.

Calcutta! ... she looked at that one with special interest, remembering how Ray Stevens had declared that all men in India got frightfully fat and bad-tempered. It was certainly not true of Wilfred!

Bombay! ... she sighed, for it seemed as if this man had visited all the places of which she dreamed, and she wondered wistfully whether there was a remote possibility that as he was her guardian, he might some day take her with him to visit them.

She was back in her corner seat when he returned.

"Enjoy your lunch?" he asked.

"Yes, thank you."

"We're nearly at Calais," he told her. "Is anyone meeting you?"

"At Dover, Mr. ... someone is meeting me at Dover."

"We shall have a smooth crossing."

"I'm a good sailor," she said. "I love the sea."

"So do I."

"Is that why you travel so much?"

He shrugged his shoulders.

"Partly, I suppose—but I find it impossible to settle down. Home life has never appealed to me. A few days in one place and I want to be on the move again."

"Won't you ever settle down?" she asked a little shyly. "I mean—you might get married—if you're not married already," she added hurriedly.

A little frown crossed his handsome face.

"I'm not married," he said rather shortly, but he did not answer the first part of her question.

At Calais he collected her luggage with his and gave it to a porter to put on board, and then he warned her that there was a cold wind blowing and that she had better wrap up.

"I've got a thick coat," she said.

He helped her into it, turning up the big collar for her as if she were a child.

"Got your ticket?" he asked.

"Oh yes."

The spring sun was shining brightly in spite of the chilly wind, and as the boat steamed out to sea, Wilfred said: "Wouldn't you rather go downstairs? It's pretty fresh on deck."

"I like it," she told him. "But please don't stay with me if you'd rather not." She was glad now that she hadn't gone by plane.

"I'd like to stay with you, if I may," he answered, and together they paced up and down the deck.

"What part of London are you going to?" he said.

"It's Kensington."

"Not quite the place where I should expect you to live," he said.

"It's Hobson's choice," she answered. "But when I'm twenty-one——" she stopped, and he said:

"It's an amazing thing how, before one comes of age, one imagines that life will be a totally different thing—but, of course, it never is."

"But at least when you're twenty-one you can do as you like," she reminded him quickly. "Though perhaps you have always been able to do as you like."

"Perhaps," he agreed, and then after a moment he went on: "Though from all appearances I am about to have my wings very definitely clipped—so that for the present, at all events, I shall not be able to fly away." His voice was ironical, and she thought with a sense of panic:

"That must be me again!" And there was something a little pathetic in her voice when she asked:

"Who is going to clip your wings, Mr. Clifton?" But instead of answering he said quickly:

"How do you know my name is Clifton?"

She flushed crimson. "I saw it on the label," she faltered.

"Oh!" he said, laughing, but still he did not answer her question, and once again she thought: "Ought I to tell him who I am? But if I do——" She looked up at him, hesitatingly, but he seemed to have forgotten her and was watching a passing ship, and with a half sigh she stopped by the rail, following the white trail of foam with wistful eyes.

Where was it going, she wondered? Somewhere wonderful perhaps . . .

Clifton had stopped too, and although she did not know it, he was looking down at her, summing her up.

Pretty, was she? He could not decide; but again he was conscious of the feeling that she was different—more innocent, did he mean? More natural and unspoilt that the majority of youngsters of her age.

He said suddenly:

"As you have discovered my name—may I ask yours?" It was a moment before she answered, and then she did not look at him. "My name is Dorothy."

"Only Dorothy?" he asked, but she was spared the difficulty

of a reply because at that moment a short, squarely-built man stopped beside them and spoke to Clifton.

"Well, I'll be hanged! And what in the wide world are you doing here? I thought you were in India."

Wilfred laughed. "Willie Guest, by all that's wonderful!" And as the two men gripped hands, Dorothy moved quickly away, with a sharp breath of relief.

And the squarely-built man said with a grin:

"And what's bringing you to London? A woman, I'll bet. How long since you honoured us with a visit?"

"Oh, a couple of years or so; and even this visit is made under protest, and won't be long if I can cut it short."

"Business?" his friend asked.

Wilfred laughed.

"Well, hardly! And what have you been doing all this time?"

"Working—trying to keep the wolf from the door. I'm not like you, you know—one of the idle rich."

"*Rich!*" Wilfred laughed.

Willie Guest smiled.

"Well, well," he said tolerantly. "And how's the ward you were telling me about when we last met? The unwanted kid you were cursing about. Have you managed to abandon her yet?"

Clifton frowned.

"I've never seen her," he answered shortly, and then he added. "As a matter of fact I'm on my way now to try and make some arrangement to shelve the responsibility. Rachett's been looking after her—you remember Rachett?"

The other man nodded. "Um! Rather a dry old stick to be in charge of an attractive girl, eh?"

"Who said she was attractive?" Wilfred growled.

Guest patted his arm.

"My dear fellow, all modern girls are attractive," he said placidly. "And you look out that she doesn't swing the halter round your neck. You can't always escape, you know."

"I've escaped so far," Wilfred answered, and suddenly he was thinking of a girl's fair face which only a few hours since had smiled good-bye to him in Paris.

Guest said suddenly: "Well, we're almost in—but the white cliffs of old England don't give you a thrill, I suppose, eh? What are you looking for?"

Wilfred answered hesitatingly:

"I had a girl with me—— No, nothing of the sort!" he added hastily as his friend laughed. "She's only a schoolgirl. I suppose she's gone to look for her luggage."

"Don't let me spoil things," Willie said affably. "See you in London, eh? You know where to find me—same address." And with a wave of his hand he walked away.

The passengers were already collecting on the landing side of the ship, and Wilfred pushed his way amongst them to look for Dorothy.

She had certainly told him that she was to be met at Dover—still ... it would only be courteous to say good-bye ...

He found her seated on a pile of luggage, looking towards the shore.

"I thought I'd lost you," he said; he sat down beside her. "Well, now for England, Home and Beauty!"

"You don't seem very pleased," she objected.

"Are you?" he asked. She looked up at him and for a moment his eyes held hers before she answered slowly:

"I'm not sure—Paris already seems so very far away."

They were alongside now, and as usual, people were pushing to get near the gangway.

"Can you see your friends?" Clifton asked, and then he laughed. "Stand up on this trunk and you'll be able to see over other people's heads. You'll have to grow."

"I don't think I want to see." But she clambered up as he suggested, steadying herself against his shoulder as the ship bumped the stone dock-wall.

"Can you spot anyone?" Wilfred asked.

"No," She jumped lightly down again, and presently they were off the ship and walking towards the customs house.

"Anything to declare?" Wilfred inquired. "No scent, watches, jewellery, spirits?"

She laughed.

"Nothing nearly so exciting. Have you?"

"No—I'm a scrupulously honest traveller."

The customs officer presented no difficulty, looked at their pile of suit-cases, scratched something unreadable on each one in chalk, and let them go.

"That's soon over," Wilfred said. "The train goes in a quarter of an hour—I expect your friends will be waiting for you."

"It's only—one friend," she answered uncertainly, and even as she spoke she saw the lean figure of Mr. Rachett standing patiently against the bookstall.

He saw her at the same moment and came hurrying forward—and then suddenly, as his eyes turned suspiciously to her companion, his expression changed to one of blank astonishment and he quickened his step almost to a run.

"Wilfred! My dear boy! And Dorothy—how in the world ——?"

He stretched a hand to each.

"But you're together," he said. "Really this is most amazing."

She looked up at Wilfred. He was staring down at her blankly, the colour deepening on his brown face.

Her lips quivered into a wavering smile.

"I'm very sorry, but I'm Dorothy Little," she almost whispered.

The guard's whistle, sounding shrilly above the clatter around, awoke Mr. Rachett to the fact that it is possible, even for the methodical, to miss a train. He took her hurriedly by the arm.

"Come along, my dear—come along!" he said fussily. "And you, Wilfred, will you travel with us?"

Clifton looked down at her with a cynical smile.

"You permit me, Mademoiselle?" he asked in French and she answered mischievously, as she had done at the Gare du Nord:

"I'm English."

"Hurry up there! Hurry up, please!" cried a porter, and Mr. Rachett almost pushed her into a first-class compartment.

"My luggage!" she gasped.

"It's all in," Wilfred said.

Mr. Rachett subsided into a corner seat and mopped his brow, and then as the train began to move slowly out of the station he started up again:

"There's no air—I can't breathe——" and he departed into the corridor where he promptly let down a window.

Silence followed until Dorothy said:

"I'm very sorry, Mr. Clifton. I suppose I ought to have told you it was me."

He looked at her, puzzled.

"And how did you know it was me?" he demanded.

"I saw your portrait—in Mr. Rachett's study."

He pouted.

"That frightful daub!"

"I like it," she told him. "And I think you look—great in uniform."

He laughed at that.

"My soldiering days are over."

"Why?"

"Why?" He seemed surprised. "Well—for one thing, the Army bored me—a peace-time army is a monotonous thing, but my father was a soldier and his father too, and he wished me to keep up the tradition."

Dorothy said, "I've never met a soldier before."

"I thought you were a peace-loving little soul."

She flushed. "So I am—but I like men to be—well—you know, tough."

The silence fell once more until he said:

"And so you recognized me from that portrait! I am not sure that's a compliment."

"It is," she told him earnestly. "And you haven't altered at all."

"Not in ten years?" he asked with faint sarcasm.

She made a rapid calculation.

"Then you're thirty!" she said, thinking he didn't look it.

"Thirty-three," he answered, and presently he added a little formally: "I feel that I owe you an apology, Miss Little."

"Mr. Rachett calls me Dorothy," she said.

"I feel that I owe you an apology, Dorothy."

"Why?" she asked simply.

He half shrugged his shoulders.

"I was not very polite—about my mission to London."

She laughed at that. "I knew it was me—all the time I knew it was me," she said, "and I think that's why I didn't tell you that I knew who *you* were." And then as he did not speak: "I shan't really be a responsibility," she told him earnestly. "I'll try not to be, as you hate it so much."

He looked embarrassed and she said with a hint of laughter in her voice:

"If that suit-case had hit me, it might have finished me once and forever, but I suppose the luck was out!"

"Whose luck?" he asked suspiciously.

"Why, yours," she answered. And then to her surprise he suddenly leaned forward to offer her his hand.

She blushed with pleasure as she laid her hand in his.

"It won't be long before I'm twenty-one," she said hopefully, "and then I shall be on my own, won't I?"

He shook his head.

"Didn't I warn you that coming of age is a delusion and a snare? My own was, anyway."

"Why?" she asked.

He did not answer at once, and then he laughed as if at himself. "Well, for one thing, there was someone with whom I was involved. My father said I didn't know my own mind and all the usual things which elderly people always tell to romantic youngsters, so I—or rather—we, agreed to wait." He laughed again. "But when my twenty-first birthday arrived, she'd changed her mind—said she didn't want to marry a soldier."

"How *awful*!" she protested. "And is that why you left the Army?"

"Good heavens, *no*! I didn't leave it until some years later—eight years to be exact."

She looked at him sympathetically.

"And did you—mind?" she asked.

"About the Army? I left it to please myself."

"I meant—about whoever it was."

Wilfred frowned a little. "I suppose I did at the time," he admitted, "but the world is full of attractive young women." And then as she turned her head away to look out of the window, he asked quickly: "Have I said something to offend you?"

She answered, with her face still averted:

"I don't like you to talk—about—us like that!"

"Us?" he echoed, not understanding.

"Women," she explained.

Fortunately, she did not see the sudden upward tilt of his mouth which was instantly controlled before he answered. "If you knew as much about the subject as I do——" and then stopped as her steady, disconcerting eyes returned to his face.

"I do," she said. "About the nice ones, anyway."

"They are not all nice," he reminded her.

24

She flushed. "Perhaps men aren't, either," she said in quick defence.

Wilfred looked amused.

"What can you know about men! A child like you—" and then he stopped with an apologetic gesture. "Why do you look so young?" he reproached her.

"You're not very old yourself," she answered spiritedly. "Not nearly old enough to be—anyone's guardian."

"Hobson's choice again!" he submitted. "I'm afraid I've been a bad guardian—shockingly neglectful."

"*Very* bad," she agreed, and then suddenly she was laughing. "If you knew the fantastic stories I used to tell the girls at school about you!"

"Such as?"

She gave a little sigh.

"Well, I had to say *something*! They were always asking why you never came to see me—so I told them you were in India. And then they asked what you were like—were you old? And I said no, quite young—though I hadn't the slightest idea, really! ... and then they asked, didn't you like me?" She stopped abruptly, remembering her own reply with some confusion.

"And what did you say?" Wilfred asked.

There was a little gleam of defiance in her eyes as she answered him: "I said that of *course* you liked me!"

He did not speak for a moment, and then he said a little bashfully: "I do—like you. I hope we are going to be good friends."

She answered ruefully: "We shan't have much chance if you're going away again so soon." And then, very earnestly: "What are you going to *do* about me, Mr. Clifton?"

His handsome face was serious.

"*Do* about you?"

"How are you going to get rid of me, I mean?"

The sliding door which led to the corridor opened and Mr. Rachett entered.

"*That's* better," he said, as if he was sure that their entire conversation had been about his breathlessness.

"And now tell me how you two met," he invited cordially. "I was amazed when I saw you together."

"I was *more* amazed to find that Miss Little was my ward,"

Wilfred told him dryly. "It was just a coincidence—we travelled from Paris in the same carriage, that's all."

"And I recognized him from the portrait in your study, Mr. Rachett," she added.

Mr. Rachett said "Dear me!" in a rather disbelieving tone of voice, and then he looked at Wilfred. "I did not expect you until next week," he informed him severely. "You said in your letter——"

Wilfred laughed.

"The things I say in letters and the things I do, seldom have any relation to one another," he answered lazily. "But all the same, I apologize for being a little premature."

Mr. Rachett looked at him uneasily, wondering whether he ought to offer the hospitality of his own house and sincerely hoping that it was not expected, for the little he had seen of Wilfred since his father's death, had done nothing to increase their mutual understanding, and he shrewdly suspected that he rather bored the younger man and that he was considered old-fashioned.

"Mr. Clifton won't be in London very long," Dorothy said, and both men looked at her.

"Is the wish father to the thought?" Wilfred asked lightly, and she answered:

"You said you wouldn't stay long, didn't you?"

Mr. Rachett coughed. He did not like to be hurried, and he had been fully prepared for the discussions on her future which he himself had prompted, to be comfortably spread over at the very least, several weeks. He both looked and felt highly embarrassed when she said quietly:

"I seem to be a dreadful nuisance to both of you."

Mr. Rachett said: "Not at all, not at all! My dear child, who ever put such an idea into your head?"

"Mr. Clifton did."

There was a slightly embarrassed silence before Wilfred said comically: "My ward is determined that I shall be in the wrong you see, Rachett."

"Dorothy is joking," the elder man replied firmly. "I am sure she is delighted—I am delighted myself—that we should all have met in this—er——" He paused, and Wilfred supplied the words for him with great seriousness—"Auspicious manner."

Dorothy chuckled, and immediately bit her lip and cast a scared glance at Mr. Rachett.

"I hope, my dear Clifton," he said in his best legal manner, "that you will be able to spare us a considerable amount of your valuable time—limited as it may be. London, I think, is at its best at this time of the year——"

Dorothy broke in eagerly: "The flowers in Paris were simply wonderful! The woman at the Madeleine ... great baskets of mimosa——"

She met Wilfred's eyes and was surprised at the momentary wistfulness of his expression.

"Mimosa——" he said reflectively, but Mr. Rachett, who refused to believe that any country could even be catalogued as a poor second to his own, interposed firmly:

"In town there will be great baskets of daffodils and tulips —in fact, *all* the spring flowers."

Wilfred's eyes twinkled.

"We must go and view them, Dorothy" he said, and at once she took him seriously:

"May we? Oh, how lovely! ... There are so many places in London I have never seen—only just the British Museum and St. Paul's—but I went there with the school and it wasn't much fun! Oh, will you *really* take me, Mr. Clifton?"

"It seems to be unavoidable, Wilfred," Mr. Rachett remarked with a vague approach to humour, and Wilfred said lightly:

"As I seem to have left undone those things which I ought to have done, I hereby promise to do my utmost to make amends during my brief sojourn in this country." And then once again he looked a little abashed as she said fervently:

"Oh, *thank* you!"

There was a little silence before Mr. Rachett said:

"I gather from your letters that you have enjoyed your year in Paris, Dorothy?" He smiled at her rather stiffly.

"I loved it," she replied.

"I hope you made some friends," he submitted, but at that she shook her head.

"I'm not very good at making friends—and there's only one who really counts—Cecilie Jepson—she wants me to stay with her when she comes home—but that's another three months yet," she added regretfully.

"Jepson!" Mr. Rachett ruminated. "I wonder if by any chance she is the daughter of Ralph Jepson the barrister. If so —I know the family well.'

"I don't know," Dorothy answered. "They live at Highgate —but I don't know what her father does."

"And how did you fail to inquire about such a necessary matter?" Wilfred demanded with pretended severity.

"Necessary?" she echoed doubtfully.

Mr. Rachett coughed. "Madame Suggia assured me that she only accepts the daughters of professional men," he said.

She said: "They were all very *nice* girls, Mr. Rachett."

Mr. Rachett picked up *The Times* and opened it rather noisily and for a moment there was silence until Wilfred asked her:

"And are you fond of the theatre?"

"Yes, I love the theatre—I haven't been to many—we sometimes went to the Opera in Paris, but never to the Folies Bergères or any places like that, and I've only been to one play in London—and that's a long time ago." She paused. "Will you take me?" she asked.

Wilfred passed a hand across his thick dark hair and laughed. "Is theatre-going included in the duties of a guardian?" he inquired, but as nobody answered, he went on: "Silence giving consent—certainly, it will be my pride and pleasure to escort you anywhere and everywhere—while I am in London."

Mr. Rachett looked pleased, no doubt because he realized that such an arrangement would mean less responsibility for himself and his wife.

"Perhaps you will dine with us to-morrow night, Clifton?" he suggested, and Wilfred answered formally that he would be delighted.

"Why do people always say they will be delighted when they don't really mean it?" asked Dorothy.

There was an uncomfortable silence until Mr. Rachett murmured: "My dear Dorothy!"

"She's right," Wilfred declared. "Most of us are humbugs— saying one thing and meaning another—but in this case," he went on, looking at her, "I am sincere—it will give me great pleasure to dine with Mr. Rachett to-morrow, and perhaps afterwards, to take you to a theatre. Will you and Mrs. Rachett join us, sir?" he asked courteously.

"My wife is, as you know, unfortunately an invalid," the elder man answered. "She seldom goes out—and I—well, the theatre is not very much to my taste, but I am sure Dorothy will be delighted to accept your very kind invitation. Shall we say dinner at seven, if that will suit you?"

"Thank you."

Conversation flagged and it was Wilfred's turn to pick up a paper, though after the first few minutes his eyes closed and he let it fall sleepily.

Dorothy watched him from the opposite corner, conscious of a new and strange excitement.

She had dreaded this return to London, fearing that she would find life with the Rachetts a colourless thing and dull, but now her sudden encounter with Wilfred Clifton had cast a most unexpected glow over everything—or would it be more correct to say that it was as if someone had opened a window to surprisingly let in the sea breeze?

Her experience of men was naturally very limited. There was, of course, Mr. Rachett, and at the school in Wiltshire there had been a music-master, a nervous young man whom some of the girls had secretly admired although she had never found him at all interesting. Then there had been Canon Johnson of the booming voice—she smiled faintly as she remembered him—and in Paris there had been a dancing master named Monsieur Roulière, a very sleek person with a trim black beard and, of course, from time to time she had met various brothers and uncles and relations of the other girls who were "finishing", but in Wilfred Clifton she had found an entirely different kind of man.

As he sat half asleep in the opposite corner, his head drooping forward on his broad chest, big shoulders hunched rather ungracefully, she thought what a very handsome guardian he was!

She liked his voice which was deep without having Canon Johnson's impressive boom—she liked his smile and especially the uplifted crooked corner to his mouth, and she admired his brown face and strong hands.

She liked the things he said, too—especially when she could not be quite sure whether he was in earnest or not; in fact, although she was not aware of it, she liked him chiefly because he was her exact opposite and the very last man she would have thought it possible *for* her to like!

In spite of her cleverness, her mind was still very young, which was, of course, due to lack of experience, and she found herself wishing now as the train sped on towards London, that Wilfred had still been in the Army, so that she could have seen him in uniform.

Would they really be friends? Somehow it seemed impossible when one thought of those labels on his suit-cases, and his extensive travelling, and the difference in their ages.

Could such a man of the world really like the company of someone who—well, after all, she had only *just* left school even if she was no longer actually a schoolgirl? Suddenly she found herself wishing that she was tall like Cecilie—and more grown-up in appearance, so that he would have treated her more as an equal and less as a child.

But perhaps all guardians treated their wards in the same way! for a guardian really took the place of one's father, even though the majority of them were probably much older than Wilfred. But still, he was twelve years her senior!

"I like you!" she told him silently. "I like you very much, and I wish you'd come home years and years ago."

And then suddenly she realized that his eyes were open and that they were looking at her with the queer expression of someone who is only half awake, and then before she could turn away he moved his hand a little towards her and unexpectedly spoke a name—a woman's name—"Pauline——"

Dorothy stared at him, the delicate colour mounting to her face, and then suddenly Mr. Rachett (who had also dropped to sleep behind his paper) gave a terrific snore, and instantly Wilfred was wide awake and had started to his feet.

For an instant he still seemed a little dazed, and then he laughed and rubbed his eyes, and yawned.

"Whew! . . . I thought I was back in Paris," he said; he gave himself a shake. "We must be nearly at Victoria," and he walked out into the corridor, yawning again.

She looked after him wonderingly.

"Pauline!" . . . and suddenly, without knowing why, she was sorry for him, sorry! as if she had looked on while someone hurt him—someone! this Pauline perhaps.

Presently he turned and stood with one shoulder leaning

30

against the framework of the open door, looking down at her.

"Little and Good, we have arrived!" he said dramatically.

Mr. Rachett must have heard the words through the mists of sleep, for he suddenly came to life and began to collect his possessions.

"Where are my spectacles? I know. I had them—now where on earth are my spectacles?"

"Here!" She dived down to recover them from the floor before she pulled on her gloves and took a look at herself in the mirror.

Not very beautiful, she decided regretfully, and she felt younger and smaller than ever when she was standing on the platform between the two men; for although Mr. Rachett stooped, he was nearly six feet when he drew himself up fully.

"I'll see to the luggage," Wilfred said. "How many thousand trunks have you got—*Dorothy*?" he added deliberately.

"Only two and a suit-case and a hat box."

Dorothy stood silently by while her belongings were piled on to and into the cab, and then Wilfred said:

"Well—it must be au revoir until to-morrow night. By the way, you didn't tell me which show you would like to see."

"*You* choose." She had no idea what was on.

He laughed. "My choice may not be your choice!" he warned her, but she only smiled and said again that she would like him to choose.

"See you to-morrow, Wilfred," Mr. Rachett called after him.

Wilfred nodded as he raised his hat. "Yes, thanks," he said. And was it her imagination, or did she fancy that he gave her a special kind of look, just before he turned away? But a moment later he was lost in the crowd.

She sighed as he disappeared and hurriedly preceded Mr. Rachett into the taxicab.

"Well," he inquired with a touch of irony, "and what do you think of your guardian?"

"I like him," she answered unhesitatingly; she turned to look at him. "Don't you like him?" she inquired.

Mr. Rachett rather obviously hesitated.

"I have seen very little of him," he admitted. "He has always been rather—wild, shall I say! Very different from his father who was one of the old school—and an English gentleman to use an old-fashioned expression."

31

"Don't you think Wilfred is a gentleman?" she asked.

Mr. Rachett smiled deprecatingly.

"He was educated at a very good school," he told her, "and he went to Oxford but as I have said, I really know very little of him, except that he bought himself out of the Army, which I consider a pity—he is just the type of man for a soldier—and since then—well, I really know nothing of his life since then."

"He's not married," she said.

Mr. Rachett cast a sidelong glance at her.

"To the best of my belief Wilfred is single," he answered. "Which is a fortunate thing."

"Why?" she asked disconcertingly.

"Why?—well——" Mr. Rachett hesitated before he continued. "A rolling stone is seldom faithful for long to the same person or to the same ideal."

She made no comment, but she seemed to hear again the whispered sound of a woman's name:

"Pauline!"

Who was Pauline, she wondered? Surely not the girl whom he had wished to marry when he was twenty-one, for he said he had forgotten her; but then he had said also that the world was full of attractive young women . . .

She had not liked that—or was it the slightly sarcastic way in which he had said it, that displeased her?

"But then I know he doesn't mean everything he says," she thought. Oh dear, if only she were older!

She was silent for the rest of the way until Mr. Rachett said with an effort at cheerfulness:

"Well, here we are, Dorothy! Home—and may I be the first to welcome you back?"

She thanked him shyly, but her spirits sank a little as she looked up at the gloomy building.

It was one of a row of houses with curtains drawn right across the windows, a highly polished doorknocker and a flight of steps leading up to the front door; they were evidently expected for it was opened immediately by a girl wearing blue jeans and a yellow polo sweater.

Dorothy said "good afternoon" rather shyly as she stepped into the hall which she remembered so well.

Its polished floor—expensive-looking rugs, rather heavily

framed pictures, and the big grandfather clock which stood in a recess opposite the hat-rack—all as dull as ever.

A bright fire was burning in the big grate in the drawing room, for the spring evenings were still chilly, and Mrs. Rachett lay stretched before it on a couch with a light rug over her knees.

She held out a very white hand in greeting.

"Forgive me for not rising," she said, "but this has been one of my bad days. How are you? I hope you had a good crossing."

"Yes, thank you."

"Would you like some tea? Or did you have it on the train?"

"We should certainly like some tea," her husband answered, relieved to find that Dorothy's reception was cordial. "You would like some tea, Dorothy?"

"Yes, please."

Her bedroom was the same—and it looked just the same, Dorothy thought, in faint surprise, though why she had imagined it would look different she did not know—except that somehow it seemed so long ago that she had slept here.

A large room, at the back of the house, a large wardrobe in which, on her last visit, her few clothes had seemed to be almost pathetically lost, a large bed too, with a pink eider-down and frilly pillows.

"Sue will help you unpack," Mrs. Rachett had said. Sue was the girl in blue jeans who came in to help occasionally. But Dorothy preferred to put her own things away, and when she had unpacked she washed and tidied her hair and went downstairs again to find that Mr. Rachett had already given his wife a detailed account of their meeting with Wilfred Clifton.

"And what do you think of your guardian, Dorothy?" Mrs. Rachett inquired with the air of one who hopes for an adverse criticism, and Dorothy answered as she had done before:

"I like him."

"*All* women like him," was the reply. "Will you pour out, my dear?"

While they were occupied over the tea-table Mrs. Rachett scrutinized her.

Not very different, she decided—a little older, of course, and better dressed—yes, *much* better dressed! She was growing up.

Pretty?—some people might think so, but Mrs. Rachett who was built on rather generous lines herself, did not admire small people, though she realized that there was something oddly attractive about that serious face and straight hair, something "different", as Wilfred had also realized.

"She looks well-bred," she thought, and of course, that was something! Mrs. Rachett was a snob at heart.

"So Wilfred Clifton is dining with us to-morrow," she said aloud. "Have you something formal to wear, Dorothy?"

"Oh yes, we often dressed in Paris—some of the girls had lovely things."

"Indeed!"

"Shall we dress to-morrow night?" she asked.

"Certainly—we always dress for dinner—my husband prefers it."

It was not the truth, for Mr. Rachett was often very tired when he came home at night, and would have preferred carpet slippers and an arm-chair, only his wife who held the belief that she was—very vaguely and indirectly—descended from William the Conqueror—as indeed are most people—declared that she could not enjoy her dinner if she was condemned to sit opposite either to a lounge suit or dinner jacket.

"And I am so seldom able to dine downstairs," she would add plaintively whenever the position needed an explanation.

When tea was over Dorothy escaped on the pretext of sorting out her things as soon as the door had closed behind her little form Mrs. Rachett turned to her husband.

"And *how* much money will Dorothy receive when she is twenty-one?" she inquired.

Mr. Rachett, engrossed in a letter said: "Eh?" very vaguely, and then suddenly remembering his manners added quickly: "I beg your pardon, my dear?"

The distant and indirect descendant of William the Conqueror repeated her question:

"I asked how much money Dorothy will receive when she comes of age?"

He considered the point. "Well, roughly—probably something in the nature of seven thousand a year. You see—the money has been accumulating for some time—and I pride myself that it has been well invested."

"Seven thousand a year!" Mrs. Rachett picked up her smelling salts. "And she looks to me as if a couple of hundred will be all she will require," she said bitterly.

Her husband rubbed his chin.

"She seems a nice, quiet little girl," he ventured, and then as if fearing he had been too enthusiastic: "Inoffensive, anyway."

"*Dull!*" Mrs. Rachett said. "And I am not at all surprised that a man like Wilfred Clifton does not relish his guardianship. It would be different if she were a pretty and attractive girl."

Mr. Rachett could have replied that unfortunately Clifton was a bad judge of most things, but he wisely held his peace, and Dorothy going slowly up the great wide staircase looked at the many not at all beautiful portraits, and thought with a sense of amazement:

"I suppose they are all relations—funny they've got so many —when I haven't even one!"

It was a depressing thought, and her face was a little sad as she shut her bedroom door and walked over to the window.

Not a very cheery outlook there either! Just dingy, narrow gardens where things tried in vain to grow—very different to Madame Suggia's garden outside Paris, surrounding a house which had once been a chateau . . .

She sighed and turned away to look through the wardrobe in which she had stored her clothes, even the wardrobe seemed to frown at her disapprovingly, perhaps because her clothes were not up to the standard of William the Conqueror.

She took out her evening frock—and suddenly she smiled.

"I'll wear it to-morrow."

To-morrow! And she realized happily that although to-day might be rather cheerless, to-morrow would be altogether different because Wilfred Clifton was coming to dine!

CHAPTER TWO

Dorothy's first day with the Rachetts was uneventful; Mrs. Rachett stayed in bed in preparation for the evening's entertainment, sending her guest an apology and expressing the hope that she would make herself at home!

Dorothy shared a somewhat silent breakfast with Mr. Rachett, who, as he was usually accustomed to eating his eggs and bacon alone with the paper propped up before him, felt rather at a loss.

He had remarked that it was a fine morning—which it was—he had asked whether she had slept well—which she had, and then he asked the question which had been in his mind for some time—"I—er—how are you situated financially, Dorothy?"

She smiled.

"I haven't very much," she admitted. "About two pounds in English money and a few francs——"

"You should change those," he answered quickly. "They will be of no use to you now——" which she already knew —and then he went on: "You understand, of course, that until you are of age your money is controlled—by your guardian and myself—but any amounts, within reason, which you require I shall of course be pleased to supply."

"Thank you."

Mr. Rachett eyed her above his spectacles. The width of the table was between them, but somehow it pleased him to see her sitting there with the morning sunlight shining on her grave face, and almost for the first time in his busy life he found himself wishing that he had been blessed with a family.

But—well, Lydia was delicate, so perhaps Providence had decided for the best.

He drained his coffee cup and rose.

"Well, I must be off. Don't hurry on my account, Dorothy —and...." He produced a pocket-book from which he extracted a five pound note. "Just in case there is any little thing you require," he said, wondering as he laid it beside her whether he was encouraging her in undue extravagance.

She said: "Oh, *thank* you," very gratefully, whereupon Mr. Rachett, who was scrupulously honest, informed her that it was merely money to which she was entitled, or rather—to which she would be entitled when she came of age.

"Was it my father's money?" she asked.

Mr. Rachett replied that it was, and that unlike many fathers, Major Little had amply provided for her future, and then with a hurried: "Well, good morning, Dorothy," he departed.

From the window, Dorothy watched him hurrying down the

road carrying a black leather case, without which she had seldom seen him, and then, tucking the five pound note casually into the pocket of her cardigan, she went into the library.

But it was not the books which attracted her this morning —though the high steps stood invitingly in their accustomed place against the shelves. Without a glance in their direction she crossed the room to look again at the portrait of Wilfred Clifton.

She had told him that he had not changed since it was painted, but now she realized that she had been mistaken, for he looked older and broader than the youth in the uniform— more determined, perhaps less care-free, and then suddenly she was remembering Pauline. . . .

A lovely name which seemed to breathe romance! But who was she? Had she been in Cannes with Wilfred, she wondered? And did she love him? Because somehow it was a foregone conclusion that Wilfred must love Pauline, or had loved her.

Love was a subject about which Dorothy was a little reserved and shy, although even at the school in Wiltshire the girls had talked about their boy friends, and the men they had met, while in Paris . . . she frowned, remembering their outspokenness about things which she considered too important for public discussion.

And yet Wilfred too had spoken about it in a lighthearted sort of way—saying that the world was full of attractive women and rather pooh-poohing the idea that at twenty-one he had suffered because the girl he wished to marry had changed her mind.

"I wonder if I shall ever be in love?" Dorothy thought, and she raised her hand to touch the portrayed hand of Wilfred Clifton, and as she did so, she imagined that his eyes, which really looked straight ahead, turned down as though to smile at her. . . .

She took great pains with her toilet that night, turning and twisting in front of the mirror, feeling a little dissatisfied.

Her dress was all right, she decided, and she wore on her wrist a plain gold bracelet which Cecilie Jepson had given to her as a parting gift.

A clock somewhere in the house struck seven, as she turned from the mirror, conscious of a growing excitement.

Wilfred would be here soon.

She went downstairs and into the drawing-room where Mrs. Rachett was lying on her usual couch looking quite distinguished and perfectly well in a black evening gown.

Dorothy went towards her, feeling a little self-conscious.

"Do I look alright?"

The elder woman's eyes travelled slowly over her dainty figure. "It is a very charming frock," she said at last a little grudgingly. "But perhaps just a little—too smart for a simple dinner party."

"I thought—I thought I ought to wear my best," Dorothy apologized, and just then Mr. Rachett appeared, looking rather harassed and with his black bow tie crooked, an offence to which his wife promptly drew attention.

"I know, my dear, I know," he said patiently, "but my sight is not too good, and——"

Dorothy stepped forward.

"Let me do it for you," she said, and with her slim fingers she straightened it.

Mr. Rachett looked down at her preoccupied face with a softened expression in his eyes, but when she had finished he only said: "Thank you, Dorothy," and moved away from her.

"I suppose Wilfred will be late," Mrs. Rachett said resignedly, and he answered:

"I do not see *why* you should say that, my dear!" and almost before the words had passed his lips the door opened and in came Wilfred.

Dorothy's eyes shone with approval as she looked at him.

He was more handsome in evening dress than he was in uniform, she thought quickly—and then remembered that she had never seen him in uniform!

Wilfred bowed over Mrs. Rachett's extended hand before he turned to Dorothy:

"How are you? All ready for the fray?"

"The—fray?" Mrs. Rachett echoed.

He smiled, charmingly.

"We're going to a show," he told her casually.

"Well, well——" her husband said consolingly. "Will you have a cocktail, Clifton? and you, Dorothy?"

She nodded. And as she sipped her pink gin, she noticed that Wilfred was looking at her over the rim of his glass.

At dinner she sat opposite to Wilfred while Mrs. Rachett languidly presided at the head of the table.

"You must forgive me if I eat very little," she apologized, but Dorothy noticed that she seemed to enjoy the good things she had provided.

"And what theatre are you going to?" Mr. Rachett asked.

Wilfred glanced at Dorothy.

"I've booked for the revue at the New."

"I know the music," Dorothy told him eagerly. "They used to play it in Paris—we had a long player of it."

"And how long will you be staying in London, Wilfred?" Mrs. Rachett inquired.

He half shrugged his shoulders.

"I don't know—my plans are, as usual, rather vague."

"It will not be too short a visit, I trust," Mr. Rachett said affably.

"I hope not too," Dorothy said warmly.

"Coffee in the drawing-room," Mrs. Rachett announced, and her husband hurried round to give her his arm.

When they had left the room Wilfred asked in an undertone:

"Is she really an invalid?"

"I don't know, I suppose she is."

Mr. Rachett returned.

"We will waive all ceremony," he announced. "It is already eight o'clock, so we will take coffee with the ladies."

"Have you a car, Wilfred?" Mrs. Rachett inquired.

"Not of my own," he answered, "but I've hired one for the short time I shall be in London. It's outside."

"I'll get my coat," Dorothy said.

She raced upstairs in great excitement and took it out of the cupboard.

She flung it over her arm and paused for a brief glance in the mirror.

"You're going to have a lovely evening," she whispered, smiling at her reflection. "The best of your life."

Wilfred was waiting in the hall.

"Ready?" he asked, smiling.

"Yes—haven't you got an overcoat?"

"It's not cold enough," he said.

She half turned: "I must just say good-bye——"

"Enjoy yourself," Mrs. Rachett murmured. She looked up at Wilfred: "Take care of your ward," she said.

"Enjoy yourself, Dorothy," Mr. Rachett echoed; he followed them to the front door, where the big headlamps of the waiting car sent a long shaft of light down the deserted street.

"Isn't it thrilling?" Dorothy said excitedly as they drove away in the Jaguar.

Wilfred turned his head to glance down at her.

"Thrilling?" She was really very young.

"Going out together like this," she answered impulsively, and then quickly: "But of course it can't be very exciting for you—I forgot. I suppose you often go to theatres——" It was on the tip of her tongue to add: "with other girls" but she stopped in time.

Wilfred laughed.

"Not very often! I am so seldom in London."

"Yes, but in Paris—and Cannes?" she hazarded.

"There are other—more exciting things to do in Paris and in Cannes," he said.

She leaned a little forward. "What things?" she asked.

"What things?—perhaps they would not appeal to you if I explained. I imagine our tastes are very different."

She felt chilled.

"You mean—that I have never been anywhere and don't know anything, I suppose," she submitted.

"Your life has only just begun," he reminded her. "You're not a hardened sinner like me. You're only a kid."

She laughed.

"You do say some funny things," she said.

"That wasn't intended to be funny," he objected.

"*Not* funny?" And again she tried to see his face. "Then are you a hardened sinner?"

He gave a mock sigh. "In some ways—yes, I suppose I am, Little and Good!"

She was silent for a moment and then she said, rather unexpectedly, he thought:

"I expect I shall be the same, when I've had your experience."

"Heaven forbid!" he answered quickly. "I should be sorry to thing it is possible for you to get into some of the—scrapes —which lie to my credit."

"What sort of scrapes?"

"Oh—just—scrapes! Rachett could probably give you a complete list, if you are interested."

"I should never think of asking him," she said with dignity.

It was his turn to be silent now, and then suddenly he asked: "And what do you think of old Rachett?" She hesitated.

"They've been very kind to me. Mr. Rachett came to see me when I was at school—not in Paris! He couldn't spare the time for one thing, and besides he's such a bad sailor."

Wilfred chuckled, and she went on:

"But when I was at school in Wiltshire he always came once during term-time, and before that—when I lived with Nuggie——"

"'Nuggie'?"

"My nurse—she brought me up, and I loved her. You see —she was the only real friend I had when I was young."

"And what became of Nuggie?" he asked.

"She died—and then I was sent to boarding school."

"Where you found lots of other people to love," he said.

"No," she answered, "I don't really love anyone—except perhaps Cecilie."

"Why not?"

"There doesn't seem to be anyone to love——" she told him simply.

"Would you have preferred to be one of a large family, with dozens of relatives?"

She considered the point, and then she said: "Yes, I think I should! It wouldn't have been so lonely."

"Is that intended for a rebuke for me?" he asked.

"For you? Why should it be?"

"I am your guardian—at all events, nominally."

"But that isn't your fault," she said kindly.

Wilfred laughed.

"Probably not—all the same, I have shirked my responsibilities."

"You're making up for them now," she told him and he said again with some feeling—as he had said once before:

"You're a sportsman, Little and Good."

And then they were at the theatre.

"I must park this mouse-trap somewhere," Wilfred said comically, and she laughed.

"It's a lovely car."

"A car is a nuisance in London," he answered. He stretched an arm in front of her and opened the door.

"Wait for me in the foyer, will you? I won't be a moment. I'm sorry to have to leave you. It may take time to find a parking place. But we're early."

"I shall be all right," she assured him happily.

She stood back a little, near the box office, watching the people around her; everyone apparently very gay and happy; though she thought there was not a man who looked so imposing as Wilfred—and then she saw him making his way towards her.

"Stalls this way, sir."

"I've got a box," Wilfred said. "All the stalls were sold out."

"How smashing," she said.

"Do you like chocolates?" he inquired.

She nodded, her eyes dancing—she liked everything tonight, and nothing could disillusion her.

"Take the chair facing the stage," Wilfred ordered. "Will you wear your coat, or would you rather take it off? I think you'll find it rather warm."

"I'll take it off."

He took it from her and laid it across a chair-back, then he put the box of chocolates on the ledge beside her.

She looked down at the crowded house, and her heart beat fast with excitement.

"It's evidently a popular show," Wilfred said.

She turned to him suddenly.

"Do you know that this is the first time in my life I have ever been out alone with a man?"

He looked intensely amused.

"You are unique," he said.

"I suppose so," she agreed. "All the girls in Paris——" she broke off as the lights were lowered. . . .

"Like it?" Wilfred inquired when the interval came.

Her cheeks were flushed and her eyes shone like stars, and he thought in faint surprise that she was really quite a pretty girl. Terribly young, but with very attractive eyes. And there was something so charming about her innocence.

"It's *wonderful!*" she said with a little sigh of happiness. "I should love to dance to that number about the balloons."

"Why not?" he asked lazily.

She clasped her hands in excitement.

"Will you take me? I mean—*could* we go out and dance somewhere?"

"I am very fond of dancing," he told her. "We'll go to the Savoy one night—to-night, if you like."

"*Oh!*" she said softly, and for a moment she could say no more.

Wilfred looked at her with a faint smile.

Twenty-four hours ago his one aim and object had been to shelve his responsibility and to get rid of this girl as quickly as possible, and yet here he was—committed to all kinds of promises and feeling quite content!

Of course she was a novelty—and that was the obvious explanation. He found her simple enjoyment and natural charm refreshing after the more sophisticated women of all ages to whose society he was accustomed.

All the same, his visit to London could not be prolonged indefinitely, for he had promised Pauline ... and then at the thought of her his face sobered, and he turned his eyes away from the girl by his side.

He and Pauline had laughed together about this girl—she had teased him and had called her his "one good deed."

She had not believed him when he declared that he had never seen her, neither had she believed him when he described her as a mere schoolgirl.

"There is no such thing nowadays," she said lightly. "I prophesy that you will be met by a highly sophisticated young woman with whom you will probably fall head over heels in love—and she with you." And he had protested in vain:

"A man does not love two women at the same time."

But to-night Pauline seemed very far away—so that it was surprisingly difficult to conjure her face, and with a half sigh he turned again to the girl beside him.

She had opened the chocolate box and was offering it to him. "The nutty ones are best," she said.

Wilfred did not care for chocolates, but he took one and bit it in half to discover the contents.

She peered forward to look.

"It's marzipan," she said. "Don't you like it?"

"I am in the mood to like everything," he told her.

"So am I," she agreed, and then impulsively she added, "I'm so glad I've met you at last."

There was something warm in the expression of his eyes as they met hers, but he only said lightly:

"The reciprocity of that sentiment is unbounded."

She laughed.

"You do say funny things," she said.

Wilfred drew himself up with mock dignity.

"I am delighted to cause you so much amusement, Miss Little." But Dorothy gave a warning: "Hush!" ... for the curtain had risen once more.

When the show was over, and the crowd was leaving the theatre, Wilfred said:

"And now, what about supper?"

"Supper?"

"Aren't you hungry?"

She hesitated. "Not really—but——"

"I *am*!" he said firmly and he took her arm to guide her across the road. "It's only a few steps to the car."

As they were driving away again Dorothy said dubiously:

"You don't think Mrs. Rachett will expect me to go straight home, do you, Mr. Clifton?"

Wilfred stopped at a traffic signal.

"I refuse to allow the memory of Mrs. Rachett to spoil my enjoyment," he declared firmly. "And—one more point! If I can unbend to call you by your christian name—I see no reason why I should be addressed as Mr. Clifton. Wilfred is a perfectly respectable name, Saxon I believe—correct me if I am wrong!"

He stopped and she said breathlessly:

"But you are my guardian!"

"Let us forget that unhappy fact," he retorted. "And for the future, if you dare to address me as Mr. Clifton, I shall not reply."

" 'Wilfred'," she said softly.

"That's better," he answered. "And now we are all friends together!"

They had turned on to the Embankment.

"Where are we going?" she asked.

"The Savoy—I can park the car somewhere near—do you think that's a good idea?"

"I have never been there. But I imagine it's terrific."

"Then you must wish," he told her cheerfully. "Wish before you set foot within its sacred portals—but don't tell me what you wish, or it won't come true."

"I shouldn't dream of telling you," she answered sincerely, but she knew what her wish would be—that it might be a long, long time before Wilfred left London.

It seemed like stepping into a dream world as they entered the big lounge.

"Have you been here before?" she asked.

"Hundred of times," Wilfred answered. "Ladies' cloak-room on the left—I'll meet you here."

When she rejoined him he was talking to the short, squarely-built man whom they had met on the cross-Channel steamer.

Wilfred introduced him.

"This is Willie Guest—my ward, Miss Little."

Guest bowed rather awkwardly.

"I have heard about you already—from Wilfred," he said. "I am delighted to make your acquaintance," and his eyes were clearly admiring her face.

"Sly dog!" he said in an undertone to Wilfred.

"See you later," Wilfred answered calmly. "I've booked a table in the centre of the room."

"That's the man you met on the boat," Dorothy said as they crossed the crowded room.

"It is," Wilfred replied. "We were at school together, and he's been a good friend."

He picked up the menu from the table.

"What shall we eat?" he inquired.

"You choose, please."

Wilfred spoke to the waiter and gave his order before he turned to her.

"Shall we dance now? Or would you rather wait?"

"Oh, now! . . . please."

"You dance very well," Wilfred said presently "And may I say how much I like your dress?"

"Do you? I'm so glad I bought it in Paris. But Mrs. Rachett thought it was too elaborate."

"Mrs. Rachett!" he echoed with pretended anger. "Why will you persist in mentioning that name when I am straining every nerve to forget her existence!"

"Yes, but I mustn't forget her existence," she said. "I may have to stay with them for a long time."

It was when they were back at the table that Wilfred said suddenly: "Have you ever thought what you would like to do with your life? Any plans, ambitions?"

She looked at him seriously.

"No, I haven't, except. . . ." she stopped.

"Except?" he prompted gently.

Her colour rose sensitively.

"Except that I don't want to be a nuisance to you, or to anyone," she said.

He flushed a little and averted his eyes.

"That was deserved," he said presently.

"Oh, but I didn't mean anything," she explained. "But I know you don't want to be bothered with me! why should you? And I don't think Mrs. Rachett likes me staying with her very much—but Mr. Rachett says that until I'm twenty-one, I can't live alone—and anyway . . . I don't think I want to——" she added with unconscious pathos.

"Has there ever been any question of your living alone?" Wilfred asked sharply.

"Yes—at least . . . I suggested it before I left Paris, but only because I didn't know what else to suggest."

He was silent for a moment and then said gently:

"Look here, my dear, you must get it out of your head once and for all that you are, as you put it just now, a nuisance to me. I am—I am proud to feel that perhaps I can be of some use to you—if you will let me be——" and then suddenly he raised his eyes and the corner of his mouth went up in his oddly attractive smile. "In fact, quite frankly, I am sorry we did not make one another's acquaintance long ago, and I mean this sincerely and not as an apology."

"I am sorry, too," she answered, and then a little sadly: "But you will be going away again soon."

Wilfred picked up the menu card, and stared at it interestedly, regardless of the fact that he was holding it upside down, before he answered:

"I may even change my mind about that," he laughed. "When you know me better, you will understand that it does not do to take anything I say too seriously! Therefore, it is quite on the cards that I may settle down in London, and become the ideal respectable, orthodox guardian. Would you like that?"

"You couldn't!" she said, laughing.

He looked at her with pretended severity.

"Is that a challenge?" he demanded. "Because if so I may accept it!" And then he laughed with her. "How would you like me if I suddenly developed into a kind of Second Rachett? Bringing you up in the way you should go—ordering your life and your love-affairs ... by the way...." and again he assumed his air of severity, "have you had any love-affairs?"

She shook her head.

"I don't know any men except you and Mr. Rachett."

"Oh!" he said rather blankly. "Then that does not give you a very wide choice."

"None at all," she agreed. "But you said once that the world is full of attractive women, so I suppose it's full of attractive men too, isn't it?"

Wilfred waved a hand towards the other tables.

"Look around you!" he said. "All the youth and beauty and riches of London are gathered here!"

She glanced towards the other tables.

"I can see Mr. Guest," she said.

Wilfred chuckled.

"Poor Willie! ... he is hardly a lady's man."

"He is not so nice as you are," she answered simply.

He looked at her quickly, and away again, with a slightly abashed feeling because, just for a moment, he had doubted the innocence of her words, and then the waiter arrived with supper and put an end to the conversation.

It was nearly two o'clock when they arrived home.

"I don't know how to thank you," she said. "It's been a perfectly lovely evening—the best I have ever had."

"And if I were to say that it is also the best I have ever had, you would not believe me," Wilfred answered. "Therefore, I will content myself by agreeing that it has been great fun."

He was still sitting at the wheel of the car and had not yet made any attempt to open the door, and Dorothy said presently:

"Aren't you *ever* really serious?"

"What do you mean?"

"I mean," she explained, "that you always seem to be—a

47

little—sarcastic ... or perhaps it's because I don't understand."

"Understand?"

"People like you," she said. "Of course, you're older, and I'm just—nobody."

She stopped and Wilfred thought ironically: "Nobody! With seven thousand a year," though aloud he said gently:

"I am not conscious of having been sarcastic with you! In fact, you are very much a girl who demands sincerity."

"I am not sure if that is a compliment," she told him slowly, "or if it means that I'm merely—stupid."

His hand suddenly fell to hers.

"It means that you are the most—real person I have met for many years," he said sincerely, "and there are enough shams in the world, Heaven knows!" And then he leaned forward and opened the door. "Have they given you a key?"

"Yes."

"Sure you haven't lost it?" he asked teasingly.

"Quite sure! Here it is."

He took it from her and went with her up the flight of steps to the door which he opened, standing aside for her to pass.

"Good night, Little and Good," he said.

She gave him her hand.

"Good night, Big and Bad!" she answered, laughing. "And thank you a thousand times."

He turned away and she shut the door quietly and crept upstairs to her room.

A lovely, lovely evening, she thought dreamily—and then with a sudden sense of shock she realized that she had not asked Wilfred when she would see him again!

CHAPTER THREE

Although, had she been asked, Dorothy would have said that she did not mind a quiet life, she found the first week of her stay with the Rachetts a little tedious.

For one thing it was lovely spring weather, and although each morning she walked in the Park, or took a 'bus to Hampstead Heath, she began to realize that loneliness was not really a thing to be desired.

Mr. Rachett did his best but he was seldom at home, and his wife, like Dickens's Mrs. Dombey, found it impossible to make an effort to entertain her guest. But then they had little in common.

"You are free to do as you like," she told her graciously, "but, as you know, I am unfortunately far from strong, and with the greatest will in the world it is impossible for me to lead the life of an ordinary woman."

Dorothy said she was sorry but, as in Mrs. Rachett's company she was always conscious of being at a disadvantage, her sympathy was not quite so sincere as it might have been.

And then one evening Mr. Rachett arrived home with a draught-board.

"It's a good game, Dorothy," he told her. "A game which was very fashionable when I was a young man. I will show you how to play."

But he had reckoned without his guest, for after the first trial Dorothy gave him a sound beating, which was not at all his idea of the fitness of things.

"That's one game each," she said generously. "Shall we play the conqueror?" And she was cleverly proceeding to allow him to win when Wilfred was announced.

Dorothy looked up eagerly and Mr. Rachett, who imagined he had just seen a clever move by which he could sweep the entire board, said "Dear me!" in rather a vexed tone of voice.

He was not particularly pleased with Wilfred, who he considered had shown extreme unwillingness to discuss the problem for which he had ostensibly come to London, and he would have been amazed had he known that as he stood hesitating in the doorway neither was Wilfred feeling particularly pleased with him—for he thought that the little scene upon which he had intruded was a pathetic one.

For why should this girl spend a lovely spring evening in a prim drawing-room playing draughts with an old man?

Probably he himself was partly to blame, he thought ruefully, and yet—surely he could not be expected to spend his entire life as a kind of professional entertainer to a ward who —to put it mildly—was a doubtful blessing?

And yet he liked her! And there was genuine pleasure in his smile as he crossed the room and took her hand.

"How are you? I hope you're winning."

"We've each won a game," she told him, "and this is the conqueror."

"Don't let me interrupt," Wilfred said. "I'll watch."

But Mr. Rachett had forgotten his masterly move, and with an impatient hand he swept the draughts back into their box.

"Some other time," he said, and then: "I'm glad to see you, Wilfred—I have been expecting you to call at the office."

Mr. Rachett went reluctantly away.

"Well?" Wilfred said as the door closed.

"Well?" Dorothy echoed.

"What sort of a time are you having?"

She hesitated.

"They mean to be kind, but. . . ." She stopped and Wilfred said:

"Not a very exciting game—draughts—is it?"

"It's better than nothing." She smiled, and then, afraid that he might think the words were a reproach, she asked hurriedly: "What have you been doing?"

"I went to a show with Guest last night. By the way, he wants us to dine with him one evening."

Her eyes brightened.

"You mean—me?" she asked.

"*And* me," Wilfred answered, smiling.

"It's very kind of him," she said.

"Yes, he's not a bad chap."

He looked down at her thoughtfully.

"What can I do about it?" he asked.

She raised her eyes to his face.

"About what?"

"About you——It's all wrong—you being here, I mean!"

"I suppose I shall have to get used to it," she submitted. "It is kind of them to have me."

He walked away from her to the window which was a little way open, for the night was mild, and above the house-tops he could see a pale crescent moon.

"There's a new moon, Little and Good!" he said quickly. "Come and wish. Got any money?"

"No—not here."

He dived into a pocket. "Here's half a crown—turn it over and wish—Wait! . . . You mustn't see the moon through glass—I'll open the window a bit wider."

50

She laughed ruefully. "You're too late—I've seen it through glass already."

Wilfred said: "Humph! ... Well, have a wish all the same."

She carefully turned the half-crown, her thoughtful eyes on the little moon, and then after a moment she said:

"I've wished! Did you?"

Wilfred laughed. "I've given up wishing long ago."

"Why?"

"Why?— Oh, because nothing I have wished for has ever come my way, I suppose, and that makes it an uninteresting sort of game."

"It's the second time you've told *me* to wish," she reminded him. "You did at the Savoy the other night."

"Perhaps you'll be luckier than I," he answered.

She gave him back the half-crown.

"I should have said that you were a very lucky person," she said.

"You would, would you?" he submitted in amusement. "On what grounds, may I ask?"

"Well—you can do just as you like, for one thing."

There was a short silence before he said rather bluntly:

"But not—with whom I like, and that makes all the difference."

"I suppose it does," she agreed. "All the same," she added after a moment, "I should have thought that if you wanted to go out with someone, it would have been quite easy."

"Funny kid!" he said. "But that isn't quite what I meant."

Mr. Rachett returned.

"If it is convenient for you to call at the office to-morrow morning, Wilfred," he said tentatively, "I shall be very happy to see you, and to discuss the matter we have under consideration."

"Me," Dorothy said, and then bit her lip, wishing she had not spoken.

"I'll be there at eleven, if that will do," Wilfred answered. "And—by the way—may I take Dorothy to dine with a friend of mine on Tuesday night?"

"If Dorothy wishes, certainly," the old man answered. "May I ask who the friend is?"

"He's quite respectable," Wilfred said carelessly. "A man named Guest."

"I should like to go," she ventured.

"Then it's settled," Wilfred declared. "And now I must be off. Good night."

"A very short visit," Mr. Rachett said when he had gone. "So typical of Wilfred! He turns up at the most unexpected moments and disappears again before one hardly has time to realize he is there!"

"Shall we have another game?" she asked, and presently they were facing one another again across the draught-board. But this time it was easy for Mr. Rachett to win, for her thoughts were far away, and when the match ended in her ignominious defeat she suddenly asked: "Mr. Rachett, what does Wilfred *do* all the time?"

The old man pushed his spectacles up over his forehead.

"My dear, I have not the slightest idea," he said rather dryly. "He has a certain amount of money, and—I imagine—many friends. He is quite an attractive young fellow."

"Would you call him young?" she asked.

"Young? Why certainly," he answered in surprise. "Young in comparison with myself, perhaps I should say."

"I wonder he isn't married," she ventured.

Mr. Rachett shook his head.

"I imagine that Wilfred's love affairs have been many and varied," he said. "I fancy that he was engaged once—some years ago—but I have heard his name coupled with that of so many different people at one time and another."

"Perhaps he thinks there is safety in numbers," she said seriously.

Mr. Rachett said: "Humph! ... And now, if you will excuse me, Dorothy, I have letters to write. We will have another game to-morrow"

"Thank you," she answered, but somehow it was not a very exciting prospect.

As she was going to bed that night Mrs. Rachett called from her room "Is that you Dorothy?"

"Yes."

"Come here—I have something to tell you."

She tip-toed into the room and Mrs. Rachett indicated a letter lying beside her on the bed.

"It is an invitation to a dress show," she said. "My friend, Mrs. Greenley, has asked me to go with her—it's to-morrow—

but as, of course, it is out of the question for me to accept, I suggested that perhaps it might interest you."

She waited with the air of one who has conferred a great honour. "Well?" she asked, "Would you like to go? It's bound to be a good collection."

Dorothy said: "Thank you, I should like to go—if I shan't be a nuisance to Mrs. Greenley."

"I think you will like her," Mrs. Rachett said. "She is quite a charming person—but a little too interested in clothes to *quite* suit my tastes! She will call for you to-morrow at half-past two."

"Thank you."

Dorothy was not looking forward to the adventure, but to her surprise she took an instant liking to Mrs. Greenley.

She was a tall, slim woman, very well dressed, with golden hair which obviously owed something to art, and a cheery laugh.

"Why, what a mite you are!" she said in amusement. "I could put you in my pocket and run away with you! Are you interested in clothes?"

"I don't know much about them," Dorothy admitted.

Mrs. Greenley laughed. "And you've just come from Paris!" she challenged her. "Well, I'll try not to bore you—come along."

There were some expensive cars drawn up outside the imposing-looking establishment in Mayfair at which they presently stopped.

"Our seats are reserved," Mrs. Greenley said. "I buy most of my clothes from these people, so they look after me."

The big salon was crowded, but an attentive assistant made way for them and escorted them to two seats in the front row.

Mrs. Greenley seemed to know quite a lot of people, and now and then she smiled and bowed to someone, informing Dorothy in an undertone who they were.

"You see that girl opposite? Well, she is here to choose her trousseau—Lorna Dean her name is—and hers will be one of the most important weddings of the season. The fat old thing two seats away is the Honourable Mrs. Lint—she's nice, but she *will* wear clothes which are much too young for her—such a mistake."

Dorothy listened and tried to be interested, but she thought it all seemed a lot of fuss about a very little, though the clothes worn by lovely slender models were certainly most attractive.

"If there is anything you fancy," Mrs. Greenley said, "write the number down and we'll have a look at it afterwards."

"They all look terribly expensive," Dorothy answered. "And you see, I never go anywhere."

Mrs. Greenley glanced down at her, surprised.

"I shall have to take you under my wing," she said kindly.

"Have you any children?" asked Dorothy.

"No—I should have liked a daughter. It would have been such fun buying her pretty clothes."

"Fun for the daughter, too."

A murmur went round the room as a tall, red-haired model entered, wearing a magnificent mink coat.

"Perfect! Wonderful!" Mrs. Greenley said in ecstasy. She turned to Dorothy. "Mink! Probably worth two thousand pounds, at least.

"I like the white ermine one better," Dorothy whispered.

When the show was ended tea was served.

"I never take tea," Mrs. Greenley said. "But you have yours, Dorothy—I just want a word with the buyer—I shan't be long." And she hurried away, leaving Dorothy alone at the tea-table.

Someone spoke beside her.

"Is this chair taken? Or may I have it?"

She looked up quickly into a face which she thought the loveliest she had ever seen.

Brown eyes—as brown as Wilfred's—Titian coloured hair —and a gloriously pale complexion.

For a moment she could only stare in admiration until the girl asked again: "May I have this seat?"

Dorothy came to life then.

"It *is* taken really—but Mrs. Greenley won't be back yet —so please have it—I know she won't mind."

The girl laughed.

"Well, if you are sure! I came late—and I'm rather tired of standing."

"It's so crowded," Dorothy said.

The lovely eyes searched Dorothy's face, half interestedly, half in amusement.

"The clothes are a dream, aren't they?" she said.

"Yes—which did you like best?"

"I liked them all," was the answer. "It's difficult to make a choice."

"I've just come from Paris."

"Have you? So have I!—I only came back two days ago. Do you like Paris?"

"I love it—I was at school there."

"I see." But after that piece of information the girl seemed to lose interest. She took a cigarette from a blue enamelled case and lit it, leaning back in her chair with rather a bored air.

Who was she? Dorothy wondered. Somebody very well known, she was sure—and what lovely shoes she was wearing! Lovely everything if it came to that—a lovely person for whom surely all these smart, expensive clothes were intended!

Across the crowded room she could see Mrs. Greenley in deep conversation with a big woman in a black high-necked frock—the buyer, she supposed, and she wondered whether they were discussing the mink coat.

Two thousand pounds! It seemed a terrible amount of money. Dorothy suddenly realized that her head was aching —owing to the rather stuffy atmosphere, she supposed, and the incessant chatter of voices—and then above the babble one insistent voice made itself heard.

"Pauline! Pauline! ... Are you ready? Because I must go."

Pauline! Dorothy's heart seemed to miss a beat as the girl beside her rose and waved her hand to someone across the room.

"I'm coming."

The enamelled cigarette-case had fallen from her lap to the floor and Dorothy bent hastily to recover it.

"Thank you so much." And a moment later the lovely figure was lost in the crowd.

Pauline! ... *Wilfred's* Pauline? Could it be?

Her heart was thumping with excitement. It was such an uncommon name—and yet there must be more than one Pauline in London!

Mrs. Greenley returned.

"Have you had your tea? Shall we go?"

"I'm quite ready."

"I tried on the mink coat," Mrs. Greenley said as they drove away. "It's a *dream*! But two thousand pounds!" She half sighed before she added: "Perhaps they'll take less, though, of course, the buyer said it was quite impossible!"

"You would look lovely in it."

"*Anyone* would look lovely in it," Mrs. Greenley declared, and she became lost in thought until Dorothy said:

"There was such a beautiful girl—she asked if she might have your chair—I have never seen anyone so beautiful."

"What was she like?" Mrs. Greenley asked disinterestedly, her mind still on the mink coat.

"Dark! Brown eyes and hair like the women in Rossetti's pictures."

"In *whose* pictures?"

"Rossetti's—Titian hair."

"Oh!" Mrs. Greenley said vaguely, and then: "I shall offer eighteen hundred and fifty for the coat. These people are too greedy and expect too high a profit."

Dorothy had no opinion to offer on the subject, and noticing her silence Mrs. Greenley said in concern: "I hope you haven't been bored?"

"Oh no! It was very kind of you to take me—I enjoyed it. I have never seen such lovely clothes."

"We must see each other again," Mrs. Greenley said warmly. "There are many interesting places I can take you to if you care about it"

"Won't you come in?" Dorothy asked a little shyly when they reached home, but Mrs. Greenley refused.

"I won't now—thanks—Give my love to your aunt—Oh, but of course, she's not your aunt, is she? Good-bye—we shall meet again" She was a breezy woman—rather self-centred and yet kindly. "Poor little girl! I expect she's lonely," she thought as she drove away. "I must see what I can do." And then she returned to thinking about the fur coat.

"And how have you enjoyed your afternoon?" Mrs. Rachett inquired. She was lying on her couch in the drawing-room, and she seemed a little disappointed because Mrs. Greenley had not come in.

"It was very interesting," Dorothy told her. "Such lovely clothes! And hundreds of women," she added.

"Naturally," Mrs. Rachett said. She sighed. "I should have enjoyed it myself, but—it was out of the question. Did Mrs. Greenley admire anything in particular?"

"A mink coat."

"She has two fur coats already!" the elder woman objected. "But still, when there is no need to consider expense it is quite easy to have half a dozen."

"Is Mrs. Greenley rich?"

"Her husband is—though I really don't know how he made his money. Some people seem to be able to amass a fortune without the least trouble, whilst others——" She paused, no doubt visualizing her husband hurrying down the road with his little black bag.

The dress show was Dorothy's only excitement until Tuesday evening came, and with it Wilfred Clifton.

A few days previously she had asked Mr. Rachett whether Wilfred had kept his appointment at the office, and had been told "Yes" in a tone of voice not calculated to encourage further questions, and so, although she longed to ask, she knew nothing of the decision that had been made—if any!

"So I suppose my fate still hangs in the balance," she thought with a sigh, as she dressed for dinner with Mr. Guest.

She wanted to wear the dress which Wilfred had admired that night at the Savoy, but Mrs. Rachett said: "No—unless you have no other."

"I'll show you what I have," Dorothy volunteered, and she returned to Mrs. Rachett's bedroom with a simple white dress and a plain blue dress.

Mrs. Rachett voted for the white one.

"She would!" Dorothy sighed as she departed; it was the one she liked least, because she fancied that it made her look even younger and more childish than she was.

But it was her obvious duty to please Mrs. Rachett, so she dutifully tried not to mind.

Wilfred's first words did much to cheer her.

"Like someone from the top of a Christmas tree!" he said, but somehow she fancied that his voice sounded preoccupied, and he was silent for a little as they drove away in the taxi until he asked, almost with an effort, she thought:

"And what have we been doing for the past few days?"

She told him about Mrs. Greenley and the dress show, but somehow she hesitated to mention Pauline.

"Wasn't it rather a bore?" he asked, and Dorothy said no, she found it interesting.

"You see," she explained, "I've never seen one before."

"I envy you," he said dryly. "There are so many things you have never seen before—so many places you have never visited. I suppose there were millions of old dears admiring the clothes."

"Yes—some of the things were lovely." And then again she hesitated with the name Pauline on her lips.

"Where are we going to dinner?" she asked.

He told her. "Guest thought it would interest you—it's the latest and most fashionable haunt of the idle rich."

"Just we three?" she asked, for somehow she was rather dreading a party.

He looked down at her and laughed.

"Just we three," he agreed.

She was silent for a moment before she asked:

"And is my fate all signed and sealed?"

"Your fate?"

"Yes; Mr. Rachett told me you went to the office, but he didn't tell me what happened."

Wilfred made a little grimace.

"Oh, we talked! We talked all round the subject in the way that lawyers do, and after nearly an hour we arrived back at the point from which we started—and then I said good morning—and that was that!"

"So I've got to stay where I am," Dorothy said blankly.

"I'm afraid so," he agreed. "At any rate, for the present. You see, it's a difficult position, Little and Good!"

"Why?"

"Because—well, if you were twenty-one it would be fairly simple—or more so—but as it is——" He stopped, rather helplessly, and after a moment she said:

"Why can't I come with you? When you leave London, I mean!"

"With—*me?*" he echoed blankly, and then he laughed. "My dear child! What in the world should I do with you?"

"I wouldn't be any trouble—I can amuse myself quite easily, and I should love to travel—to see all the places you have seen. . . . Oh, Wilfred, couldn't I?"

It seemed a long time before he answered with unusual gentleness: "It's impossible—For one thing, Mr. Rachett would never consent."

"But if you're my guardian, what does it matter whether Mr. Rachett consents or not? I thought guardians could do as they liked with—with people like me." She paused hopefully, and as he did not reply she said: "Of course, I know you would much rather be rid of me altogether—but——"

Wilfred broke in sharply:

"I've told you before that you are not to say that or even think it! I don't *want* to get rid of you, so put that idea out of your head once and for ever. But—my dear, you must see that it's impossible for me to take you abroad—or anywhere!" He laughed grimly. "A nice scandal there would be!"

"A—*scandal*!" she said blankly.

"Yes, a scandal," he said again, firmly. "I am not Methuselah, remember! Or even a middle-aged, fatherly bachelor—and you are a young and attractive girl—Be sensible, Little and Good!"

"I *am* being sensible," she insisted. "And—and—nobody has ever told me before that I am attractive—and of course you don't mean it."

Wilfred gave a sigh.

"Oh, dear," he said in a long-suffering voice. "Tell her the truth and she doesn't believe you! Tell her a lie and she will swear it's the truth." He glanced down at her. "And I imagined you were so different from all the rest."

"I imagined *you* were, too," she said, and her voice trembled and fell into an unhappy silence.

"And I thought this was to be another pleasant evening," Wilfred complained, and then more seriously: "Don't worry, my child! . . . The right solution will come along sooner or later, and we shall all live happily ever after."

"I shan't be happy—if I have to live alone," she said.

"If you talk in that depressed voice," he insisted cheerily, "I shall set you down here—right in the heart of Piccadilly—and leave you to walk home! . . . *You* won't live alone at least, not for long! . . . Before you know where you are, and before I can warn them off, you'll have half a dozen admirers swarming round you. How does that appeal to you?" he inquired. "Like bees around a honey-pot."

"I don't want half a dozen admirers swarming round," she protested. "I'd much rather have just you."

There was a constrained silence before Wilfred said lightly:

"I thought I was a bad picker myself—but now it seems as though you are even worse!" ... And then more seriously: "Don't put your money on me, Little and Good! I'm not a stayer—if you know what that means!"

"What does it mean?"

"It's a racing term," he explained. "It means a horse which starts off well and then changes its mind and either slacks off or stops altogether."

"You mean—you change *your* mind?"

"Frequently," he insisted breezily. "Ask anyone who knows me well! Ask old Guest! And he will tell you that although the poet says 'Inconstancy, thy name is woman'—*his* version is 'Inconstancy, thy name is Wilfred'." And then, with rather a clumsy attempt to turn the conversation into lighter channels, he asked: "And did you buy any of the beautiful clothes at the dress show?"

She suddenly sat very upright, staring at the many lights ahead, and there was something very deliberate in her voice as she answered:

"No—but I saw someone there—the most beautiful girl I have ever seen."

Wilfred said dryly: "It is not often that one woman admires another. Tell me what she was like."

"She had brown eyes and Titian-coloured hair," she told him slowly, and she turned to look at him. "She sat next to me—and she was beautifully dressed, and someone—another woman who was with her, called her Pauline."

There was the faintest possible pause before Wilfred said casually: "A most romantic name!"

"She was a most romantic person," Dorothy answered. "I think you would have thought so, too."

For a moment there was silence, and when next he spoke it was merely to say: "We are apparently in for a wet night. I hate rain."

And then they were at their destination and Guest was waiting for them just inside the flower-decked porch.

"Jolly nice of you to come!" Willie Guest said as he took her hand. There was something very boyish about him in spite of his somewhat middle-aged portliness.

"It was very kind of you to ask me."

"Hope you'll like this place," he said. "It's the rage at the moment—always packed to the roof—but it will be all right till the theatre crowds come in."

He looked at her admiringly, for Willie Guest liked little women.

"How are you getting along with old Wilfred?" he whispered.

"Very well, thank you."

"He's one of the best," he murmured. "A bit wild, of course, but none the worse for that."

There was a bunch of lilies-of-the-valley lying on the dinner table beside Dorothy's plate, and she picked them up with a little exclamation of surprise and pleasure.

"Are they for me?"

"I thought you would like them," Guest said rather awkwardly.

"Oh, lovely!" she said gratefully. "Thank you so much."

"Our Willie is quite the ladies' man," Wilfred informed her. "Even though so far he has managed to escape being led to the altar!"

"So have you," Dorothy said.

Both men laughed.

"That went home, eh, Wilfred?" Guest chafed him.

"For your insolence," Wilfred replied haughtily, "I shall ask Miss Little for the first dance, and leave you in solitary state at the table. Come along, Dorothy."

But surprisingly she shook her head.

"I don't think I want to dance yet—thank you."

Wilfred stared at her.

"Don't want to? But you're a very good dancer."

Guest chuckled. "Snub number two, my boy!" he said in amusement and he called a waiter. "We'll have dinner now—I ventured to order without asking what you would like," he apologized to Dorothy.

"I don't know anything about food," she told him.

She sat between the two men, and Wilfred half turned in his chair looking away towards the dance-floor where as yet only half a dozen couples were dancing.

Annoyed with him, was she? Little monkey! Oh well, it only proved that no matter how confidently a man might believe that he understood women, he didn't really know the first thing about them! Presently he glanced round at her, wondering whether it was only his imagination that she looked rather pale, and then he was thinking: "Poor kid! It's not much of a life for her!" And the frown vanished from his handsome face and he turned round again, determined to be very nice to her for the rest of the evening. Guest was saying mischievously:

"If you won't dance with the noble Wilfred, I suppose it is useless to hope that you will dance with me?" But to his surprise and to Wilfred's chagrin she rose at once.

"I should like to dance with you."

Wilfred looked after them, puzzled. She was not so simple and unsophisticated as he had imagined evidently, he thought with vague dissatisfaction, and yet—she looked little more than a schoolgirl in her white dress, and with Guest's spray of lilies fastened against her breast she could have been only sixteen or seventeen.

Guest was a rotten dancer, anyway, he remembered with satisfaction—serve her right if he trod on her feet—and then he was laughing at himself.

Absurd to feel annoyed because a slip of a girl had snubbed him! Oh well—there were very few scores which he was unable to settle to his entire satisfaction, sooner or later!

He sipped his wine, conscious of a sudden boredom.

He had done this sort of thing so many hundred times before and it all led nowhere. He had never settled down.

Flowers, pretty women, good music, good food, wine, laughter, empty talk! The frown came back.

Funny that Little and Good should enjoy the things which to him were just a way of killing time. Still, it was her fault that he was in London! But for her he might still have been in Paris.

And then he was remembering what she had said about the girl at the dress show—Pauline. But the Pauline he knew was still in the Paris for which he was suddenly feeling homesick.

And she hadn't written to him since they parted . . . possibly that was why this surprising attack of the blues had so suddenly descended upon him.

He lit a cigarette, but almost immediately it went out and he made no effort to re-light it.

She was an ungrateful little monkey, he thought as his eyes fell again on Dorothy across the floor.

It was only for her sake that he was here to-night—because

62

he wanted her to have as good a time as possible while he was in London! And then he smiled—his odd, crooked smile—as he recalled the words she had spoken in the car.

"Why can't I come with you? When you leave London, I mean!"

An innocent request? Yes, he knew it had been—but such a crazy suggestion. Did she really know what she was saying?

He tried to picture himself with her in Cannes—no doubt she would be perfectly happy, but he . . .

It was not that she would bore him—there was always something refreshing about her—something unexpected—still, he pictured old Rachett's dismay at such a plan . . .

"But my dear Wilfred! Really!"

The music stopped and Guest and Dorothy came back—Willie mopping his face, but Little and Good looking as fresh and unmoved as a flower in the moonlight.

"That was fine!" Guest said with enthusiasm. "But it's thirsty work. Waiter!"

"It's a lovely floor," she said. "Oh, my flowers!" For they had suddenly fallen from their insecure fastening.

Wilfred stooped to recover them for her—one lily-spray had broken from the rest, and he stuck it in his buttonhole.

"To add to the collection?" Guest asked mischievously and Wilfred answered:

"To wear next my heart, naturally."

"Does he talk like that to every girl he knows?" she inquired, and Wilfred grinned.

"To every girl," Guest declared positively. "He is the biggest fraud . . . never believe a word he says."

"I don't," she said calmly.

"Your collar, my poor friend, seems to be in rather a deplorable state," Wilfred remarked sarcastically.

Guest wriggled his neck uncomfortably.

"Collars always collapse on me when I dance," he apologized. "But I brought a supply—I'll go and change."

"His dancing is rather elephantine, don't you think?" Wilfred asked mildly when his friend had gone.

"He doesn't dance so well as you do," she agreed calmly. He shot a suspicious glance at her.

"Is that a compliment? Or do my ears deceive me?" he demanded, and then, as she did not answer, he bent a little towards her. "I'm sorry—if I've done anything to annoy you."

She met his laughing eyes steadily.

"Perhaps I am easily annoyed," she answered. "But then, I told you that I don't always understand you."

"I don't always understand myself," he said in an odd voice.

There was a moment's silence before she said simply:

"I think—don't you sometimes—*pretend*?"

"What do you mean?"

"I mean," she explained hesitatingly, "that sometimes—you're not really so—happy—as you pretend to be—or—or so heartless," she added.

She expected that he would laugh, but instead he said:

"Heartless! . . . those innocent eyes see a great deal further than one would imagine—perhaps too far!" And she answered quietly: "Perhaps I am not such a child as you imagine, Wilfred!"

He was not looking at her now, but she saw his hand which was resting on the table, suddenly clench, though almost immediately he was laughing.

"We are very serious to-night! . . . Why is it, I wonder?"

She shook her head. "I don't know!" and then suddenly she laid her hand on his arm. "Look!" she said breathlessly.

Wilfred glanced up.

"What is it?"

She answered eagerly, her seriousness of a moment ago quite forgotten.

"The girl I told you about!—the one I saw at the dress show —over there!"

But it was Wilfred whom she watched as he half turned to look in the direction she indicated.

She saw the blank amazement which flashed into his eyes— saw him make a half movement as if to rise, as involuntarily a name leapt to his lips—"Pauline!"

So she *was* Wilfred's Pauline! Dorothy was conscious of her quickened heart-beats as she turned her eyes from his face to the radiant figure across the room, for the band had ceased to play and the dance-floor was empty, but at that moment Willie Guest returned—looking slightly self-conscious in a fresh collar, and his stocky form completely shut out the girl upon whom Dorothy was concentrating with passionate eagerness as he said cheerily:

"Well, here I am! Richard's himself again." He beamed down at her. "Will you honour me once more?" he inquired. "Or will it be too much of a penalty?"

Dorothy hesitated, and then suddenly she thought—if we dance Wilfred can go and talk to her, for somehow she knew that it was what he was longing to do, and with a half sigh she rose.

"Frightful mob, eh?" Guest said.

"Yes," Dorothy agreed, but her eyes were turned back towards Wilfred, who had already risen to his feet.

They finished the dance—not altogether with success—and returned to the table, and presently Guest said with a chuckle:

"Hullo! Our Wilfred has found a beauteous dame."

"She's *very* beautiful," Dorothy said wistfully. "Do you know who she is?"

Guest shook his head.

"Never seen her before! ... But she's a good-looker all right."

"I think she's lovely," Dorothy said again.

He glanced at her in amusement.

"Jolly little kid," he thought. "Honest too—no nonsense about her." And then, as unconsciously she sighed, he asked: "Tired?"

"I think I am—a little, and it must be getting late."

"One o'clock," he told her.

Guest glanced across the room to his friend.

"I'll fetch Wilfred, if you like," he said, but she answered quickly:

"Oh no—please don't do that."

There was a short silence until Guest said:

"And so you live with old Rachett?"

"Yes, do you know him?"

"Only slightly—he's a dull old dog, isn't he?"

She hesitated—for somehow the words seemed a little disrespectful.

"He's very kind to me," she said at last.

"I should imagine that everyone is kind to you," Guest answered bluntly. "Ought to be if they're not. Ah! ... here comes the truant."

Wilfred dropped into the chair on the opposite side of the

table, and he frowned when Guest began to sing the chorus of the song which the band was playing.

"But nobody goes through the market-place crying—
    Any broken hearts to mend."

"Call that singing?" he inquired shortly.

Dorothy picked up her handbag.

"I think—if you don't mind—I ought to go home," she said apologetically.

Wilfred roused himself.

"Yes, it's time little girls were in bed," he agreed. "Can we give you a lift?" he asked of his friend, but Guest said no, and that for him the night was still young.

"I'm coming back," he told the waiter.

Dorothy fetched her cloak and rejoined them in the foyer. "Wilfred's gone for the 'bus," Guest said, and then: "I hope you're not too tired?"

She smiled and shook her head.

"Oh no, it's been lovely—thank you so much."

"Nothing to thank me for," he answered.

She glanced back and waved her hand to him as they drove away. "He's nice," she told Wilfred.

"Not a bad old chap," Wilfred agreed, and then they were both silent until she asked shyly:

"Who was the beautiful girl Wilfred?"

"Her name is Pauline Charteris."

"She *was* the one I saw at the dress-show."

"Evidently."

She looked up at him but it was too dark to see his face, and presently she said: "I should like to know her—if you wouldn't mind."

He laughed then. "Why should I mind?" And as she did not answer he said: "I'll introduce you some day."

"Thank you," she answered gravely.

He suddenly covered her hand with his own and pressed it. "You're rather a darling, Little and Good," he said with some emotion, and then hurriedly: "I'm afraid the evening's been rather a wash-out, hasn't it?"

"Oh no," she assured him eagerly. "I enjoyed it very much."

"And am I still in your black books?" he asked.

She was silent for a moment, and then she said:

"I think you might take me with you, that's all—I mean—when you go away—instead of leaving me here."

They were outside the Rachetts' house then, and Wilfred answered shortly as the taxi stopped:

"It's not possible—though I almost wish it was." And without waiting for her to speak he got out and came round to open the door for her.

"Good night," Dorothy said a little constrainedly, and she ran up the steps to the front door.

"Got the key?" he called after her, but she had already fitted it in the lock.

"Yes, thank you—good night," she said again, and was gone.

The following day he sent her the biggest box of chocolates she had ever seen.

"So bad for you," Mrs. Rachett said disapprovingly.

"But I love chocolates," Dorothy protested.

"Young people usually love the things which are bad for them," was Mrs. Rachett's reply.

"Because they are always the nicest things, I suppose," Dorothy answered thoughtfully.

She wrote a little note to Wilfred, thanking him, and saying that she hoped to see him again soon, but the rest of the week went by and he did not come, and the only excitement she had was when Mrs. Greenley took her out to lunch and afterwards to a matinée.

"Did you buy the fur coat?" Dorothy asked interestedly, and Mrs. Greenley laughed.

"Yes, I am afraid I did—very silly of me, of course, but I *adore* mink."

And then she questioned the girl about herself—how long she was staying with the Rachetts? Was she happy? What did she mean to do in the future?

"You ought to be amongst young people," she said in her breezy way. "Why doesn't your guardian do something about it?"

"I don't know."

"I hear he is rather an odd sort of person," Mrs. Greenley said. "What do *you* think about him?"

Dorothy turned her face away.

"I like him," she said with a touch of defiance.

Mrs. Greenley laughed.

"I am told that all women like him," she said dryly. "I have never met him myself, but from all accounts——" And then she stopped, but Dorothy had nothing more to say.

"And how do you spend your evenings?" Mrs. Greenley inquired presently. "It can't be very exciting for you."

"Sometimes I play draughts with Mr. Rachett," Dorothy told her. "But sometimes he's too busy."

"Draughts!" Mrs. Greenley sounded horrified. "What a terrible game! . . . I should be bored to tears."

"It's a shame," she told her husband over the dinner table that night. "I call it cruelty to children to shut the girl up with a middle-aged couple. If I knew her guardian I should give him a good talking to, and tell him exactly what I think."

Mr. Greenley laughed.

"Wait till you meet him!" he warned her.

"Do *you* know him?" she asked interestedly.

"I've met him—he was in Rachett's office one morning when I was there."

"And what is he like?" his wife demanded.

Mr. Greenley shrugged his shoulders.

"Oh—quite a nice young fellow."

"Young!" she said disbelievingly.

"Yes—somewhere in the early thirties, I imagine."

"And Dorothy's *guardian*? I never heard anything so preposterous."

"My dear," her husband answered. "It really is not your concern, or mine—so why worry?" And he very definitely closed the conversation.

But over his own dinner table Mr. Rachett had started on the very same topic.

"No sign of Wilfred," he informed his wife. "I have written to him and telephoned without result—it is really most annoying."

"You speak as if it was something new," she answered. "And you know perfectly well that he has always been the same irresponsible creature. It would not surprise me in the very least to hear that he has left London without a word to any of us."

"Oh *no*!" Dorothy said quickly. "He wouldn't do that."

Mrs. Rachett looked at her coldly.

"I happen to know Wilfred a little better than you know him," she retorted. "And I repeat that it is quite on the cards that he has left London, and that we shall hear no more of him for some time."

"Well, well," her husband said soothingly. "Dorothy is very welcome to stay with us for as long as she pleases—very welcome, my dear," he added, smiling at her across the table, and then as she flushed sensitively he said: "I am afraid we shall not be able to have our usual game to-night—I have important letters to write, but to-morrow perhaps."

He departed to his study as soon as dinner was over and as Mrs. Rachett excused herself on the plea of a nervous headache, Dorothy was left alone.

She tried to read, but the silence of the big drawing room oppressed her, and she put the book aside and wandered over to the window.

Nearly a month now since she had left Paris—and another two months before Cecilie Jepson would return.

She looked out at the gathering darkness and her heart sank at the thought of the unknown future.

Were there other girls in the world in such an unenviable position? With nobody of their own to whom they could turn? Unwanted guests in a strange house? Sudden tears rose to her eyes and she brushed them hastily away.

No use getting miserable. The only thing was to look forward to the time when she would be her own mistress and free to do as she pleased.

Madame Suggia had always said when any of her young ladies were depressed: "Occupy yourself—that is the cure! Idle thoughts are the sad thoughts."

Dorothy sighed and turned from the window to get the draught-board. There was nobody to play with her to-night, but she set the draughts in position and looked down at them disinterestedly, her chin sunk in the palm of her hand.

Perhaps things would be better when Cecilie came to England—or had she a new friend now and forgotten all about the plans they had made together? It was another depressing thought and one less easy to push aside, for she had counted so much on Cecilie although she had only heard from her once since they waved good-bye to each other at the Gare du Nord.

Only once in a whole month! Surely she could have found time to write more often!

Dorothy closed her eyes and tried to imagine that she was back in Paris; tried to hear the noise of the traffic which was somehow quite a different noise to that of the London streets; tried to visualize the little steamboats chugging up and down the Seine, the flower girls at the Madeleine—the tall towers of Notre Dame.

She had been happier then than she was now, for this house seemed oddly unsympathetic and in spite of Mr. Rachett's clumsy attempts to be kind it was impossible not to feel that she was unwanted.

And now Wilfred—whom she had looked upon as a friend— had deserted her too! Perhaps he was spending his time with Pauline, perhaps—as Mrs. Rachett had suggested - he had left London without a word of farewell, unless one counted the big box of chocolates!

Was she really only a child to him? And was that why he had sent her sweets instead of something more grown-up? Somehow she was sure that to Pauline he would send flowers—long-stemmed roses, perhaps, tied with ribbons and packed in an exciting box.

On the opposite side of the room she could see her own reflection in a square mirror—the reflection of a little girl sitting forlornly at a table, with an empty chair facing her, and she thought with a sudden passionate resentment, I wish I wasn't so small—I wish I were tall like Pauline—because if I were, perhaps Wilfred would like me better.

And she so badly wanted someone to like her—someone of her own, to whom she would mean more than all the rest of the world—in whose regard she would come first for ever and ever.

Just *one* person of whom she could be quite sure! Was it *very* much to ask of a world in which other people seemed to have so many friends.

Pauline, of course, never felt lonely, but then she was so beautiful that everyone must want to be with her—to watch her lovely face, and listen to her voice.

Dorothy suddenly remembered the blue enamelled cigarette-case which had fallen from her lap at the dress-show. Had Wilfred given it to her, she wondered? And then suddenly she knew that she was jealous of Pauline—not so much of her beauty but of her power to attract, of her power to attract Wilfred!

She was conscious of the quick thudding of her heart, and of the hot colour beating to her face, so that she put her hands to her cheeks with an odd feeling of shame.

Jealous! ... The door behind her suddenly opened, and she started guiltily and turned her head.

"All alone?" Wilfred asked cheerily.

She tried to smile, but her lips trembled too much, and then as he closed the door behind him and came towards her she suddenly, unexpectedly, started to cry.

He stopped half-way across the room, and there was a painful silence broken only by her stifled sobbing, till at last she stammered in an agony of shame:

"I'm so—so-sorry ... so s-sorry."

And Wilfred answered as he had once before:

"I'm sorry—too, my dear," and without looking at her he took the empty chair on the other side of the little table and absently began to straighten the draughts which had got disarranged, and when her sobbing ceased and she had brushed away the tears he said gently: "*Your* move—if you care to play."

She looked at him pathetically.

"Isn't it—yours?" she asked in a shaken voice.

Wilfred raised his eyes, and it was a moment before he answered: "Yes, it is—but I don't know what move to make. I only wish I did."

She brushed her hand across her eyes and tried to smile.

"I thought you were never coming back," she said. "I thought ... you'd gone away without saying good-bye." And then as he did not speak she asked: "What have you been doing? I expect you've been busy."

"Busy!" he laughed. "Yes, busy racing round London trying to believe that I was enjoying myself. Dancing—eating——" he made a swift gesture of repudiation, and the silence fell in again until once more he said: "Your move, Little and Good."

She made a gallant effort at gaiety.

"I shall beat you," she warned him.

"I am sure you will," he answered sombrely.

Her hand shook a little as she made the first move.

"Mr. Rachett and I always play three games," she said. "He says it's the fairest way."

"The legal mind should know," Wilfred answered dryly. Dorothy won the first game easily, and as she re-set the pieces in place he looked at her searchingly.

Why had she cried like that, he wondered? Because she was unhappy? Lonely?

He glanced round the room with a feeling of distaste, and yet by contrast with the noisy stifling night clubs and ballrooms in which he had spent so many hours during the last week, it gave him a certain sensation of restful homeliness.

Dorothy touched his hand:

"Your move, Wilfred," she said.

He roused himself with an effort.

"And this will be my game," he said briskly, but he lost again.

"You're too clever for me, young lady," he told her, and then abruptly: "By the way, Mrs. Charteris would like you to lunch with her one day."

"*Mrs.* Charteris!" Dorothy said involuntarily. "Oh, is she married?"

His colour rose a little as he answered briefly:

"Yes—she's married. Her husband is in Paris."

"Oh!" said Dorothy.

He began to pile the draughtsmen one on top of the other and she watched vaguely until suddenly—down they all toppled.

"And that's the end of all castles in the air," Wilfred said grimly.

She collected the scattered pieces.

"You didn't build it properly," she told him gently, and she began to build them together again, until they were standing eight high.

"*There!*" she said proudly.

"I told you that you were too clever for me," he reminded her. "Will you have a cigarette?"

"No, thank you."

She glanced towards the mirror on the opposite wall, but now she could no longer see her own reflection for Wilfred's broad shoulders shut it out.

"When are we to lunch with Mrs. Charteris?" she asked.

"She said any day this week would suit her. To-morrow?"

"Yes—if Mrs. Rachett doesn't want me, and I don't suppose she will."

Wilfred blew a cloud of smoke into the air before he said abruptly: "What am I to do with you, Little and Good?"

She bit her lip to steady it before she answered very quietly: "Nothing! . . . I can stay here."

"I know, but"—he took the cigarette from between his lips and stared back at it before he asked with some emotion— "what made you cry—like that?"

She turned her face sharply away.

"I think I was feeling—miserable—but I don't—very often. And—when you came—I was so surprised . . ."

"Did you really believe that I had left London without saying good-bye?"

"Mrs. Rachett said . . . it wouldn't surprise her if you had," she answered hesitatingly.

"Oh, *that* woman!"

Her eyes came back to his face.

"I think she means to be kind," she said simply. "But it can't be very nice for her as she's ill, having me always in the house."

"*Ill!*" he said, and there was a short silence before he went on ruefully: "If I were married it would be easy—you could live with us."

"Could I?—but your wife might not like it," she told him quaintly.

"She wouldn't be asked," he retorted. "However, as I'm *not* married. . . ."

And then Dorothy said something which she would at once have given anything in the world to recall:

"I thought perhaps you liked—Mrs. Charteris. I mean— she's so beautiful—but of course as she is married, it can't be, can it?"

Her eyes were on his face and she saw the hot blood rise slowly to the very roots of his hair before he answered in a queer voice: "And why should—the fact that she is married prevent me from liking her?"

She felt suddenly confused.

"I didn't mean that, at least. ... If she's got a nice husband——"

"He's a brute," Wilfred said sharply, and he pushed back his chair and rose to his feet. "However—that's neither here nor there! The question is—what about you?"

He looked down at her from his great height—at her grave face and serious eyes, and his own softened.

"I can't leave you here," he said.

Her eyes dilated. "Leave me! ... then you *are* going away——"

He shook his head. "No, not yet, anyway—but when I do——" He laid his hand on her shoulder. "I shan't be very happy to know that you are still here, Little and Good—and sometimes perhaps feeling miserable."

She said hopefully: "Perhaps by that time Cecilie will be back—Cecilie is my friend—or she was—when we were both in Paris——" she added a little painfully.

"Was?" he echoed. "Don't you believe that friendships last?"

Dorothy shook her head.

"I'm not sure. You see, she's got a home and a mother and father and lots of friends, but I——" She stopped and he said rather grimly:

"You've got only me."

Her eyes fell as she answered him:

"That would be all right—if I was sure."

"Sure? What do you mean?"

"Sure that I had really got you," she explained simply. "But I know I can't expect it. I'm just nobody—and you must have lots of friends, and it wouldn't be any fun for you, if there was only me."

He moved away and stood with his back to her, staring at a very flattering portrait of Mrs. Rachett which occupied the most prominent place on the mantelshelf, and presently he said abruptly:

"And it wouldn't be any fun for you either, Little and Good —you see, I'm such an unstable sort of fellow—unreliable, as no doubt you have heard from the estimable Rachett. I've got the wanderlust—badly! ... I can't settle anywhere—and it wouldn't be the right sort of life for anyone—much less you."

She looked at him with a faint smile.

"I think that's because you're not really happy," she said with simple wisdom. "I read in a book that people who wander about the world are generally the unhappy ones— trying to get away from unhappiness; do you think that is right?"

Wilfred laughed rather mirthlessly.

"I did not know you were a philosopher, Little and Good," he said.

"I don't think I am," she answered, "and I expect I explain things badly—but there is a little verse I know which does it so beautifully—perhaps you know it?"

"Tell me."

She repeated the lines a little shyly and without looking at him:

> "Then stay at home, my heart, and rest;
> The bird is safest in its nest
> O'er all that flutter their wings and fly
> A hawk is hovering in the sky,
> To stay at home is best."

Her voice died away, and Wilfred said:

"But if one hasn't a home?"

"You could have one if you wanted," she told him. "Men can always have what they want."

"Not always," he said. "Sometimes—even a man wants the things which are beyond his reach."

"Do they?"

He turned round and looked down at her.

"Why is it that you and I are always so serious with one another?" he asked in amusement.

She smiled. "Sometimes we quarrel," she reminded him, and he answered: "But surely that is a serious matter too?"

She began to put the draughts away in their box, and presently Wilfred said: "So to-morrow we go to lunch with Pauline—with Mrs. Charteris." He hesitated. "I hope you will like her, Little and Good."

Dorothy nodded.

"Is she living in a hotel?" she asked.

"No—she has a flat just off Park Lane."

"A beautiful flat, I expect," she said confidently.

"A very expensive flat," he said with a smile. "Her husband is very rich."

"Why don't you like him?" she asked impulsively.

Wilfred shrugged his shoulders.

"Must I like everybody?"

"Oh no, but if you like her——" She stopped, confident that she knew what his answer would be.

"Perhaps that is why."

There was a long silence until she asked slowly:

"Isn't her husband—kind to her?"

"Kind?—I told you that he is a brute—he doesn't know the meaning of the word kindness. If I—if I——" He stopped, controlling his voice with an effort before he said more quietly: "Don't let's talk about him. What about another game before I send you to bed?"

She obediently tipped out the draughts which she had packed neatly away.

"I shall beat you again," she said gaily, but there was a strange feeling around her heart—as if someone had hurt her —was still hurting her.

Wilfred came back to his chair.

"Your move," she said, but this time he did not answer.

They were half-way through the game when Mr. Rachett appeared. "Bless my soul !" he said in amazement. "I didn't know you were here, Wilfred." He glanced at his watch. "Do you know what the time is, Dorothy? It's almost twelve."

"We've nearly finished," she answered.

The old man stood silently by, watching while they played and presently he chuckled.

"She's beaten you, Wilfred!"

"Not for the first time," Wilfred answered.

"And it won't be the last," Mr. Rachett said confidently. "And now, my dear—supposing you run away to bed. I want to talk to Wilfred."

She rose at once and said good night.

"I'll call for you to-morrow," Wilfred reminded her.

"Yes," she answered. "I'll be ready."

"A very nice little girl," Mr. Rachett said when she had gone. "Always the same—and never gives the very slightest trouble to anyone."

"More's the pity perhaps," Wilfred answered.

The old man stared at him.

"And what, may I ask, does that mean?" he inquired.

Wilfred laughed. "Only that it would be better for her if she was more go-ahead—more able to fight for herself."

Mr. Rachett answered with dignity that he considered Dorothy's greatest charm was her simplicity, and he added somewhat to his own surprise, that the man who won her for his wife would be exceedingly fortunate.

"And I am not referring to the question of finance," he said severely. "Although I know that in your estimation, Wilfred, it is a thing of great importance."

"How well you understand me!" Wilfred mocked him.

Mr. Rachett looked a little complacent.

"And now sit down," he invited. "It is not often I get the opportunity to talk to you. As a matter of fact I had made up my mind that you had already left London."

"I intend to go—shortly," Wilfred answered, and he wondered irritably, why the lines which Dorothy had quoted should suddenly come back to him:

> "Then stay at home, my heart, and rest;
>   To stay at home is best. . . ."

CHAPTER FOUR

Pauline's flat was all and more than Dorothy had imagined it would be. Magnificent decoration and upholstery—cunningly concealed lighting—the smartest of furniture, and curled up in a blue-lined basket, a white toy Pekingese who promptly set up a terrific yapping.

Wilfred said: "Shut up, Ming," and pulled its silky ear as Dorothy gasped out:

"Oh, but isn't it lovely! The room and—everything! But of course you've seen it before."

"Often."

Dorothy tiptoed to the window and looked out at a wide-spread view of the park.

"Does she live here always?" she asked.

"She has a house in Paris as well, and a place in Somerset."

The girl sighed.

"In Paris! ... how lovely."

Wilfred was pacing up and down impatiently, and he swung quickly round as the door opened and Pauline came in.

"So here you are!" she said rather unnecessarily. She held out both hands to Dorothy. "I am told we have met before! ... Why, of course—you're the little girl who sat next to me at the dress-show! ... What a strange coincidence! Wilfred made such a mystery about it, and refused to give me any particulars."

She laughed, her lovely eyes on the girl's face. "So you're the little ward! ... I've heard so much about you—'Wilfred's One Good Deed' I christened you long ago! ... and tell me, what do you think of him as a guardian? Does he come up to expectations?"

"I far exceed them," Wilfred answered quickly. "And Dorothy will tell you that I am the world's most perfect guardian."

But she didn't. Instead, she said, "What a beautiful flat you have."

"And how do you like Ming?" Pauline stooped to pick up the little peke clamouring at her feet.

"I think he's lovely," Dorothy said.

"He's perfectly adorable," Pauline declared. "Come along and we'll have lunch," and she led the way across the hall to a dining-room which was furnished in red lacquer with windows hung with Chinese embroideries.

They sat at a round table on which there was a magnificent silver bowl of red roses.

"From Wilfred," Pauline said lightly as Dorothy admired them. "He knows that red roses are my favourite flowers."

"Have you heard from Paris?" Wilfred asked, and Pauline nodded.

"Yes—Bertram is flying over on Saturday." She turned to Dorothy. "My husband is in Paris," she explained, "Wilfred, of course, knows him well. Oh, do have a little wine!" she pleaded as Dorothy shook her head. "It's quite a light wine—and I think you will like it."

"Just a little then, thank you," she answered.

She looked shyly round the room which was so unlike the Rachetts' dining-room—realizing its beauty, and yet wonder-

78

ing how anyone could really feel quite at home in such elegant surroundings, for it looked as if nothing was ever disturbed, as if nobody would dare to move an ornament out of place, or to knock out a pipe in the grate as she had often seen Mr. Rachett do when his wife was not present.

Pauline was the perfect hostess and devoted most of her conversation to Dorothy but once when she appealed to Wilfred about something he answered a little absently and yet as if it was the most natural thing in the world: "Yes, darling."

Pauline flushed faintly, though she laughed.

"Wilfred calls everyone darling," she said lightly. "I do myself—in fact, nowadays darling means nothing at all!" and she laughed again when Dorothy said:

"I always thought it meant everything."

"How sweet!" Pauline murmured, and she touched the girl's hand with a caressing gesture. "She's rather adorable, isn't she, Wilfred?" she appealed. "So unspoiled."

"She is my ward," he answered, "so how could she be less than adorable?"

"Conceited fellow!" Pauline scolded him, and she turned again to Dorothy.

"And what are you going to do, when Wilfred has started off on his travels once more?—or have you managed to reform him and to persuade him to stay at home? He's such a terrible wanderer! . . . one dines with him one night, and the next he is—heaven alone knows where! . . . but of course I'm used to it, and it never surprises me when he suddenly does one of his vanishing tricks."

"You generally know where I have gone," Wilfred said rather shortly.

"Which means," Pauline explained, "that occasionally he sends me a post card from Japan or from some other distant spot. I have quite a collection of them!"

And then suddenly she transferred her attention to Wilfred to speak of some mutual acquaintance, and Dorothy watched her with almost painful interest.

Lovely? Yes—as a Botticelli angel in modern clothes would be lovely! She wore her golden hair in little flat curls across her forehead, and bunched high on her head.

Her dress was of the very simplest, in a midnight shade of

blue—exquisitely cut to show the graceful lines of her slender figure, and she wore no jewellery.

Was she happy, Dorothy wondered? And then was surprised at the sadness of Pauline's eyes when she was not smiling.

Not happy, with so much! ...

Then, what constituted happiness? The girl's eyes turned to Wilfred's face, and she found the answer written there.

To love and to be loved by the one person who mattered.

"A penny for your thoughts, Little and Good," Wilfred said suddenly, and the colour rushed to her face as she answered:

"I was thinking about something you wouldn't understand."

"What impertinence!" he protested, laughing, but Pauline said quickly:

"Dorothy is quite right. I am sure from the expression of her eyes that she has many thoughts which neither you nor I could understand. She doesn't live in our world, Wilfred—you and I said good-bye to youth long, long ago." And then as if regretting her sudden seriousness she laughed and changed the subject.

"You must come and stay with us in the country, mustn't she, Wilfred? We shall go down when my husband arrives. Do you like the country?"

"Better than London," Dorothy answered, and her eyes shone. "I was at school in the country before I went to Paris."

"And you still look just a babe," Pauline declared, and she sighed as she rose from the table. "Coffee in the other room. Bring the cigarettes, Wilfred."

Did she love him, Dorothy asked herself? But of course she must love him—for he was the dearest. ...

"Come and sit beside me," Pauline invited. "Wilfred—your nose is about to be put out of joint very completely, because I feel that Dorothy and I are going to like one another very much indeed! What have you to say to that?"

"That I am wracked with bitterest jealousy," he answered lightly.

"You hear that," Pauline demanded. "But I hope you don't believe a word he says—Wilfred's loves are as the sands of the sea—that's why he's still a bachelor."

She rattled away, talking in the same strain until at last Wilfred declared they must go.

"Yes, I am afraid you must," Pauline agreed. "I have an appointment with my dress designer at half-past three—and you know what a martinet he is! . . ." She took Dorothy's hand. "I am so pleased to have met you," she told her again, and now her voice was very sincere—"I hope we shall be friends."

"I think we shall," Dorothy answered and impulsively she lifted her face and they kissed.

"And you'll come down to Somerset?" Pauline repeated as they parted. "Mind you bring her, Wilfred?" She gave him her hand and Dorothy hurriedly averted her eyes as she saw him raise it to his lips.

And then they were being whirred downwards in the lift.

"Well?" Wilfred asked with a smile.

"She's beautiful," Dorothy answered, and in her heart she added: "I don't wonder you love her." But she didn't say it.

As they drove away she asked:

"But why isn't her husband nice to her? How can he help being nice to her?"

"Wait till you see him," Wilfred answered grimly.

There was a little silence, until Dorothy said: "It was kind of her to ask me to her country house, but I suppose she will forget all about it."

"She won't forget." And then as a quick sigh escaped her he said again: "Another penny for your thoughts!" and this time she told him.

"I was wishing that I was as beautiful as she is."

He glanced down at her.

"Why?"

"Because then—people would love me."

"Don't they love you now?"

"Who?" she asked.

"Well——" but he did not continue, though presently he said: "Don't envy Pauline, there is no need to envy her."

"I think there is," she answered gently, but he did not press for an explanation.

"It's a lovely flat," she said as they turned into the Park. "But somehow . . . I think I would rather have just a little house of my own—with a garden."

"You can have anything you want when you are twenty-one," he reminded her. "Lots of money to spend——"

She frowned above her serious eyes.

"I don't think I want a lot of money," she protested.

"Then you are the first woman who doesn't," he declared. "It's all the majority of them think about—that's why they marry middle-aged brutes."

"You mean—did Pauline marry Mr. Charteris for money?"

"I imagine so."

"Did you know her before she married, Wilfred?"

"No."

Dorothy said quietly:

"I don't think I envy her after all."

He laughed. "It is a woman's privilege to change her mind," he said casually.

"I don't change mine very often."

"I believe you," he agreed. "I am sure you are a very constant little soul."

There was a short silence before she said with a touch of impatience: "I wish you wouldn't always talk to me as if I was still in the nursery."

"Weren't you happy in the nursery?"

"Not very——"

"Nor at school?"

"Not very—the other girls didn't like me very much."

"Nor in Paris?"

"Happier there than anywhere else."

"Which, from the tone of your voice, was not a very great happiness either," he said gently.

"No, it wasn't," she agreed.

"Perhaps it's all to come," he suggested cheerfully. "The little house in the country and the garden—and a knight in shining armour—Is that by any chance your idea of happiness?"

"Is it yours?" she countered.

"Mine?" He shook his head. "I'm content as I am."

She looked away from him across the Park in its spring dress of vivid green.

"What did Mrs. Charteris mean, when she said that you and she had said good-bye to youth? You're not old."

It was a moment before he answered.

"I suppose she meant that we are both sophisticated and grown-up, compared with you."

"And do sophisticated people always pretend?"

"What do you mean?"

"I mean—pretend as you do—that nothing matters, when all the time you know that there are some things which do matter tremendously."

"Would you prefer me to wear my heart on my sleeve for daws to peck at?" he asked frivolously, and then as she did not answer: "You're such a child, Little and Good," he said. "You don't understand."

She laughed uncertainly.

"Then how soon do you think I shall grow up?" she inquired.

"I hope—not for many years—not until you fall in love with the knight in shining armour, and then unless he is a very suitable person, it will be my painful duty to warn him off the course."

"Didn't *you* grow up till you fell in love?"

"I've been in love so many times," he declared flippantly. "Everybody is—only they won't admit it. It's a favourite boast with many people—especially with women—that in all their lives they have only ever cared for one man. Sheer sentimentality, of course." He glanced down at her with a smile. "Don't look so disbelieving—some day you'll realize the truth of my philosophy!—although it may not be until you have had various love affairs yourself, Little and Good."

"No," she said positively. "I won't—ever."

"No?" Wilfred laughed. "Have you made up your mind to die in single blessedness?"

She shook her head.

"But I shall only love one person—all my life."

"A rash statement," he declared breezily. "Some day I shall do myself the pleasure to remind you of it, and to contradict it."

"No," she said again.

Wilfred laughed.

"Obstinate, is she?" he said teasingly, and then as she looked a little hurt he touched her hand in affectionate apology. "Well, whoever the lucky man may be, I envy him," he said.

Her lips moved to say quickly: "You needn't," but she

closed them firmly against the words, and against others which were echoing in her heart: "You needn't—because it's you." She wanted to say it, but she daren't.

Had she always loved him? Right from the very first? This man who treated her as if she were a child? This man who loved Pauline Charteris, a married woman?

The discovery gave her no surprise for it seemed the most natural thing in the whole world that she—who had never had anyone of her own to love, should suddenly love this man; as natural as falling asleep, and as waking to the morning light.

She could think of him as her own now for ever and ever—and the thought brought only happiness.

Wilfred said suddenly: "I am prepared to risk another whole penny to be told what you are thinking about—and that will be threepence I owe you."

Dorothy laughed softly.

"You wouldn't be interested," she told him. "And, anyway, a penny isn't nearly enough."

CHAPTER FIVE

When Dorothy awoke the following morning it was with a strange sense of happiness and peace.

She lay still for a long time with her face turned towards the window, looking at the chinks of sunlight round the edges of the curtains, feeling as though since last night someone had said to her confidently: "It's all right—everything is all right, and you are going to be very happy."

"I know," she answered in her heart, even while she wondered why she should be so sure, for nothing was changed; she was still in the Rachetts' house, she had slept in the same rather ponderously furnished room, and she knew that soon she would get up and go down to breakfast, just like on any other day.

But this morning Dorothy was not depressed at the thought of the same things happening at exactly the same moment every day; she felt rather as she had done years ago at her first boarding school, when, after a week of toothache, she had been taken to the dentist to have the offender removed, and the following morning she had awakened with the delightful knowledge that there could be no more pain. A lovely feeling! though why she should experience it to-day she could not understand, unless. . . . She suddenly closed her eyes to the little chinks of sunlight, remembering that yesterday had given her the greatest emotion of her life—the knowledge that she loved Wilfred Clifton.

It was something so utterly different to anything she had imagined. She had heard other girls talk light-heartedly about falling in love; she had known one who had made a great trouble of it, and who had shed copious tears in private and had lost her appetite and had taken to writing sentimental verse, and Dorothy had thought, well I hope if that is falling in love it will never happen to me, but now it *had* happened, and it was something quite different from anything else in the whole world—a warm, comforting thing to hug to one's heart and to feel glad about.

Dorothy opened her eyes again and smiled at the sunshine which meant the beginning of a new day—the beginning of an entirely new chapter of her life, the happiest she had ever known.

She felt with exhilaration that never again would she be depressed, that henceforth it would be easy to make the best of everything, because of her new and wonderful secret.

She did not even trouble because her love was not returned; it was enough to know that she had given it, that at least she had found someone on whom she could expend the wealth of affection upon which in all her life no demands had ever been made.

She would be so good to him—she would never be hurt or angry again, no matter what he might say or do; she would show him that there was one person in the world in whose eyes he was always right; one person who would stand by him, no matter what happened.

And then she laughed at the thought—picturing her diminutive self as a bodyguard for the man whose six feet something towered above her. He would laugh too, she was sure, if he could know her thoughts, only of course she would never tell him—it would for ever be her own secret.

She was too young and inexperienced to realize that the time must come when even the most selfless love demands a return, and that one day she would be better able to understand poor Jessica's tears. For the moment she was wrapt in a dream of happiness and could find supreme satisfaction in the knowledge that there was someone who meant all the world to her.

She hurried with her bath and her toilet and crept downstairs to find Mr. Rachett standing rather helplessly at the dining-room window.

He turned as she entered:

"Oh, good morning, my dear. I'm afraid Mrs. Rachett—my wife, is not too well this morning."

Dorothy answered, "I'm so sorry. If there is anything I can do . . . ?"

He shook his head.

"The doctor has been, and he says she must be kept perfectly quiet—so if you will remember——" He broke off with a faintly apologetic smile. "But I know you are always as quiet as a little mouse," he said, and then more cheerfully: "Well, we must have breakfast. Will you pour out the coffee?"

He had never asked her to do it before, and she was conscious of a new importance as she carefully filled his cup and passed the sugar basin.

"Are you going to the office?" she asked presently, and Mr. Rachett answered that certainly he was, business must be attended to, but of course, if he was wanted. . . .

He looked so lost and worried that she hastened to reassure him. "I am sure she will be all right, I am sure she will."

He smiled at her across the table.

"You are very kind, Dorothy," he said. "I am glad you are here—you are a comfort to me."

She flushed gratefully at his words, realizing that it was the first time anyone had said they were glad of her presence.

"I'll do everything I can to help," she told him gently.

She followed him to the front door when he left the house. "You haven't got your little bag," she reminded him.

"Dear me!" Mr. Rachett apologized. "It's the first time I have forgotten.

"I'll get it," she said quickly.

He thanked her absently when she came back, but he turned at the gate to smile at her and to raise his hat, and impulsively she blew him a kiss.

"Dear me!" Mr. Rachett thought in perplexity as he hurried down the road, but he was not at all displeased.

She shut the door and went back to the dining-room where Sue, the girl in jeans, was clearing away the breakfast things.

"Is there anything I can do to help?"

Sue looked grateful.

"There's the flowers," she said. "I generally do them myself, but if you wouldn't mind. ..."

"I'd love to do them,' Dorothy answered gladly, and there was a little song in her heart as she busied herself sorting them out and re-filling the vases, for she was of use to someone at last—and Mr. Rachett had told her that she was a comfort to him.

And then suddenly she was thinking of the bowl of red roses which had stood on Pauline's lunch table.

Did Pauline know that red roses meant love? She remembered the look of sadness which she had surprised in Pauline's eyes, and the flippancy of Wilfred's voice which now her awakened love for him told her was only because he too had been unhappy and would not as he had said—wear his heart upon his sleeve!

Would these two ever know the happiness she was sure they desired? She tried to picture Wilfred married to Pauline, but it seemed impossible. Wilfred, who had declared that he was quite happy as he was—as somebody's husband? Somebody *else's* husband her thought had really been, but she bravely ignored it.

He and Pauline would make such a handsome pair, for Pauline was tall for a woman, and would reach to Wilfred's shoulder, whereas she ... "Just as high as my heart".

The words floated into her mind and gave her a strange feeling of pleasure; nice to be just as high as Wilfred's heart!

Sue came into the room.

"You ought to go out this lovely morning," she said reprovingly. "If you've done the flowers——"

"I've just finished."

Sue said. "A lot better than I could do. But a walk before lunch would do you good. It's a smashing day."

"If there's nothing else I can do for you?"

"Nothing, thanks."

The Park would be lovely this morning she thought, so she

walked to the end of the road and took a 'bus to Hyde Park Corner.

Lots of people about—elderly couples on the seats enjoying the warm spring sunshine, cars drawn up against the railings.

"I wish I had a car," she thought suddenly, and then remembered that Wilfred had told her that she would have plenty of money when she came of age. Enough to buy a cottage in the country and everything else she wanted.

But not *every*thing, surely? The tiniest shadow fell across her happiness, and she blinked her eyes quickly to dispel it. Nobody had everything they wanted! Not even the richest people or the most beautiful—like Pauline!

And then suddenly she saw Pauline, sitting alone at the wheel of a stationary car under the trees, with Ming perched perkily beside her. Her first impulse was to run forward but she checked it as the quick thought flashed into her mind—perhaps she is waiting for Wilfred. . . .

She would have turned in the opposite direction, but Pauline suddenly caught sight of her and beckoned.

"All alone?" she asked gaily, as Dorothy went up to her.

Ming immediately began yapping a protest, but finding himself ignored, he calmed down.

"Such a lovely morning," Pauline said. "I adore the sunshine. Where are you going, all by yourself?"

"Only for a walk. Mrs. Rachett is ill—we've had the doctor, and she has to be kept very quiet."

Pauline shivered. "I do hate illness!" she murmured. "I suppose I've never had a day's illness in my life! It must make you very depressed—doesn't it?"

Dorothy shook her head.

"Oh, no. I'm only sorry; but she'll soon be better, I am sure she will."

"Nice to be such an optimist," Pauline smiled, and then her face changed subtly and she bit her lip to steady its sudden trembling before she said lightly:

"All the world and his wife seem to be in the Park this morning! Here comes your devoted guardian."

So she *was* waiting for him!

Dorothy said quickly: "I'll go,"—but she was too late, for Wilfred had already joined them.

"Good morning," he said; he leaned his arm on the door of

the car, but although he looked at Dorothy she felt that it was because he could not for the moment trust himself to meet Pauline's lovely eyes.

"Is this an assignation?" he inquired smiling.

"It's a pure accident," Pauline told him. "We both chose the same spot in which to enjoy the sunshine—and you seem to have had the same idea."

"I must have known I should meet you," he answered lightly, and then again he looked at Dorothy. "And how are we this morning?" he asked.

She smiled up at him. "Very well, thank you."

"She looks radiant," Pauline declared gaily. "I am beginning to think that somebody must have left her a fortune!"

"*Another* fortune," Wilfred corrected dryly.

"Has she one already?" Pauline asked. She touched Dorothy's shoulder. "Lucky you! You'll be able to do everything you want to do—and be quite free as well."

"Her idea of happiness is a cottage in the country," Wilfred said.

Pauline sighed. "And perhaps she is right," she submitted. "I am beginning to think that the happiest people are those who haven't too much of this world's goods."

"Would you like to live in a cottage?" Dorothy asked.

Pauline laughed.

"Sometimes I *think* I should, but then, when autumn comes and foggy days ... ugh!" she shivered.

"But the country is lovely in the autumn," Dorothy reminded her. "Isn't it, Wilfred?" she appealed.

He looked down at her with an amused smile.

"It isn't everyone who likes solitude," he answered, and Dorothy said quickly, "I don't like it either. I hate being by myself."

"Poor wee thing!" Pauline said sympathetically, and Dorothy flushed. "I'm really quite happy," she said earnestly.

"Lucky you!" the elder girl answered, and then nobody spoke for a moment until Dorothy said: "I must go."

"I shall drive you home," Pauline declared. "Wilfred, you get in at the back, and Dorothy can sit beside me—if Ming will allow her to," she added laughing. She picked the little peke up and held him while Dorothy got in, and then she put him down on the girl's lap. "And just behave yourself, sir," she admonished him. Ming cast a suspicious eye upwards and snorted, but seeing there was no help for it, he condescended to settle down.

Pauline cast a smiling glance backwards at Wilfred.

"Can you manage to fold your long legs?" she inquired, for there was not much room at the back of the car, and Wilfred answered:

"I would do far more than endure the tortures of mere cramp for your sake."

"Of course, we ought to have stayed out to lunch," Pauline said as she drove away. "It's a shame to go home on such a glorious morning."

"I must go home. You see, Mrs. Rachett is ill and I might be wanted."

"She's always ill, isn't she?" Wilfred asked indifferently.

"This time she's really ill."

"Oh!" he said apologetically.

"Wilfred is like me," Pauline remarked. "He's never had a day's illness, so he can't sympathize with those who have."

"I've never been ill, either," Dorothy admitted. "Except once—when I had whooping cough, and that was horrid."

"Childish ailments for the children!" Wilfred said banteringly. "When will you grow up, Little and Good, and leave all such things behind?"

She half turned to smile at him. "I *am* grown-up," she said seriously.

Such a lovely smile, Wilfred thought, and although he did not answer he watched her a little sadly while she talked to Pauline.

Totally different, these two girls, and yet—yes, he realized with faint amusement that he loved them both.

Pauline . . . he knew every changing expression of her lovely face so well, and Little and Good . . . a child in spite of her dignified assertion that she was grown-up; a pathetic child in many ways, and back came the old disturbing feeling—it's my fault, but what on earth can I do about it?

"Which way now?" Pauline inquired over her shoulder, and he roused himself to direct her.

"First to the right, round by the island," and then his attention returned to Dorothy.

Not attractive in the way that Pauline was attractive—and

yet ... perhaps a man would find greater happiness with her quiet sincerity than with Pauline's tantalizing allurement.

Wilfred was seldom given to retrospection, but now he was realizing grimly that the three years which had passed since he first met Pauline had never brought him any real happiness.

Excitement, restlessness, uncertainty; moments of bitterness, when he determined not to see her again—even months during which he had neither written nor heard from her, but chance always seemed to bring them together again, and then —the whole miserable business started once more.

Dorothy had said quaintly: "I thought perhaps you liked Mrs. Charteris ... but of course if she's married, it can't be."

Her words had amused him at the time by their simple unsophistication, and yet—probably she was right, for what peace or happiness was there to be found in loving another man's wife?

Once, quite at the beginning of things, he had urged Pauline to ask her husband to set her free, and she had refused because she had dreaded the thought of a scandal. That, he supposed, should have ended the affair, but—well—it had dragged on until he had grown more or less accustomed to their intermittent meetings, and to the long wearisome business of pretended friendship.

Strange that for the first time to-day, he should feel slightly ashamed and irritated.

"*Your* fault, Little and Good," he accused the girl sitting beside Pauline; yes, entirely her fault for being so honest and childlike. To be in her company was like walking away from the glaring lights of a ballroom into the freshness of a spring morning. "My boy, you're getting poetical," he told himself grimly. "And that's a bad sign. Time you were off on your travels again."

"Which house?" Pauline was asking, and Dorothy answered with quick agitation: "The one with the car outside—it must be the doctor's car. Oh, I hope Mrs. Rachett isn't any worse."

Pauline drew to the kerb and stopped.

"I'll come in with you," Wilfred said, and he flung open the door and got out.

Dorothy turned a troubled face to Pauline.

"Good-bye, and thank you," she said hurriedly.

"Good-bye, darling," Pauline answered sympathetically. "I

hope you'll find that everything is all right." But Dorothy was already running up the steps and Wilfred followed quickly.

The front door was open, and Sue stood at the foot of the stairs with tears in her eyes.

"Oh, *Sue*!" Dorothy said agitatedly. "Oh, Sue what is it?" But she knew before she was told, that the illness in which nobody had quite believed had suddenly proved fatal.

Wilfred said presently: "I'll just go and tell Mrs. Charteris. I'll be back in a moment."

And Pauline said at once: "That child can't stay in the house, can she, Wilfred? Ask her to come to me. There's plenty of room, and I should really like to have her."

Wilfred's eyes softened. "It's very good of you, my dear. I'll ring you later, if I may ... I can't leave her just yet."

To his surprise she said a little wistfully:

"You're very fond of her, aren't you, Wilfred?" And then, without waiting for a reply: "Very well—ring me any time. I shall be in all day. And please give her my love and tell her how welcome she will be. Good-bye."

He watched her drive away and then returned to the house.

Dorothy was alone in the drawing-room.

"Mrs. Charteris has gone," he told her. "She sent her love, and asked me to say that she will be pleased if you care to go and stay with her, Little and Good; you can't stay here, of course."

"Can't stay here?" Dorothy echoed. "Why not? I can't leave Mr. Rachett alone; how can I? It's very kind of Pauline but I can't leave Mr. Rachett alone."

"My dear child," Wilfred began, and then stopped to add quietly: "Very well, we'll talk about it later on." But there was a worried look in his eyes so that Dorothy said gently:

"If you think this will make things more difficult for you, it won't, because I shall be quite happy here, and you needn't worry at all." And again she remembered with a sense of gladness that Mr. Rachett had told her that she was a comfort to him.

Sue came to the door.

"Dorothy Mr. Rachett's just come in," she said.

Dorothy said, "Oh, wasn't he here?" and then added quickly: "I'll go to him at once."

Wilfred made a hurried movement as though to prevent her, but she was already at the door.

"In the library," said Sue.

Mr. Rachett was sitting at his writing table looking blankly before him, unconsciously still grasping his little black bag, and the morning sunlight played about his head with its thinning grey hair, and his face with its lined severity.

And Dorothy thought in infinite compassion, that it was almost like looking at a portrait instead of at a real man, for he seemed so still and lifeless, and he did not move as she came towards him.

"Mr. Rachett," she said softly, and she knelt down beside him and gently took the little black bag from his unresisting hand, but still he did not stir or seem to be aware of her presence.

She looked at him with sorrowful eyes, at the stern compression of his mouth, and the little weal over the bridge of his nose made by his spectacles, and then impulsively she leaned up and put her arms round his neck, pressing her soft cheek to his, as if he had been a child whom someone had hurt.

She felt the little shiver which passed through him, and heard a broken sound like a sob before he said in slow bewilderment:

"And now I'm all alone."

The words were so infinitely pathetic that the tears rushed to her eyes as she answered:

"I'll stay with you if you want me—please let me stay."

He raised his hand slowly to her shoulder, and for a moment it rested there, before he said again, brokenly:

"You are a great comfort to me, Dorothy."

"I'll try to be," she whispered back.

Everybody said that it was an impossible arrangement.

"It's not the right thing at all," Mrs. Greenley protested. "A young girl like you, alone with an old man. My dear, you will find it terribly depressing—it must have been bad enough before! But now!" She looked at the girl's quiet face in perplexity. "Come and stay with me—at any rate for the present," she urged. "You will be much happier. I know you mean to be kind, but indeed you will regret it."

"Thank you," Dorothy answered. "But if Mr. Rachett wants me to stay, I shall not leave him."

Whereupon Mrs. Greenley appealed to Wilfred, whose acquaintance she had recently made.

"Such an handsome creature," she informed her husband reluctantly. "But not in the least the type to be anyone's *guardian*! That child Dorothy will be falling in love with him if he's not careful. I shall talk to him very plainly, and tell him it is his duty not to let her stay with Mr. Rachett."

But she did not find Wilfred easy to manage; he listened politely and answered that even he could not order Dorothy to do anything against her will.

"But you are her guardian?" Mrs. Greenley protested. "And she is under age! What are guardians for, if they cannot exercise a little authority?"

One corner of Wilfred's mouth went up slightly higher than the other as if he was politely checking his amusement, as he replied that he really had not considered the question but that he would do so.

"Then I wash my hands of the responsibility," Mrs. Greenley declared, whereupon Wilfred answered diffidently that he was not aware that the responsibility had ever been hers, anyway.

"It is just his artful way of shelving things," Mrs. Greenley told her husband afterwards. "In my opinion the whole thing is a perfect disgrace."

When Wilfred gave an account of the interview to Pauline he was surprised to find that she shared Mrs. Greenley's views.

"I agree with her that it is cruel to leave the girl in that house," she said. "Don't you think so, Wilfred? I know I simply couldn't *bear* it myself—it would be too depressing for words! Do persuade the poor little thing to come to us —we shall go down to Somerset as soon as Bertram arrives —and I think she would be happy there." She sighed as she looked at his obstinate face. "If anyone can persuade her, *you* can," she added.

"There seems to be a sudden great affinity between you and my ward," Wilfred answered, and then perhaps because it was the last thing he intended to say: "Are you trying to make me jealous, Pauline?"

She raised her lovely eyes.

"I think it is I who should be jealous," she said simply, and then as he frowned: "But I'm not, darling! Because surprisingly I am very fond of Dorothy and there are not *many* people I care—much about," she added slowly, but although the words were just a little provocative Wilfred made no reply.

And Pauline thought with a pang—once you would have asked whether I cared much about *you*! and with a rather pathetic gesture she slipped her hand into his.

"You will do your best to persuade her, won't you?" she said again. "I don't know why—but somehow—I shan't feel happy if I know she is alone in that depressing house."

"It's not such a bad house," Wilfred protested slightly to his own amazement, and suddenly he visualized the big drawing-room and Dorothy sitting alone at the table with the draught-board before her.

Pauline gave his hand a little tug.

"Promise?" she urged again, softly.

Wilfred raised her hand to his lips.

"When you look at me like that there is nothing I will not promise," he said, but he spoke absently. . . .

But in his turn Wilfred found Dorothy difficult to persuade.

"I *want* to stay with Mr. Rachett," she said earnestly.

"And if I say that I would rather you did *not* stay?" he asked abruptly. Her colour rose a little as she realized how hard it was to refuse him anything, but she answered gently:

"I shall still stay, though—please don't be angry with me."

Wilfred began to pace up and down the room, and presently he said: "You were not very happy here before Mrs. Rachett died, were you, Little and Good? So won't you be less happy now? The house will be more lonely—nobody at home all day! You must see that it will be more lonely."

"It's different now," she answered. "It's quite different, because then there was nothing for me to do, but now—I know Mr. Rachett wants me to stay—and besides. . . ."

"Besides—what?" he asked.

"It's nice to feel that somebody wants me," she answered, and then as he frowned she went on quietly: "And supposing I don't stay, Wilfred, where can I go afterwards? Because nobody will want me for very long, will they? Not even Pauline?"

He smiled ruefully and came back to where she stood by the window.

"It's a pity you're not ten years older, my child," he said only half seriously, "or that I am not ten years younger."

"Why? she asked.

Wilfred laughed. "I was thinking that then I would marry you and so settle the question of your future once and for all."

He looked down at her questioningly with his crooked smile, but she did not answer, so presently he said with a slight trace of embarrassment: "Well, what about it?"

She raised her eyes to his face with disconcerting suddenness.

"But that *wouldn't* settle the question of my future," she said.

"Why not?"

"Because—you wouldn't be happy—and you would want to go off again—abroad somewhere, and leave me behind." She did not say: "*I* shouldn't be happy either."

Wilfred laughed a little constrainedly.

"You evidently haven't much opinion of me as a possible husband," he said, and she answered: "I don't think you would marry anyone you didn't love."

"It *has* been done," he submitted dryly. "And when you arrive at my mature years of discretion, you will realize that there are so many degrees of 'love' as you call it."

"What do *you* call it?" she asked disconcertingly. Wilfred looked a little taken-aback but he answered bluntly :

"I call it a most overrated emotion. It's a nuisance while it lasts—but thank heavens it doesn't last for ever."

"You don't mean that," she said quickly. "You're just pretending—as you always do when——"

"When—what?" he asked.

"When we talk about anything—serious," she explained.

There was a short silence before he answered with forced flippancy: "You are such a great reader, Little and Good, that you must know the lines—'There are three things a wise man will not trust—The wind, the sunshine of an April day, and a woman's plighted faith'—Author forgotten!"

"What about a man's plighted faith?" she asked.

"Ah!" Wilfred said darkly. "That's an entirely different matter." There was a gleam of mischief in his handsome eyes as they rested on her face. "You're only begging the question, you know," he accused her.

"What question?"

"I remarked—with all humility—that if you were ten years older, or I ten years younger, I might ask you to marry me."

"You didn't say you would 'ask' me to marry you," she corrected him. "You said you *would* marry me, and settle the question of my future that way."

"And you very rudely contradicted me, and said it wouldn't settle it," he reminded her.

She drew a quick breath.

"But I'm not ten years older," she said. "And you're not ten years younger, and you think I'm only a child anyway—don't you?"

Her voice was gently mocking, and Wilfred answered sharply: "If I thought you were only a child I would make you obey me."

A little flush crept into her cheeks.

"You couldn't," she said.

A look of surprising anger came into his eyes.

"Couldn't I?" he answered. "Don't be too sure, my child. And if that's a challenge——" He suddenly took her by the shoulders, turning her round to him. "Now then—I order you —*order* you, to do as I wish and to accept Pauline's invitation. Do you hear?"

"Yes, I hear," she said breathlessly.

Wilfred laughed. "Then that's settled. Will you write to her or shall I tell her?"

Her lips trembled a little as she answered:

"I'm not going—I didn't mean that I was going, even though you—ordered me."

They looked at one another steadily, and her eyes pleaded with the anger in his.

"I'm your guardian," he said shortly, "and you're under age. The law is on my side."

She tried to laugh. "It sounds very grand," she submitted. "But—all the same I shall stay with Mr. Rachett."

He turned sharply away from her and at once she was pleading.

"Oh, Wilfred, don't be angry—but if you were alone and unhappy—I would stay with you too—if you wanted me—but you can't understand because—I don't suppose you've ever been lonely or unhappy, have you?"

He asked dryly: "And would it break your heart if I said yes?"

She looked at him with something of tragedy in her eyes.

"I should be—very sorry," she said at last.

"And if I tell you you will make me—unhappy if you insist upon staying here?" he submitted.

It was a moment before she answered: "That's different! Mr. Rachett only has me, and you—you've got lots of people who would be kind to you—if you wanted them to be."

"I see," he agreed dryly, and then: "Well, then I suppose I must take it that you defy me—and that in spite of all my tears and pleading," his voice was cuttingly ironical, "you intend to go your own way."

"Yes," she agreed. "And, Wilfred—there isn't any need for you to bother about me at all now—because——" she laughed a little uncertainly—"I've settled the question of my own future."

He paced restlessly away from her again before he answered:

"Rachett is an old man, and don't forget, Little and Good, that it is not so very long ago that you wanted me to take you with me when I left London. You seem to have changed your mind very suddenly."

She said slowly: "I can see now that it was a—silly thing to have asked you to do—no wonder you didn't like it." An odd little smile crossed her face. "What a nuisance I should have been, shouldn't I?"

"Would you?" he stopped beside her again. "I'm not so sure about that," he admitted reluctantly. "And though you probably won't believe me, I like being with you—you're—well, like a breath of fresh air—a double brandy—a . . . my eloquence fails me!"

"I like being with you, too," she said simply. "But I expect if we knew we had got to be together for ever—it wouldn't seem quite the same thing." She smiled with great sweetness: "You're not angry with me any more, are you?"

"Angry?" Wilfred held out his hand and she laid hers in it. "Old Rachett is a lucky man," he said.

"I think I'm very fond of him," she answered, and Wilfred repeated:

"Then again, old Rachett is a lucky man." And as she drew her hand shyly away, he suddenly put a hand beneath her chin and tilting her face upwards, bent and lightly kissed her lips.

"You're rather a darling—as I believe I have told you before," he said with deep sincerity.

Dorothy jerked her head sharply away.

"You shouldn't—have done that," she almost sobbed, and before he could stop her she had fled past him and out of the room.

Wilfred stared blankly after her, then he half shrugged his shoulders and groped for his pipe.

Odd little creature, he thought, adorable too—for wanting to stay with a grumpy old beggar like Rachett. It was a good deal more than most girls would have done, Pauline, for instance! he could not picture her alone in this house, sacrificing everything rather than that an old man should feel lonely.

Pauline! . . . a little frown of weariness clouded his brow at the thought of her. Charteris would be home to-morrow —and then—"Time I was off," he told himself philosophically but there was no pain in the thought of leaving Pauline as once there used to be, unless in itself that was a pain?

Wilfred returned the unlit pipe to his pocket as Mr. Rachett came into the room . . .

"I didn't know you were here, Wilfred," he said absently. He glanced round. "Where is Dorothy? I thought——"

"She was here a moment ago, sir," Wilfred answered.

The old man's eyes came back to Wilfred's face.

"Well, and have you persuaded her to leave me?" he asked.

"No, sir."

Mr. Rachett sighed. "It's a difficult question," he said rather helplessly. "And one which I have purposely left to you and to the child herself. If she leaves me—where is she to go? And if she stays—you know as well as I do—that it is not the right environment for any young girl."

He paused, but as Wilfred did not speak he said again: "You do not answer my question, where is she to go if she does not stay with me?"

"I wish I knew," Wilfred answered.

Mr. Rachett shook his head.

"*You* seem to be the only alternative," he said presently. "And that, of course, is quite out of the question, from your point of view at all events."

"Why from my point of view only?" Wilfred asked bluntly.

"Because," the old man explained, "I can imagine that

Dorothy would be quite happy were such an arrangement possible." He smiled thoughtfully. "I must admit, Wilfred, that you have risen a great deal in my estimation because of Dorothy's good opinion of you. She may be only a child, but in many ways she is very wise, very wise indeed—I think highly of her intelligence."

He dropped into an arm-chair and began to polish his spectacles. "I have an idea to propose," he said presently. "Dorothy tells me that Mrs. Charteris has invited her to stay at her house in—Somerset, is it?—and that she has refused—for my sake, or so I imagine—but I am considering the advisability of taking a short holiday myself—probably in Scotland." He looked up at the younger man quizzically. "Do you know, Wilfred, that it is three years since I had a holiday of any sort? and I think—if I decide to take one now—it will give Dorothy—indeed all of us, the time in which to think matters over, to think them over quietly and sensibly."

"I hardly think Dorothy will change her mind," Wilfred said. "She seems very determined."

"That is as it may be," Mr. Rachett agreed. "But it will do her no harm to have a little time in which to further consider the position. Something quite unexpected may happen—I have frequently noticed that when one is most determined about a matter something will happen to alter one's entire outlook and judgment." He replaced his spectacles and carefully folded the silk handkerchief before returning it to his pocket. "Dorothy may even—marry," he added thoughtfully. "She is very young, I know, but—my dear wife was very little older when I married her, and we were very happy together, very happy."

There was a short reminiscent silence before he continued mildly: "And if such a thing should occur, it will rid us both of our responsibility, will it not, Wilfred?"

Wilfred groped for his pipe once more and began to ram the tobacco into the bowl with rather unnecessary force, as he answered:

"She is not your responsibility—though I am profoundly grateful to you for all you have done for her. . . . Will you tell Dorothy yourself—about this proposed holiday?"

The old man nodded.

"It will be three weeks at the most," he said. "Possibly less, but a great deal can happen in three weeks." His keen eyes were on Wilfred's hands. "Don't you find it difficult to smoke a pipe if you ram the tobacco down so tightly?" he inquired, with interest.

Wilfred laughed. "Oh, I don't know——"

Mr. Rachett said presently: "I understand that this Mrs. Charteris is a friend of yours, Wilfred. I have only met her once, but I thought she was a very charming lady. Has she extended the invitation to you, also?"

Wilfred frowned.

"She has—yes—but I may not go—it depends. Why do you ask?"

"I was merely thinking," Mr. Rachett explained, "that it would be more pleasant for Dorothy, if you were there. She is a little reserved with strangers—or so it appears to me."

"She seems to like Pau—Mrs. Charteris," Wilfred said rather shortly.

Mr. Rachett rose from his chair.

"I will speak to Dorothy," he murmured and wandered to the door, turning to ask: "Will you stay and dine, Wilfred?"

"Not to-night, sir, thank you. I have another engagement. I'll just wait to say good-bye to Dorothy."

He smiled as he spoke the name—it seemed so odd and unsuitable. But Dorothy did not come, and at last Wilfred impatiently went in search of Sue.

"Where's Dorothy?" he asked.

"She has a headache and is lying down, so will you please excuse her." She hesitated before she added: "She asked me to give you her love."

"Oh! . . . very well—thanks."

Sent her love, did she? . . . she would, bless her heart!

Wilfred sighed and smiled together as he drove away from the house, remembering how soft and innocent her lips had felt beneath his kiss, and then incongruously telling himself again—"Time I was off on my wanderings."

But the thought brought with it a strange reluctance, and as he drove on it was not Pauline's fair face he could see in the sunlight, but a solitary little figure sitting alone at a table, with the draughtsmen spread out before her.

"*Your* move, Wilfred——" but he could still only give the same worried reply:

"I don't know what move to make! I only wish I did!"

CHAPTER SIX

Dorothy pushed her bedroom window wide, and leaning her elbows on the sill, looked out over the Charteris' lovely garden in Somerset with dreamy eyes.

She had been with them a week—a queer sort of week, she felt, an odd jumble of happiness and vague discomfort, mingled with a surprising longing for Mr. Rachett and for the peaceful monotony of his home. Dull, so she had once considered her life there—which only showed how altogether different things appeared when one viewed them in retrospection.

Distance lends enchantment! It was a very true sentiment, and yet—could one desire more beautiful surroundings than those upon which her eyes now rested?

The Fortress, the house was called, and Dorothy had discovered for herself that the oldest parts of it were medieval and that it was still possible to trace the bed of the moat—long since filled in—which surrounded its walls.

Bertram Charteris had spent a small fortune on renovating the place, and in bringing its interior up-to-date, and although she knew he was enormously proud of his achievement, Dorothy considered that he had utterly spoilt its atmosphere of tradition and antiquity. But the grounds were as perfect as money could make them, although to Dorothy's surprise Pauline showed very little interest in the velvety lawns and rose-beds and the belt of trees which shut out the road.

"We are so seldom here," she said carelessly, "that it seems a colossal waste of money, and I much prefer Town."

And yet Pauline was a very dear person! Dorothy's heart warmed at the thought of her, and once again she told herself a little sadly, no wonder Wilfred loves her.

And then she thought of the man whom Pauline had married, and she frowned.

Bertram Charteris was a thick-set, dominating creature, with sharp eyes and sandy-coloured hair which stood out in odd contrast to his bucolic complexion. He was many years older than his wife, and it had not taken Dorothy long to discover that he treated her as an expensive possession rather than as a human being. He openly criticized her clothes and the way she

102

dressed her hair, and he liked her to wear jewellery, even in the day-time.

"Not very nice," Dorothy thought now, and at once felt a little ashamed, for in his way Charteris was kind to her and had done his best to make her feel at home.

He ate and drank a good deal, and his voice was the voice of a bully, and yet Brandy and Soda, the two spaniels who lived at The Fortress all the year round in the housekeeper's charge, seemed to adore him, and were his constant companions.

"So there must be something good about him," Dorothy thought generously, "because dogs always know." So why wasn't he kinder to Pauline? Not merely kind in the way that means loading a person with expensive gifts, and beautiful clothes, but kind in the way that commands loyalty and affection?

She shrank from the admission that Pauline probably disliked her husband—but it was obvious that she feared him, and that she was an entirely different person when he was present.

Nervous—apologetic—anxious to propitiate him in every possible way, and yet in spite of all this, she stayed with him, although surely, had she wished to go, she could have done so.

Perhaps it was the money and the luxury which made her stay, Dorothy thought, and then she suddenly felt terribly sorry for Pauline, because of the false value she must put on such things; for what did money matter if one was unhappy? And if she cared for Wilfred, how could she allow it to come between them?

Of course it was supposed to be wrong to leave one's husband, or was that an oldfashioned, exploded idea? At any rate, surely it should depend on the husband and the kind of treatment one received from him!

Dorothy was shrewd enough to have discovered that there was a very definite weakness in Pauline's character; she loved ease and comfort, and she hated making an effort about anything; she shrank from anyone who was poor, just as she shrank from the thought of illness and trouble. Only yesterday when they were driving to Minehead and had seen a small boy knocked off his bicycle by another car, Pauline had not wished to stop.

"I can't bear the sight of blood," she said, and she shivered and turned her face away when Dorothy hurriedly opened the door and followed the chauffeur who had already gone to the boy's assistance.

He was not badly hurt, but his machine was damaged, his only means of getting to school, two miles away from his home. Dorothy had gone back to Pauline to borrow the three pounds he told her it would cost, because she had no money with her.

"I haven't any with me either," Pauline answered. "Tell him to give you his address and we will send it. I'll give him the money myself, but for goodness' sake come along, I can't bear to see him crying." So Dorothy had scribbled down the address, and the money had been duly despatched. "We'll send half each," Dorothy insisted, even though she knew it would mean writing to Mr. Rachett for an extra allowance.

And as they drove away, Pauline had asked with a queer note in her voice: "Do you always rush to the rescue of people in trouble?"

She flushed a little. "I try to," she admitted shyly. "Because I always think that it might have been me who wanted help, and how dreadful it would be if nobody came."

Pauline said: "I dare say the boy was to blame—people generally are when things go wrong." And then she laughed and pressed Dorothy's hand as she explained apologetically, "I suppose you think I'm very hard-hearted, but anything sordid makes me feel positively ill."

Dorothy could not quite see in what way the poor boy and his ruined bicycle were sordid, but she did not argue the point, and Pauline deliberately changed the conversation.

"I wonder what she would do if things went wrong with her own life?" Dorothy thought now, with a sense of pity, and she realized that perhaps Pauline's unnatural shrinking from trouble explained why she stayed with Bertram Charteris.

And then she was wondering whether Bertram knew about Wilfred? Knew that he and Pauline loved one another? But surely not, or he would not allow Wilfred to visit the house—and this weekend—yes to-morrow, for to-morrow was Friday—Wilfred was to arrive.

How different people's lives were! And how true it was that very few would willingly change theirs, even if such a thing were possible! Pauline was beautiful—the most beautiful woman Dorothy had ever seen—and The Fortress was surely the most lovely place in England, and yet: "I wouldn't change places with her for anything," she told herself firmly. "Not for anything! At least, only for one thing—to be loved by Wilfred."

And then for an instant she closed her eyes to the sunshine and to the wide-spread garden, and conjured his face—his oddly attractive, crooked smile—brown skin—broad shoulders —the sound of his laugh, the sarcastic tone of his voice when he was saying something he did not really mean. "Pretending" as she called it, and, this last of all—the touch of his lips on hers when he had kissed her.

She knew it was only a kiss which he might have given to a child, and yet . . . it had gone right down to her heart and had left something there which could never be erased.

"I shall always love you," she told him now with proud humility. "Whatever you do—even if you go away and I never see you again, I shall always love you."

And then that thought brought one of Cecilie—Cecilie who had written to her at last to say that she was home—that her time in Paris had been cut short by her father's illness, and that she was not to return.

"I know I should have written to you before," she apologized, "but life has been such a hectic rush, and so much seems to have happened. Father is quite well again, but he was dreadfully ill, and now I have something to tell you which is more important than anything else—I am engaged to be married—to the Lawrence Browning I told you about. I'm terribly happy, Dorothy, and I'm dying for you to meet him. Let me know how soon you can come and stay with me, and I'll fix it up."

Dorothy had answered the letter by return to say how glad she was to hear of Cecilie's engagement, although all the time she realized that it probably meant the end of their close friendship.

Cecilie had talked a great deal about this Lawrence, who was a kind of second-cousin, but she had always declared that they were only good friends and that she was not in the very least in love with him.

Dorothy had never quite believed her, although she had

hoped it was the truth, for surely love-affairs separated even the closest of friends, and made all the difference.

Oh well, she was glad Cecilie was so happy—lucky Cecilie, to have got the man she wanted. . . .

She turned from the window as someone tapped on the door.

"Are you there, Dorothy?" Pauline asked.

"Yes—come in, please," and then she gave a little cry of distress as she saw the tears on Pauline's lovely face.

"Oh, what is the matter?" she cried and she ran across the room and took her in her arms. "Oh, Pauline, what is the matter?"

"Nothing," Pauline answered in a muffled voice. "I'm just miserable, that's all . . . I am sometimes—and so I thought—well, it's nice to be with somebody kind when you're unhappy."

Dorothy thought suddenly of the boy with the smashed bicycle—perhaps that was how he had felt too!

Pauline gently disengaged herself from Dorothy's arms and dropped into a chair, carefully wiping her tears away.

"Bertram hates me to cry," she said pathetically.

"But what is the matter, and why are you miserable?" Dorothy asked gently. "You ought to be so happy, you've got everything in the world—you ought to be so happy."

"*Everything!*" Pauline echoed. She laughed mirthlessly, and there was a short silence before, very determinedly, she wiped away the last tear and tried to smile.

"There! . . . I'm all right now—I've been silly—but it's all over now. . . ." She touched Dorothy's hand. "I'm sorry I worried you—please forget all about it."

Dorothy watched her with sympathetic eyes, thinking that even tears could not spoil Pauline's beauty. "Not like me!" she thought ruefully, "I look a sight when I've been crying."

Pauline rose and walked over to the window.

"By the way," she said presently, in a voice which tried hard to be matter-of-fact. "I heard from your guardian this morning. He may not come to-morrow after all."

"Not come!" Dorothy's voice was blank with disappointment.

"No," Pauline laughed. "He doesn't say why—I expect it's someone attractive—as usual."

Dorothy felt that she must protest.

"Wilfred isn't like that," she said quickly. "At least—I'm sure that's not why he isn't coming."

"You don't know him as well as I do," Pauline answered, and then she laughed again. "What a catty speech, isn't it? But I don't mean to be catty. What are you doing up here all by yourself?" she asked with an obvious effort to change the conversation. "You ought to be out in the sunshine."

"I was looking at the garden, and—thinking."

"Funny child." Pauline crossed the room to look at herself in the mirror, and suddenly she said: "I hope you'll never marry, unless you're quite sure that it's a man you love—someone you could never be happy without——" Her voice quivered, but was instantly controlled. "There!" she said with forced gaiety. "Now I've done being miserable, and it shan't happen again. What would you like to do—go somewhere in the car?"

"Would you like to go?"

Pauline shook her head.

"Not particularly," she admitted. "You go twenty miles and have to come back again—it doesn't amuse me."

There was a little silence before Dorothy asked:

"What *does* amuse you, Pauline, when are you happiest? —really happy?"

Pauline's hand fell from the hair which she had been so carefully rearranging, and there was something of tragedy in her voice as she answered: "I—don't know." And then after a moment she hurried on: "I don't think I'm one of the people who are meant to be happy—though I always seem to be trying! ... *Always* trying, but it never comes off!" Through the mirror the two girls looked at one another silently, and then Pauline said: "You've got such honest eyes, even Bertram said that about you, and I know just what you're thinking— you're wondering why I ever married Bertram, aren't you?"

"Yes," Dorothy admitted.

Pauline sighed. "I'll tell you, if it won't be boring—I've such a horror of boring people. You see, I'd never had any money —my people were poor—and I hate poverty—I loathe what people call making do on nothing. I was only nineteen when I met Bertram—just your age, isn't it? And I was engaged to another man. ..." She stopped and a little frown crossed her face, as if with difficulty she was trying to visualize and recapture the memory of that other man, and presently she went on: "He hadn't any money either—if I'd married him it would have meant just going on in the same old way—making do on nothing, so when Bertram asked me to marry him, I broke my engagement and said yes."

"And what did—the other man say?" Dorothy asked gently.

Pauline drew her slim shoulders together with a little shiver.

"He was terribly upset, of course, I never heard a man say such bitter things. But he didn't try to persuade me—not to marry Bertram, I mean—he just said ... that he hoped I should be as—wretched—as I had made him!"

"Oh, but that was cruel!"

Pauline smiled faintly. "Perhaps," she agreed. "But you see, he loved me very dearly."

"And—did you love him, too?"

"Not as he wanted me to—I was fond of him, but ... I never loved him as I—*could* love—someone!"

She picked up a little trinket from the dressing table and looked at it vaguely, then she laughed.

"Well, as your estimable guardian says, it's only for the duration, and nothing lasts for ever, so why worry?" Her voice was harshly flippant.

"But that's not true," Dorothy urged. "There are some things which last for ever—one thing, anyway."

"Love?" Pauline queried. "True love?"

Dorothy nodded. The elder girl turned round to look at her.

"How do you know?" she asked curiously. "You're such a child—you've never been in love. Besides, it doesn't last—*I* know that!"

They were both silent until Pauline said sceptically:

"And—when it's all over, and you—die?"

"I don't think even dying could make you forget," Dorothy answered. Then she said:

"And what became of him—of the other man?"

Pauline put the little trinket down.

"He died," she said, "in a stupid motor accident. At least, people said it was an accident, but sometimes—I wonder! ... You see, it happened on my wedding day—I read about it in the paper—when I was on my honeymoon."

Dorothy said: "I think it *was* an accident—because if he loved you, he couldn't have been so cruel as to—as to——"

108

She stopped and Pauline said enviously:

"It must be nice to think so well of people as you do! You can always find an excuse for everyone! No wonder Wilfred calls you Little and Good!"

She wandered back to the window again, and suddenly she said: "There's Bertram! I think we had better go down or he will wonder where we are." She took Dorothy's hand and drew her to the door. "And what does little Wise-Acre think of my husband?" she asked gaily.

"He's kind to me," Dorothy answered shyly. "And Brandy and Soda love him, don't they?"

Pauline laughed. "When I want a reference I shall certainly come to you," she said.

"And you'll get the very best, ever!"

"So there is a doubt about Clifton honouring us with his company this weekend," Bertram Charteris said as they joined him in the garden. He looked at Dorothy. "Is he a particular favourite of yours?" he inquired.

She met his keen eyes smilingly.

"He's my guardian, so of course I like him."

Mr. Charteris grunted. "I can't see the force of that argument," he protested in his blunt way. "You'll be telling me next that all women must like the man they happen to have married, because they are their husbands."

"I am sure they do, if they're nice men."

"And if they are nice women," he added.

Her colour rose a little, and seeing it Pauline pressed her hand warningly, but her husband said at once:

"Don't prompt the child, my dear. I find her honesty most refreshing in a world of arch-humbugs." And again he looked at Dorothy. "And what is your candid opinion of my charming wife?" he asked, and the girl's eyes glowed as she answered unhesitatingly:

"I think she's great—sweet."

Mr. Charteris said: "Spoken as the perfect guest!" and whistling the dogs, who as usual were at his heels, he abruptly walked away.

"Doesn't he like Wilfred?" Dorothy asked when he had gone.

"Does he like anyone?" Pauline answered wearily, and then impulsively she added: "I am afraid Wilfred doesn't like him."

"I know, he told me," Dorothy said thoughtlessly, and hastened to add: "But I shouldn't have said that. I'm sorry."

There was a short silence before Pauline spoke again and then it was to say: "Wilfred tells you many things, I suppose." Dorothy shook her head.

"I don't see him very often, and when I do we generally seem to talk about what is to become of me."

"Poor darling!" Pauline said. "And what *is* to become of you?"

Dorothy's eyes brightened. "It's all right now," she explained cheerfully. "I'm going to stay and look after Mr. Rachett."

"But not for *ever*!" Pauline protested. "You're such a child —and later on—when you have your own money, there are so many things you ought to do!"

"What things?"

"Well! ... mix in society—make friends—go to theatres— go abroad—have a good time——" Pauline explained.

Dorothy puckered her brows.

"I'm not sure that it would be a good time," she apologized. "Not for me, I mean—you see ... I'm not very good with strangers—and they don't like me much. I've only had one real friend in my life, and she's engaged to be married now —so I don't suppose we shall see much of one another any more——" she sighed.

"Don't you count me as a friend?" Pauline asked reproachfully.

"Of course!" Dorothy answered warmly. "But—your life is so different from mine, and so I think it's lovely of you to have asked me to stay here with you—but afterwards——" she stopped.

"Afterwards?" Pauline queried, "Does that mean that you intend to cut me out of your life once you have left The Fortress?"

"You know it doesn't," Dorothy assured her. "Only—in London you won't have time for me—and I expect I shall be busy too. You see, I'm going to ask Mr. Rachett to let me do all the housekeeping and look after him."

"And—can you?" Pauline asked quizzically.

"I can try."

The telephone bell on the terrace rang, and Pauline went to answer it.

"It's for you, Dorothy," she said.

Dorothy's eyes opened wide. *"Me?"* she said disbelievingly.

She was a little breathless by the time she reached the phone. "Yes?" she said faintly.

"Is that you, Little and Good?" said Wilfred, far away.

"Yes—I was in the garden."

"How are you? Quite happy?"

"Oh yes, thank you."

She waited, and presently he said: "It's about my coming down. I had practically decided not to come this weekend, but I've changed my mind! At least, I *will* change my mind if you feel you can bear to see me."

She said delightedly: "Oh, Wilfred, of course!" And then more soberly: "But I'd better ask Pauline."

She heard him laugh. "You needn't," he said carelessly. "Just tell her that ... my other plans have fallen through, and that I shall be arriving for lunch tomorrow."

"Yes."

"You don't sound exactly overjoyed at the prospect of a visit from your devoted guardian!" he protested.

"Oh, but I am! ... Of course I am," she answered eagerly.

"And everything in the garden is entirely lovely?" he asked.

"Lovely," she agreed.

"Have you heard from old Rachett?"

"Only once—to give me his address. He's in Scotland."

"All amongst the bonny heather!" Wilfred said flippantly. "I can't exactly picture him in a kilt and sporran, can you?"

She laughed. "You are *funny*," she told him. "Why should he wear a kilt?"

Wilfred laughed too as he answered: "I haven't the slightest idea." There was a little pause before he asked: "Anything more to tell me?"

"I haven't told you anything, yet, have I?" she queried uncertainly, not quite understanding.

"Not yet——" he answered, and then: "Am I still first favourite, Little and Good?"

"First favourite?" she echoed.

"With you," he sounded quite serious.

The warm colour beat into her face, and it was a moment before she answered gaily: "I'll tell you when you come."

"Tell me *now*," he said.

She laughed. "No, I'll tell you when you come, in case you *don't* come," she said mischievously. And then quite suddenly she said: "Good-bye," and hung up the receiver. There! He had gone!

Lovely to have heard his voice, she thought happily as she ran across the garden to find Pauline; she could picture just how he had looked—the laughter in his eyes—the sarcastic twist of his lips—but she did not know that her own eyes were radiant as she joined Pauline.

"He's coming, after all!" she said joyously. "He says his other arrangements have fallen through and that he'd like to come. Wilfred, I mean—he wants to come to lunch tomorrow."

Pauline turned her head away.

"I think he might have spoken to me," she said, and then she laughed. "No, I don't mean that—how is he? Quite well and happy?"

"I think so." Dorothy looked at the elder girl and the gladness faded from her eyes as she said: "*I* think he ought to have spoken to you, too!"

"Nonsense!" Pauline declared. "Why should he? You're more to him than I am," she added deliberately.

And suddenly Dorothy was thinking pityingly: "But surely you're not—how *can* you be—even the tiniest bit jealous of me?" and she said, trying to speak cheerfully: "Wilfred thinks I'm just a schoolgirl—but I expect you saw that the day we lunched with you. I try to tell him that I'm not, and that I'm quite grown-up, but he doesn't take any notice. I suppose it's because I'm so small! And of course he's much older than I am."

Pauline said with rather forced humour: "And do you look upon him as quite a middle-aged old gentleman?"

Dorothy laughed. "Sometimes perhaps I do—when he tries to be very severe and to order me about—but at other times when he's funny—he seems—quite young."

Pauline said gently: "I expect it is you who make him feel young——" And she remembered the day when Wilfred had tried to persuade her to tell her husband that they loved one another.

"It's impossible to go on like this," he had said angrily. "I hate this—pretence—this hole-in-the-corner business. Let's be honest—as far as we can."

112

But she had refused, and Wilfred did not know how many times since she had regretted that refusal.

And yet—were he to ask her again? I suppose I should still refuse, she admitted with a sigh, I'm a coward—I can't face it, even with him! But Wilfred had never asked her again —had never been quite the same to her since, although until this moment she had not fully realized it. Wherein did the difference lie? He was always charming when they were to-gether—courteous, and tender, and yet she knew now there was something missing—something, a very indefinite some-thing upon which it was impossible to lay one's finger, and that only added to its certainty.

Dorothy slipped a hand through her arm.

"What are you thinking about?" she asked.

Pauline gave herself a little shake.

"Nothing in particular—isn't it lunch time? I'm dreadfully hungry. . . ."

Wilfred arrived the following morning in what he described as a blaze of glory and with a fanfare of trumpets, although the only sound which broke the silence as he swept round the drive was the horn of his own car upon which he kept his finger in order to announce his presence.

Dorothy who had been trying not to look out of the window too often, heard the ear-splitting sound and dashed to the front door.

Pauline was not yet up—she had told Dorothy that she was in a lazy mood and would be down to lunch, but the girl could not know that she was watching from her bedroom window with strained, pathetic eyes.

She saw the big car turn with a dangerous sweep round the spreading cedar which stood in the centre of the drive, and heard its door bang as Wilfred descended—heard his voice too as Dorothy rushed to greet him.

"Hullo! Little and Good. Top of the morning to you!" And he was up the steps which led to the front door before she could get down them, and had seized both her hands.

"I believe you've grown!" he said comically.

Dorothy laughed as she looked up into his face.

"I wish I had," she said ruefully, and then: "It is nice to see you again."

"Again!" he echoed. "Anyone would think that a week is eternity."

"It's seemed a long time," she admitted. "But it's been lovely here. This is a wonderful place, isn't it?"

"Um," Wilfred said absently; he followed her into the morning room. "Where's everybody?" he asked.

"Pauline isn't up yet," she told him, because she knew it was Pauline he meant. "She said she was lazy and that she would be down to lunch."

"How the poor live!" he remarked ironically, and then: "And Charteris?"

"He's out somewhere—with the dogs. I'm sorry," she apologized.

"Sorry?" he echoed, smiling.

"That there's only me," she explained.

"Only you!" Wilfred laughed. "It is you I came to see." She did not believe him and she laughed.

"Pauline said I was to give you a cocktail," she told him. "I know where they are—but perhaps you do too?"

"I don't want a cocktail, thanks." He caught her hand as she would have passed him. "Don't go—I want to talk to you."

They both heard Pauline's voice outside at that moment and Dorothy dragged her hand from his.

"Pauline!" she whispered, and then wondered why she had not spoken the name in her usual voice instead of making it seem like a secret. Pauline stood in the doorway for a moment, perhaps conscious of the picture she made in her smart blue slacks and high heeled sandal shoes. Her hair was beautifully dressed in its usual flat curls, and she wore a diamond brooch at her breast. Dorothy drew back a little, her eyes on Wilfred's face and she thought his expression was rather set as he crossed the room to Pauline.

"A sight to gladden a weary man's eyes," he said lightly, and Dorothy thought quickly—he's pretending again, and then because she was a little ashamed of such a thought she slipped out of the room, closing the door behind her.

"So you decided to honour us after all," Pauline said gaily. "Dorothy is delighted."

"No more than I," he answered, and then—and the words somehow seemed a little formal: "You are looking as charming as ever, Pauline."

"Why not?" she said. "*You* are here!"

There was the very slightest pause, during which it seemed as if she waited for him to speak, but as he did not she went on lightly: "Hasn't Dorothy given you a drink? I am sure after such a long drive you are dying for one. What time did you leave London?"

"With the lark—to be romantic—at half-past seven."

"Half-past seven! I was still asleep."

"So I imagine, were all good people," Wilfred said.

She looked at him quickly and away again.

"How long have you been a self-confessed sinner?" she demanded.

Wilfred shrugged his shoulders.

"All my life—as you should know."

There was a moment of silence before she asked: "And why should I know?"

"Don't you know most things—about me?" he answered.

Pauline sighed. "A week ago I should have said yes," she told him. "But now——" And then impulsively she turned to him and slipped her hand into his. "Do you still love me, Wilfred?" she asked, softly. "Really love me?"

Wilfred's grave eyes rested on her lovely face, as he quoted half mockingly:

> "How many times do I love thee, again?
> Tell me how many beads there are
> In a silver chain. . . ."

and then abruptly he drew his hand from hers. "I'm going away," he said shortly, "Moving on."

"Oh, Wilfred!"

He walked over to the window and stood with his back to her. "I'm sick to death of London—sick of everything," he said abruptly. "That's why I—decided not to come to-day— and why I changed my mind, and came, after all . . .!"

"Just to—say good-bye," she whispered. "Good-bye— again?"

Her voice was so pathetic that as Wilfred turned he felt slightly ashamed.

"I can't go on, Pauline," he said. "All this—leads no-where—— We must go our separate ways and make the best of it. The ways—*you* chose for us both."

She met his eyes steadily.

"Does that mean I am not to be allowed a second choice?" she asked slowly. "Does that mean that because I once made a mistake——"

He broke in hurriedly. "You were right, Pauline—at the time I couldn't see it, but now——"

Pauline said faintly: "You mean—you don't love me any more? . . . Oh, Wilfred. . . ." Her face was a tragedy in its sudden realization and pain, and then as there was a heavy footstep in the hall, she recovered her masklike indifference and moved slowly over to the cocktail cabinet in which her husband took such an inordinate pride.

"Made to my own design," he liked to tell people. "Have a look at it! . . . Everything you can want. I'll make a bet you can't ask for a thing that isn't there."

"So you've turned up, like the proverbial bad penny," Charteris said, as he entered the room. "Well, and how are you? Bless my soul, Pauline, what have you done now?" For Pauline had dropped a glass and it lay on the polished floor in pieces.

"I'm so sorry," she faltered. "I don't know how it happened. It was very clumsy of me. Oh dear!"

"*Very* clumsy," her husband agreed shortly. "Why didn't you leave it for me to do?" He stalked across to her. "Cut yourself?" he demanded bluntly. "Um—not much damage— go and wash it and tie it up.'

Pauline escaped gladly, and on the landing upstairs she met Dorothy.

"I've cut myself," she explained. "I was mixing a cocktail and I dropped the glass. . . ."

"Let me see to it for you," Dorothy said quickly; she followed Pauline to her room, and gently bathed her finger and tied it up with a little strip of lint.

"It's not very bad," she said encouragingly.

"No—it's not very bad," Pauline repeated, but there was a far deeper wound in her heart, and presently she said—trying to speak in a matter-of-fact voice: "Wilfred tells me that he is off on his travels again—quite soon."

Dorothy was drying her wet fingers, and it was a moment before she said: "Is he? When?"

"Soon, he said." Pauline looked at her pale reflection in the mirror. "We shall miss him—shan't we?"

"Yes."

There was a momentary silence before Pauline said slowly:

"Perhaps if we ask him to stay—or if *you* ask him! You are his responsibility, aren't you? I mean you have the right to—want him at home."

Dorothy did not answer, although in her heart she was saying:

"*You* have a better right—because he loves you."

"Well," Pauline said brightly, "we must go down—lunch will be ready." And together they descended the stairs.

Wilfred and Bertram Charteris were talking together in the polite manner in which men will talk when they are not really on friendly terms, and they both looked relieved when the two girls appeared.

"Clifton is just saying," Bertram announced, "that he is contemplating another world tour!" He looked at Dorothy. "What do you say to that?" he inquired.

"I think he is very lucky to be able to go," she answered.

"I tell him he should take you with him," Charteris said jocularly. "Show you something of the world! ... Travel is a fine education for young people. Why don't you persuade him, eh?"

"Perhaps I should not require much persuasion," Wilfred remarked, and as Dorothy saw Pauline bite her lip and turn away she said quickly: "*I'm* the one who would need persuading!—but it wouldn't be any use. I'd rather stay at home."

Wilfred frowned. "Oh dear, you girls!" he said. "Only the other day you said you would like to come."

Dorothy smiled a little constrainedly.

"I know, but you said it was impossible to take me," she reminded him, "and so, like a dutiful child, I changed my mind."

Dorothy took Pauline's arm as they crossed the hall followed by the two men, and went into lunch.

"And what do you propose to do this afternoon?" Bertram asked when they were seated; he looked at his wife. "You're very subdued, my dear—have you a headache?"

She gave a little start. "Oh no, no—thank you. I was just listening to the conversation."

"A remarkable feat!" her husband said dryly. "Seeing that nobody has spoken a word since we sat down."

Dorothy rushed into the breach.

"Let's go for a long walk," she suggested. "It's a lovely afternoon—let's all go for a long walk."

"Thanks very much," Charteris said dryly, "but I have other things to do. I'm going to ride round the estate and see what that lazy Royston has been up to while I've been away. From what I can see of it he's been taking a rest-cure."

Pauline said timidly that she thought Royston was quite a hard working man, and that as far as she could see everything looked all right. "But then, of course, I'm no judge," she added apologetically.

"No judge at all, my dear, except of clothes," her husband agreed affably; he looked at Wilfred: "May I leave the ladies in your charge until dinner time?" he inquired.

"I shall be delighted," Wilfred answered mechanically.

But when lunch was over and Bertram had whistled the dogs and had departed for the stables, Pauline said:

"If nobody minds, I think I will stay at home this afternoon and rest. I *am* a little tired! and we have people coming to dinner, so——" her eyes turned to Wilfred as if hoping he would attempt to dissuade her, but he only said:

"You were never fond of walking, were you?"

Dorothy flung him a glance which she did not know was reproachful as she urged: "Oh, do come, Pauline—it would do you good, and you haven't been out to-day." But Pauline would not change her mind.

"I'm going to be thoroughly lazy, and lie down," she declared. "And besides— you know I haven't a pair of country shoes to my name." She laughed and turned to the door. "Good-bye, children—enjoy yourselves." And she had gone.

"Why didn't you ask her to come?" Dorothy demanded as they left the house. "It's a shame to leave her alone, and besides. . . ." she stopped and he asked casually:

"Besides what?"

"I'm afraid she thought we didn't want her."

Wilfred laughed. "And did we?" he submitted. "You know the old saying two is company."

The girl flushed. "Of course we want her! I do anyway— I've a great mind to go back and. . . ."

Wilfred took her hand.

"You'll do as you're told—for once," he said firmly, and with a little sigh she gave way.

"I think it's unkind, all the same," she insisted, and she drew her hand from his and walked a pace away from him.

"Well, it's a lovely afternoon, anyway," she said with an effort.

"A lovely afternoon for a heart to heart talk," he agreed impassively.

She laughed.

"That sounds dramatic!" she said lightly. "Am I in for another lecture?"

"No, I merely wish to inquire—for the last time—whether you have definitely made up your mind to stay with old Rachett."

She flung him a quick glance.

"Must we have all that over again? I told you I had made up my mind—ages ago."

"A week, to be exact," he corrected. "And I had hoped—even in seven days, that you would have *changed* your mind."

"I never change my mind."

"Indeed!" his voice was sarcastic. "And yet a moment ago you told Charteris that you had no wish to go abroad with me—if that is not changing your mind, what is, I should like to know?"

She laughed. "Oh, but that's something quite different," she said. "And anyway, I knew you were only joking when you said you might not need much persuasion to take me."

Wilfred said dryly: "You seem to have a perfect understanding of my somewhat complex nature, Miss Little, and therefore argument appears to be useless."

He pushed open the gate which led to the road and stood aside for her to pass, and she asked as they walked on:

"How long will you be away?"

"Will it please you if I say—for ever?" he inquired.

"You don't mean that," she answered. "Of course I know you'll come back—you always do, don't you?"

There was a short silence before he said:

"Hitherto I have imagined there has been something to bring me back, but now—I am less optimistic."

She said hurriedly: "But nothing is different—the people

who—wanted you before, still want you—nothing is a bit different."

"And supposing—those people who were kind enough in the past to want me—as you express it—no longer attract me in the same way?" Wilfred asked tersely.

Dorothy stooped to pick a little celandine which was growing in the bank beside the road, and it was a moment before she answered quietly: "That's silly—if you once like someone—you always like them and are always glad to see them—aren't you?"

"Definitely, no," Wilfred answered, and he laughed. "I believe I told you once before that even a mere man may change his mind—well, I am a mere man."

She looked away from him over the fields beyond the hedge, and a sudden terrifying thought flashed through her mind.

Does he mean that he doesn't love Pauline any more? Oh, he *can't* mean that!

"Well?" Wilfred demanded. "What has our student of human nature to say now?"

She answered slowly, choosing her words with care:

"I don't think you mean what you say because—if you do —other people might be hurt, very much."

"*My* feelings evidently being of no account," he said.

"You're a man," she answered. "And—I am sure you wouldn't hurt anybody—not willingly, I mean—you're much too—kind." She stopped. "Shall we go this way through the wood?" she asked. "I've been before, and it's a lovely walk."

They went through a rather ramshackle gate leading to a mossy path with tall trees overhead, and a thick undergrowth on either side. "There's a little brook farther on," Dorothy told him, "and the other day I found some primroses there, and I saw a dabchick sitting on its nest." She looked up at him. "Do you like primroses?"

"I adore them," Wilfred answered ironically. "But I don't think a great deal of your very obvious effort to change the conversation."

She did not answer, and presently he said:

"You're an honest creature, Little and Good—so could you find it in your heart to answer me one question—honestly?"

She laughed a little constrainedly.

"Yes, I'll try. What is it?"

The old frivolous note was in his voice when he answered: "Do you, out of your vast experience of human nature—believe it is possible for a man—or woman—to love—a second time?"

The little celandine fell from Dorothy's hand and she stooped to recover it before she spoke.

"Yes, I think it is—but perhaps not in the same way."

"In a—better way perhaps?" he urged.

"I—don't know. It all depends."

She indicated a little pathway to the right.

"That's the way to the brook," she said.

They were both silent until they had reached it—a tiny stream of very clear water running over pebbles, with a few pale forget-me-nots in the grass on either side.

"You brought me here of your own free will," Wilfred announced, "and so here I stay for a well-deserved rest." He indicated the stump of an old tree. "You'll find that quite dry if not altogether luxurious—" and he stretched himself on the grass by the edge of the brook.

"Isn't it damp?" she asked, doubtfully.

He looked up at her and laughed.

"Can it be that you fear for my precious life?" he inquired mockingly, and she answered:

"I think you're quite able to take care of yourself."

She sat down on the tree stump and looked at the running water—and Wilfred quoted: " 'For men may come, and men may go—but I go on for ever'—Tennyson's *Brook*, in case you doubt my knowledge of poetry."

"It's a lovely poem," she said.

There was a moment of silence before Wilfred said lightly:

"To return to our previous conversation. I know a man who—in the words of the best novelists, loved or imagined that he loved a woman with a great and undying love!" He paused and Dorothy said:

"If you say it in that tone of voice, I shan't believe that he really loved her at all."

Wilfred laughed. "I don't know how else to say it—so you must take the will for the deed. To proceed—circumstances over which the man had no control, prevented them from marrying—but as we are told that all is not lost until hope is lost, he continued to hope that something would happen to bring about the conventional happy ending." The corner of his mouth went up in a sarcastic smile. "How does that sound?" he demanded.

She said gently: "It sounds—just like you—always making fun of the things which you know are really serious."

Wilfred picked up a stick and threw it into the stream and they both watched it whirl round and round in an eddy before he spoke again: "Years went by! and our hero—shall we call him our hero?—began to realize the truth of the saying that 'hope deferred maketh the heart grow sick'. A dozen—no, a hundred times, he—tried to cut adrift—unsuccessfully, until. . . ."

She was watching him with tender eyes, and when again he stopped speaking she said gently: "She was married, I suppose, wasn't she?"

But even then he would not be serious, and he answered lightly:

"You have solved the puzzle most efficiently!—yes—the lady was married."

"But she loved—him?"

Wilfred turned his head away as he answered:

"Yes, I believe she was—kind enough to love him—unworthy creature though he is—was!" And then suddenly he made a gesture of passionate repudiation. "But now," he said with unconscious tragedy: "It's all over, Little and Good—and he doesn't—care for her any more—not in the same way."

They looked at one another with eyes which tried in vain to hide their complete understanding, and the only sound to be heard was the voice of the running brook and the song of a bird in the trees overhead.

The little twig which Wilfred had thrown into the stream had got caught against a stone so that its journey was ended, and when at last Dorothy turned her eyes from his, it caught her attention, and leaning down she gently set it free and watched it float gaily away.

And she thought what a pity it seemed that all things could not be put right as easily, that the touch of a willing hand could not as simply unravel the tangles which people made of their lives, and set them on the straight road again.

She took her handkerchief from her pocket and wiped her

wet fingers, and the man at her feet said with rough emotion:

"I can't pretend any longer—not with you, Little and Good —so—you know who I am talking about, don't you?"

A little sigh escaped her as she answered in a whisper:

"Yes, yes I know and I wish—I wish I didn't——"

CHAPTER SEVEN

And the sunshine was so warm upon her face, and there was such peaceful loveliness around her, and yet—suddenly everything seemed to be spoilt and overcast, Dorothy thought as she averted her eyes from Wilfred's wondering why her chief emotion should be the defence of Pauline.

He had not mentioned her name, but there had been no need to do so, for while he was speaking it was as if she had been standing there between them, her lovely eyes watching.

Why had Wilfred made this confession? It was so unlike him to be really serious or to show any emotion, and besides, in what way could it help him to confide in someone whom he looked upon as a child?

"And I can't help him, anyway," was her troubled thought, for she knew it was impossible to help him, much as she longed to do so. All her heart seemed to be rushing towards him in a passion of sympathy and understanding, just as her little body had rushed to the rescue of the boy with the bicycle.

And then Wilfred said bluntly: "Perhaps I ought not to have spoken, but ... I couldn't help it." And then as she kept silent he laughed in his old careless way. "Well, that's that!" he said philosophically. "Forget it!"

"I don't want to forget it," she answered gently. "I only wish there was something I could do—to help, I mean."

Wilfred had found another little stick, and with it he was idly digging a hole in the soft turf, and his eyes were intent upon his occupation when presently he said jerkily:

"And what would—you—do—in the circumstances, Little and Good?"

It was a moment before she answered.

"I think—I think I should try to be quite honest, and— quite honest—if I was sure! ... I should try to be honest without hurting anyone—more than it was—necessary."

Her eyes came back at last to his troubled face. "*Are* you quite sure—Wilfred?"

Wilfred absently pushed a dead leaf into the little hole he had dug, and carefully covered it up with the loose earth as if he were trying to bury something of far greater importance, and she saw the blood mount slowly to his face as he answered curtly:

"Quite sure. You see—my dear—there's someone else."

Her lips moved in a voiceless echo of the last words.

Someone else! ... Why should the blunt admission make her feel as though a knife had turned in her heart when hitherto the belief that this man loved Pauline had failed to wound?

And now even the sunshine could not warm the deathly coldness which seemed to be creeping slowly through her body until it reached her lips and made speech impossible.

Somebody else!—not Pauline, whom she loved and in whose happiness she could have rejoiced, but a stranger—The realization was so unbearable that she turned her face sharply away, afraid of its betrayal. And then suddenly Wilfred sprang to his feet, brushing the bits of grass and dried leaves from his coat.

"We'd better go back," he said. "It looks like rain."

"Yes, it looks like rain," she echoed.

He glanced quickly at her.

"What's the matter?" he asked. "Aren't you well?" He touched her hand. "Why, you're as cold as ice!" he protested.

She jerked her hand away. "I am—a little cold—I think it was rather silly to stay so long. You see, it isn't summer—yet, is it?"

The colour was slowly returning to her cheeks, and the overwhelming sense of shock was lifting.

"And who warned *me* about the damp grass?" Wilfred asked.

She tried to laugh. "Well, let's run—and get home before the rain starts."

But running was not easy on the uneven narrow footpath which led back to the crooked gate, and she was forced to walk ahead of him.

What were his thoughts, she wondered? She wished she dared turn to look at him, but she could not trust herself, and suddenly the desire rose in her heart to cry out:

"Somebody else? Who is she? Who *is* she?" as if she had been cheated—as if she had the right to know.

But at once she was upbraiding herself—don't be so ridiculous! It's nothing to do with you! What right have you to be jealous? You're *not* jealous, do you hear? *Not* jealous!

"The clouds seem to have passed over," she heard him say in a matter of fact voice, and she glanced up at the bits of blue sky which were visible between the trees overhead.

They had reached the gate then, and once out on the road they could walk side by side, but for a little neither of them spoke until presently Wilfred said: "I feel that I owe you an apology for being such an embarrassing companion! But I suppose we all have mental lapses. How long are you staying at The Fortress?"

"Pauline asked me to stay until Mr. Rachett comes back from Scotland—that will be another week."

He glanced down at her. "I think you already look better for the change," he said.

"Yes," she agreed. And then as they neared the house she said gaily: "I'm dying for tea, aren't you?"

"Tea is not one of my vices," Wilfred answered.

Dorothy laughed. "Well it *is* one of mine, and I hope it's ready!" And then with an effort it seemed, she spoke his name.

"Wilfred?"

"At your service, madam."

"You won't hurt her, will you? Not more than you can help because ... she's not—very happy, is she?" And then she ran on ahead of him and into the house.

Pauline called to her from the drawing-room:

"Tea! ... tea! ... I was just going to have mine."

"Coming in a minute," Dorothy answered and she went up to her room and shut the door, flinging her hat and coat on to the bed.

Jealousy! ... so this was it; the thing she had never thought to experience, and which in others had left her a little ashamed.

Jealousy! Because there was an unknown woman in Wilfred's life. She bathed her face with cold water and smoothed her hair, and all the time she was saying over and over again in her mind—don't think about it, don't think about it—not now! Wait till to-night, when you're alone in the dark and it won't matter.

She was humming a little snatch of song when presently she descended the stairs. Through the open drawing-room door she could see Pauline at the tea-table, and Wilfred standing beside her. They looked very much the same as usual, and yet something told Dorothy more definitely than any words could have done that they were altogether different; that something had happened—perhaps an indefinite something to destroy the tenderness of which she had always been aware when she was with them.

Was *that* how love died? All in a moment! ... and without any warning? She bent to kiss Pauline's cheek before she sat down beside her, and for the first time she was aware of a cold resentment against Wilfred because of this thing he had done.

And yet, was it altogether his fault? People said it was so true that continual dropping will wear away even a stone and she knew that patience was not one of Wilfred's virtues, and then she felt sorry because she was criticizing him, and as she looked at him with remorseful eyes, she thought again that he seemed different—that his old smiling nonchalance seemed to have deserted him, and that there was a worried little line between his eyes.

"I hear you have been in the woods," Pauline said.

"Yes, it was lovely," Dorothy glanced round the room. "Isn't Mr. Charteris in yet?"

"Not yet, and he doesn't take tea anyway."

"Wilfred says that tea is not one of *his* vices, either," Dorothy said, trying to speak lightly. "But I expect he has lots of others."

"Such as?" Wilfred demanded.

"I was only joking——" she explained.

"The kind of joke I do not find amusing," he said sharply.

"Wilfred!" Pauline protested; she looked from one to the other in amazement, at the painful flush in Dorothy's cheeks and at the anger in Wilfred's eyes.

And then Dorothy laughed as if it were of no importance.

"May I have one of those cakes with the sugar on?" she asked.

There was an uncomfortable silence until Pauline said:

"Oh dear, I've left my cigarettes upstairs on the dressing table!"

Wilfred produced his case, but she shook her head.

"You know they are not my particular brand——" and she turned to Dorothy. "Will you be an angel and fetch them for me?"

They both knew it was merely an excuse, but Dorothy departed gladly, and as soon as she had gone Pauline turned to Wilfred.

"Why did you speak to her like that? She looked terribly hurt, poor child!"

"Is she the only one who is hurt, I wonder?" he said with sarcasm. "You two seem to have formed a determined alliance against me and—and——" His voice softened. "I'm sorry," he apologized. "Please forgive me."

Pauline rose and went across to him.

"Have *I* done anything to hurt you, Wilfred?" she asked.

He looked down at her with faint embarrassment.

"Nothing—I lost my temper and . . ."

She laid her hand on his coat-sleeve.

"Sure you're not cross with me about anything, are you, darling?" she whispered.

"My dear—*no*!"

She glanced quickly over her shoulder and then she raised herself on tiptoe and kissed him just as Dorothy pushed open the door.

For the fraction of a second she hesitated, and then she came forward. "The cigarettes are not on the dressing table," she said.

"Oh dear!" Pauline laughed a little nervously. "Never mind. I'll go and look for them myself."

Wilfred walked over to the window and stood with his back turned, and Dorothy picked up a magazine and began to turn the pages with fingers that were not quite steady. She would have given a great deal had it been possible to follow Pauline from the room, and she tried in vain to think of something to say which would break a silence which was growing unbearable, and then suddenly Wilfred turned.

"Sorry, Little and Good," he said, and she answered without looking at him.

"You needn't be!—it's all right."

He came back to where she was sitting.

"I behaved abominably," he apologized.

She glanced up with a fleeting smile.

"I expect you'll behave just as badly again," she said. "But I don't mind."

Wilfred frowned. "Does *anything* I do or say affect you in the very slightest?" he asked shortly.

"Oh yes," she admitted. "But you see, I don't mind because I understand."

Wilfred hunted for his pipe, looked at it and returned it to his pocket.

"No, you don't," he said brusquely. "You don't understand in the very slightest—unless *you* are pretending this time!"

"It's my turn to pretend," she told him quietly, but her heart seemed to be beating up in her throat, making her breathless.

Wilfred watched her for a moment in silence before he said bluntly: "You came into the room a moment too soon—didn't you?"

She dropped the magazine and raised her eyes.

"You don't deserve to be loved!" she said with passionate intensity. "You don't mind how you hurt us—you only think about yourself—just because you're angry——" She stopped and Wilfred said eloquently:

"Us?" He laughed. "I don't flatter myself that I could ever hurt *you*."

And then for a moment she lost her self-possession.

"Because I'll never *let* you hurt me," she answered. "I'll never let any man hurt me! Men only care for themselves—they're cruel and selfish—Madame Suggia always said so and I didn't believe her—but I do now! I know it's true, and you're just the same—just the same!"

Wilfred took a quick step forward and caught her by the shoulders. "Take that back!" he commanded. "Do you hear? Take that back or——" He released her suddenly as his name was called shrilly by Pauline: "Wilfred! Wilfred!"

Dorothy gave a startled cry: "Pauline! ... Oh, what is it!" but Wilfred was already across the room and had flung open the door. "What is it?" she heard him ask.

Pauline was in the hall, her face the colour of ashes, and a maid and two men from the stables were with her, and one of them blurted out:

"It's the master—there's been an accident——" and then as

Wilfred asked a sharp question he shook his head. "No, sir, he's alive, sir—they're bringing him in now."

Wilfred turned to Dorothy.

"Take Pauline away," he said briefly.

"Is he—dead?" Pauline whispered between white lips.

"No, no——" he answered, and then she permitted Dorothy to lead her back to the drawing-room, where she dropped into a chair and hid her face in her hands.

"Don't let me see him," she said, sobbing. "I can't bear to see him—oh, don't let them make me see him, Dorothy."

The girl knelt down and took her in her arms.

"You shan't do anything you don't want to," she comforted her. "And perhaps it's all right—perhaps it isn't really a bad accident—you mustn't be so frightened." She could feel Pauline's slender body shaking from head to foot and she held her tightly as though trying to impart something of her own courage. And then, as they heard slow, heavy footsteps in the hall, Pauline cowered down, and put her hands over her ears, whimpering again: "Don't let me see him—don't let me see him!"

It seemed an eternity before Wilfred returned and then at last Pauline looked up.

"What—is it?" she whispered.

"It's all right," Wilfred assured her. "The doctor is here, and he seems to think it's nothing very serious. He must have been thrown—but nobody knows exactly what happened—the horse came home alone—that's how they knew something was wrong. Charteris was unconscious when they found him, but the doctor says that as far as he can tell at present there are no serious injuries."

Pauline gave a little sob and stretched out her hand to him—"Oh, Wilfred!"

He took her hand in his—and Dorothy rose to her feet and stole unnoticed from the room.

The doctor was coming downstairs and as he looked at her inquiringly, she asked:

"Is it—all right?"

"He's badly shaken, of course," he told her. "I shall send a nurse—by the way, who are you, my dear?"

"I'm just staying here."

"I see—well, I don't think there is need for any great anxiety

—he's a heavy man, of course—but we must hope for the best."
He picked up his hat from the hall table. "By the way," he
added, "those dogs—we can't get them away from the bedroom door—if you have any influence——"

"I'll try," Dorothy said. She went softly up the stairs and
there on the landing were Brandy and Soda sitting side by side,
their beautiful eyes fixed immovably on the closed door of
their master's room.

Dorothy spoke to them but they did not even turn their
heads—she stroked Brandy's golden coat, but he seemed quite
unaware of it, though he growled quietly when she took hold
of his collar.

Dorothy went downstairs again and to the open front door
from which the doctor had just driven away, and presently
the groom came across the garden.

"They won't move for me," she said.

He shook his head.

"What those two dogs don't know, isn't worth knowing," he
told her. "Human, they are, except that they can't speak."

He entered the hall and whistled—very softly, and after
the barest hesitation the two spaniels came helter-skelter down
the stairs and looked up into the man's face with imploring
eyes.

The groom stooped and caressed them both.

"All right, boys!" he said encouragingly. "You just come
along with me——" and obediently they followed him, but
Dorothy noticed there was none of the usual tail-wagging or
joyous running around, they just walked soberly at his heels
through the sunshine across the lawn and out of sight.

It seemed very quiet everywhere when they had gone; the
drawing-room door was still closed, and with a little shiver
Dorothy went down into the garden.

Supposing Bertram Charteris died? She tried to dismiss the
thought but it persisted.

If Bertram died, then Pauline . . . and Wilfred! . . .

"It's all over, Little and Good—and he doesn't—care for
her any more—not in the same way."

Tragic words! hardly to be borne! . . . and yet, if Bertram
died . . . she stood still as she saw Wilfred leave the house
and come towards her.

"Pauline?" she asked.

He answered, not meeting her eyes: "She's gone to lie down
—there's a nurse coming——"

There was a little silence before she said hesitatingly:

"Do you think I ought to go—back? Home, I mean? I
don't want to be a nuisance."

"Wouldn't Pauline like you to stay?"

"I'll ask her—presently."

They stood side by side in the sunshine, both perhaps feeling that there was nothing to be said—and yet both conscious
of a grey foreboding, until at last Dorothy spoke:

"Brandy and Soda love him, don't they?"

Wilfred started. "The dogs?—yes—where are they?"

"The groom fetched them—they were outside Mr. Charteris's
door—they wouldn't come away for *me*—I tried."

"That was most ungrateful of them."

Sudden tears filled her eyes as she said: "Oh, Wilfred!
Don't be sarcastic now—when everything is so sad."

Wilfred turned in astonishment.

"My darling child! I don't mean to be sarcastic——" And
then as the tears overflowed on to her cheeks he said sharply:
"Don't cry, do you hear! ... I can't bear to see you cry."

She hurriedly groped for her handkerchief.

"I'm not crying," she insisted, "it's only—oh, why can't we
all be happy!"

There was a little line of pain between his eyes as he
answered unhesitatingly: "Because the thing which would
make most of us happy belongs to someone else—or at any
rate, doesn't want to become our own exclusive property, and
jealousy is a—pardon the word—damnable thing!"

She brushed away the last tear.

"But you've never been jealous," she said a little resent-
fully. "I'm sure you've never had any cause to be jealous."

Wilfred laughed. "Perhaps," he submitted, "in the words
of your friend Lord Byron, 'Yet he was jealous, though he did
not show it. For jealousy dislikes the world to know it'."

"It's very difficult not to show it," she said.

"How do you know?" Wilfred demanded, and then lightly:
"Don't tell me that someone has dared to pay his addresses
to you behind my back! Don't tell me that with all my care
and vigilance you have managed to escape into the Secret
Orchard!"

"I shouldn't tell you if I had," she answered. "And, anyway, I don't know what you mean by the Secret Orchard."

"It means," Wilfred began and then stopped as he saw the groom crossing the lawn towards them.

"Mrs. Charteris would like you to go to her, please," he said to Dorothy.

"Thank you, I'll come at once," Dorothy answered.

She found Pauline lying in a darkened room with the windows wide open, and she stretched out her hand as the girl entered.

"I'm so sorry I was such a coward," she said a little ashamedly "But—I told you—how illness or—anything dreadful terrifies me ... but they say Bertram is not so bad after all. Dr. Smiley has sent a nurse, so perhaps it will be all right, and Dorothy I've telephoned to my mother and she is coming to stay with me."

"I'm glad."

Pauline sighed.

"It seems funny," she said. "Mother and I are not really as devoted to one another as mothers and daughters are supposed to be, and yet—whenever anything goes wrong, she is the first person I think of and want!"

"It's lovely to have a mother you *can* send for," Dorothy said.

"Poor little thing!" Pauline whispered. "I forgot that you haven't—anyone! And I wouldn't have suggested that you went back to Mr. Rachett only—he telephoned—just before we knew about Bertram—I was coming to tell you—when I heard! He asked how you were, and said that he was back in London. He didn't say that he wanted you to go back, but —I think for your own sake, perhaps it will be best! You've had enough trouble as it is and I don't want you to stay here while things are—as they are——" She stopped, and Dorothy said gently:

"I was just telling Wilfred that I thought I ought to go! Though I didn't know that Mr. Rachett was home, and of course now I must! He can't be left alone, and if your mother is coming——"

Pauline pressed her hand.

"It isn't that I want to lose you," she said. "Please don't think it is! And later on—when Bertram is better, you'll come again, won't you?"

"If you ask me."

"You know I shall ask you. Wilfred is going back to Town to-night—he thinks it better he should—and I think so too, although——" She stopped but Dorothy did not speak, and she went on: "I thought—it would be nice—if you were to go with him—much nicer than going by train."

"Yes, if he doesn't mind ..."

Pauline gave a little sigh. "And promise that you will come again, when Bertram is better?"

"I promise."

"Kiss me," Pauline said, "and then run away and I'll get up presently, so that I can see you off."

Dorothy kissed her gently.

"And it's been lovely—staying with you," she said gratefully.

And so Mr. Rachett was home again! ... probably the holiday had not been a great success, she thought as she went down the stairs, and she realized that she would be quite pleased to see him! Although she would have liked to stay with Pauline, especially now, when there was trouble, but if her mother was coming, of course it would be all right.

She looked a little grave as she rejoined Wilfred in the garden.

"Mr. Rachett is home," she said.

Wilfred raised his brows.

"Home? Was the holiday a failure!"

"I don't know—he spoke to Pauline on the 'phone—and—so I am going back to London to be with him."

"When?"

"Well, Pauline thought—if you wouldn't mind taking me with you—do you mind, Wilfred? You see, Pauline's mother is coming and I think it would be better for me not to stay, even if Mr. Rachett wasn't there——" She glanced at him a little apologetically. "I can go by train if you like," she submitted.

He laughed. "If you can tolerate my company, I will do my utmost to tolerate yours," he answered.

They left the house about six o'clock.

"We ought to do it in about three hours," Wilfred said. "And it will be light till eight."

"And don't drive recklessly," Pauline warned him. She kissed Dorothy affectionately. "Write to me—and take care of yourself."

"I'll write to-morrow."

Pauline looked at Wilfred.

"Good-bye—I'll let you know how Bertram is."

"Please," he said.

Dorothy turned to wave as the car moved away, and she thought how lonely Pauline looked standing there in the doorway of the big house with the sunshine all about her.

"She says her mother will be there to-night," she said as they rounded the bend of the drive and Pauline was out of sight. "Do you know her mother Wilfred?"

"I have met her—yes."

"Is she—nice?"

"A bit worldly—but—yes, I think one may say that she is quite pleasant."

He squared his big shoulders. "And now for London," he said cheerfully.

"Are you pleased to be going back?" she asked.

"Yes, and no," Wilfred admitted. "I like the country, but—in the circumstances. . . ."

They talked very little during the long drive, and Dorothy's thoughts turned again and again to Pauline. Supposing Bertram died? Did Pauline really want her freedom? And if so, why had she refused when Wilfred had asked her to go away with him?

And suddenly she was thinking: "*I* would have gone!"

Yes, she was sure she would have gone, thought no doubt it would have been very wrong of her—or wouldn't it? Was it any worse to go away with a man one loved, than to stay with a man for whom one had no affection?

And who was the other girl of whom Wilfred had spoken? He must know so many—and what would Pauline say when he told her the thing which must be told?—or wouldn't he speak of it if Bertram Charteris died?

She had heard people talk of what they called 'the honourable thing' but she could not agree that it *was* an honourable thing to pretend to love someone when you didn't love them any more! For surely sooner or later they must find out! Then what would happen?

Life was so perplexing, or was it love that she meant? It ought to be such a simple, happy thing, and yet—in connection with it—there always seemed to be difficulties and unhappiness.

Even in her own case—— She looked at Wilfred, remembering that she had made up her mind only to find contentment in her love for him, and that already jealousy had crept in and spoilt that contentment.

A little smile crossed her face as she wondered what he would say if he could know! Perhaps he wouldn't believe it —perhaps he would think it was just a childish fancy!

If only he would realize that she was no longer a child! That she was just as grown-up and sincere in her love for him as he was—or had been in his love—for Pauline!

"That was a very big sigh," Wilfred said.

She sat up with a great show of energy.

"I didn't know I sighed," she protested. "How much further is it to London?"

"Another eighty miles. Does Rachett know you are coming?"

"Yes, I telephoned, and he seemed quite pleased."

"As he is, I imagine."

She asked presently: "And do you still mean to go away again—soon?"

Wilfred hesitated. "What do you think about it?" he inquired, and she answered steadily:

"It's nothing to do with me."

"A thousand thanks."

"I mean," she explained, "that if you don't go, I know it won't be because of me."

He answered with sarcasm: "Your wisdom is indeed profound! But as a matter of fact, I shall probably wait a week or two——"

To see what happens, he means, she thought quickly.

And what *would* happen? Funny that nobody knew!— that nobody could see beyond to-day and discover what was lying in wait—not even the fortune-tellers who pretended to know so much and who were very seldom right!

Cecilie had loved having her fortune told! Once at a fête in

Paris, she and Dorothy had gone together to have their hands read by a very voluble Frenchwoman who had talked so rapidly that Dorothy had hardly been able to follow what she said, but she remembered vaguely that it was something about coming to cross-roads, and having to choose which way she should go.

"You're to have a much more exciting life than me," Cecilie had sighed afterwards. "Mine is to be all plain-sailing like a duck pond," she added disgustedly. "I shall marry and have two children and settle down—ugh! It's the last thing I want to do."

And perhaps it was what she would do, and be quite content!

"I hope I shall see her soon—and Lawrence, too," she thought, and then she was remembering how Wilfred had said, when she had accused him of being sarcastic about Brandy and Soda: "My darling child!" ... But somehow the words hurt because they had been such a definite reminder that to him she was nothing more than a child!

Wilfred broke in again upon her thoughts.

"Do you think you will be happy with old Rachett?"

"Yes," she said unhesitatingly.

"Playing draughts every night?" he submitted.

"I like playing draughts," she answered.

He looked down at her with his odd, twisted smile.

"May I come one night—for another beating?"

"You know you can."

"Such an enthusiastic invitation!" he said dryly.

"What would you like me to say?" she inquired.

"I should like you to say: 'Darling Wilfred, come as often as you will, and as soon as you will,'" he told her flippantly.

She shook her head.

"I don't think I like that word 'darling'—everyone uses it."

"Can you think of a better?"

"I think I could—if I tried."

"Such as?"

"I'll keep it to myself."

"To be shared—someday—with the other fellow," Wilfred said.

She smiled a little constrainedly.

"I don't know any other fellow."

"The world is full of them," he reminded her.

"And full of other women, too," she said; she leaned a little forward to peer at a sign-board. "London forty-three," she told him.

"One more hour of my company, and we shall be there," he said. "Shall I be invited to dinner?"

"I am sure Mr. Rachett will invite you! I told him you were bringing me."

"And did he shout for joy?"

She chuckled.

"Of course he did!"

Wilfred laughed too. "I can just picture the old fellow!" he said in amusement. "Clutching the receiver in one hand and leaping up and down shouting 'Hurray!'—I don't suppose he has ever been excited in the whole of his life."

She said soberly: "I don't believe I have, either!—Oh, yes, once! When I recognized you in the train, coming from Paris."

"No much to get excited about, Little and Good," he submitted.

"It was!" she insisted. "You see, I longed to tell you who I was, but I knew you weren't very—anxious to meet me."

There was a moment of silence before he answered:

"Will you believe me when I say that I found you—most attractive?"

"After your suit-case nearly killed me?" she asked gaily.

"You evidently *don't* believe me," he said.

"You didn't expect me to!" she retorted.

Wilfred slowed down a little, and presently he said: "And yet I am more honest—more myself—with you—than with anyone else I know, Little and Good."

"Are you? Perhaps it's because I don't really matter," she answered simply.

"Don't matter?" he laughed. "Oh, well—even Napoleon met his Waterloo."

"What has Napoleon got to do with it?" she asked.

"Nothing, except that at Waterloo he came face to face with an enemy he could not vanquish."

"You mean—*you* have?"

He looked down at her.

"Yes, I mean that I have."

"The other day," she reminded him, "you said that all is not

137

lost until hope is lost, so the thing is not to lose hope, isn't it?"

Wilfred accelerated again as he answered grimly: "There was once a bee who stung a lion to death."

She looked a little puzzled, and he explained. "I mean that one of the hardest things in the world to fight is complete indifference! If someone hates you, there is always hope, but complete indifference is a soul-destroying impossibility, especially when it is accompanied by extreme honesty and too great an understanding."

"And do you know—someone like that?" she asked hesitatingly.

"I do."

"She sounds nice," she said ingenuously. "At least I suppose it is a 'she'?" she apologized.

"As usual, you are quite correct," Wilfred agreed.

Dorothy said, "Only another twenty miles."

"Are you tired?"

"Oh, no. I wonder how Mr. Charteris is?"

Wilfred frowned.

"No doubt we shall hear to-morrow."

"Yes—I wonder why Pauline is so afraid of illness and trouble?"

"We are all made differently. Some of us prefer to keep to the shallows—and some of us rush wildly out into the breakers and prefer to take a chance. What do you think about it?"

"I think I'd go wherever my friends went."

"All over the world and back again?" he asked.

"Yes—if they wanted me to."

Wilfred said: "And yet you changed your mind about wandering around with me, or am I not a friend?"

She made a little gesture of repudiation.

"I think it's a silly conversation," she said rather wearily. "And I'm sure that's London—all those houses and chimney-pots." And she felt glad that the journey was over—for to-day it was an effort to respond to Wilfred's apparent flippancy, and she was conscious of a great weariness.

"For complete respectability commend me to this neighbourhood," Wilfred said as they turned into the street where Mr. Rachett lived. "I am sure that none of its residents ever uses

138

bad language or owes money, or even knows a policeman by sight!"

She laughed at that and leaned forward to look up at the solemn windows of the tall house.

"I expect he's waiting dinner for us," she said and she was out of the car before Wilfred could move.

Sue had already opened the front door and looked pleased as Dorothy grasped her hand. "Here I am!" she said gaily, and then Mr. Rachett appeared.

"Well, my dear—so you've arrived safely."

He laid a kindly hand on her shoulder. "You must be hungry —dinner is ready when you are."

"I won't be a moment," she told him and she dashed upstairs.

"I'm glad you've come back, miss," she said. "The house has seemed so empty."

It seemed empty, although it was not nearly such a large house as The Fortress, but Dorothy missed the garden and the fresh air—she missed Pauline too, though somehow her thoughts seemed to shy away from her and from the future.

During dinner Mr. Rachett told them about his holiday in Scotland. "The weather was not altogether favourable," he said in his slow way. "Though I understand that in the West it was warm and sunny. The hotel was comfortable, but hotel life does not greatly appeal to me," he smiled. "I think the truth is that I am too old really to enjoy a holiday."

"You look much better," Dorothy told him. "You're quite sunburnt."

"The mountain air, no doubt," he agreed. "And you, my dear? I am sorry your holiday has ended so sadly. I hope Mr. Charteris is improving?"

"We don't know," she answered. "But Pauline said she would write."

It was late when they had finished dinner and Mr. Rachett had already tried without great success to stifle a few yawns, so he made no protest when Wilfred said he would not stay.

"Thank you for bringing me home," Dorothy said, and Mr. Rachett's eyes softened at the word "home".

"And when shall we see you again, Wilfred?" he asked cordially. "Come whenever you like—you will always be welcome. We shall need a little cheerful company sometimes— eh, Dorothy?"

"Good-bye," Dorothy said, and her eyes were a little pathetic as she realized that it might be a long time before Wilfred took advantage of the invitation.

He answered now with a faint smile: "In the best circles, Dorothy, we say au revoir, and never good-bye."

"Au revoir, then," she said, but she did not follow the two men into the hall.

When Mr. Rachett returned he looked at her a little dubiously, so that she said at once:

"It's nice to be back again."

The old man shook his head.

"I hope you will be happy, my dear," he submitted. "It is your own choice remember, and one for which I am—profoundly grateful."

"I *shall* be happy," she insisted.

But her smiles faded as she went up to her room. Now the necessity to appear gay had gone, she felt ineffably tired and sad.

When she was ready for bed she pulled the curtain aside and looked out into the darkness in the direction which Wilfred had taken.

"Au revoir—dearest," she whispered, and she felt a lump, coming up into her throat, almost as if she were going to cry.

CHAPTER EIGHT

"There! That's the telephone." said Sue.

She hurried off to answer it, and Dorothy listened, her lips parted and her heart racing. Was it Pauline?

Sue returned. "Mr. Clifton would like to speak to you."

Dorothy dashed to the 'phone, her eyes shining.

"Hullo?"

"Is that you, Little and Good?"

"Yes."

"Pauline has just rung through—Charteris is better."

"Oh! . . . I'm so glad."

"She asked me to tell you—she sent her love."

"Thank you."

There was the slightest pause before he asked:

"And how are you?"

"Quite well, thank you." She laughed. "I'm going to take over the housekeeping for Mr. Rachett—Sue is only part time here."

She heard him chuckle.

"I can't picture it!" he declared. "What do *you* know about running a house?"

"Not much," she admitted ruefully. "But I can learn—and it will be something to do. You must come to dinner and see what you think of my efforts—but not until after Saturday.'

"You mean that you have no desire to see me for another week?" he demanded.

"Of course I don't mean that!" she protested. "Mr. Rachett said you could come any time you like."

"My heartfelt thanks to Mr. Rachett," Wilfred said dryly, and then before she could speak he rang off.

Dorothy's face fell, had she offended him, or had they just been cut off by mistake?

"You cut us off," she told the operator.

"Sorry!" a voice answered mechanically. "Can you give me the number you were speaking to?"

"I'm afraid, I can't," Dorothy admitted.

"If you hang up the receiver, the subscriber will probably ring again," she was told.

But Wilfred did not ring again, though she waited hopefully for some time, and the next day passed and the next, but he gave no sign.

They were uneventful days, except that one afternoon Mrs. Greenley called and stayed to tea.

She seemed tremendously interested in Dorothy's future and asked so many questions that she left her a little dazed.

"It's entirely a wrong environment for you," Mrs. Greenley declared. "I blame Mr. Rachett very much, and your guardian also. A child like you, keeping house for an elderly man! It's preposterous."

"But I *like* it. I'm very fond of Mr. Rachett."

"It can't possibly last," Mrs. Greenley said. "Mark my words, it can't possibly last." And then, struck by the chilled look in the girl's face, she patted her shoulder. "Well, well," she said in a more kindly way: "It's no use expecting to find old heads on young shoulders—and we all have to learn by experience. Come and see me when you feel like it," and she took her departure.

Mr. Rachett smiled when Dorothy told him about the visit.

"She means well," he said, "but she never realizes that there are two sides to every question." He looked at the girl a little wistfully. "All the same, there is something in what she says," he admitted. "And the majority of people, no doubt, would agree with her."

Dorothy answered spiritedly that she did not mind what the majority of people thought, and that she was perfectly happy, and then in order to change the conversation, she suggested a game of draughts.

It was the following afternoon that she came face to face with Willie Guest in Regent Street.

"Hul-*lo*!" he greeted her delightedly. "I was thinking of you only a moment ago. Where have you been all this time? And where is that scoundrel Wilfred?"

"He's somewhere in London, I think," she answered "And I'm still with Mr. Rachett."

"What about a cup of tea?" he suggested. "I'm so pleased to see you again that you're not going to escape easily."

They found a near-by teashop and a corner table.

"And now tell me about yourself," Guest commanded. "I hear you went down to Somerset to stay with some friends of Wilfred's."

"Yes, Mrs. Charteris—we met her that night—don't you remember—when you took me out to dinner?"

Guest nodded. "Um, I remember—and how did you enjoy yourself?"

"It was lovely until Mr. Charteris had an accident—he was thrown from a horse, and so I had to come home."

"And was Wilfred there too?"

"Yes; he came back with me. Haven't you seen him lately?"

Guest shook his head.

"No—but he's like that—disappears for weeks at a time, and then turns up smiling. And this man, Charteris—how is he?"

"He's better. Why?" she asked a little defensively.

"No reason," he answered airily. "Just a civil question."

But Dorothy felt there was another and deeper reason behind the inquiry.

"And so you've decided to stay with old Rachett?" Guest said presently.

"Yes." Her voice was a little defensive, but he merely said:

"Sporting of you, Miss Little. Not many girls would make such a sacrifice."

"But it isn't a sacrifice!" she protested. "I'm very happy—and besides—where can I go if I don't stay with him?"

Guest rubbed his chin thoughtfully.

"No relations?" he asked with a smile, and then as she shook her head: "Well, perhaps you're lucky," he said. "The trouble with most of us is that we've got too many."

"Have you got too many?" she asked.

He laughed. "I could dispense with a few of them," he admitted frankly, and then he asked if some day he might again have the pleasure of taking her out. "Do you like the theatre?"

"I love it."

"Well, any night you are free, I shall be only too delighted. Just give me a ring or drop me a line."

"Some night when Mr. Rachett is out," she said. "Thank you very much."

"We won't take Wilfred this time."

"Won't we?'

He looked at her comically. "Must we?" he questioned, and she laughed.

"Not if you don't want him. And besides, he has so many engagements."

"Of a temporary character only," he agreed.

She looked at him quickly, but she made no comment, until presently she said she must go.

"And I shall hope to hear from you soon," he reminded her as they parted.

She felt a little perturbed when he had departed.

"He's nice," she thought, and yet she could not rid herself of the feeling that had she given him any encouragement, he would have said a good deal more about Wilfred.

Perhaps he knew about Pauline, she thought, and yet surely Wilfred would never have spoken about her!

An eager voice suddenly broke in upon her thoughts, and

turning sharply, she looked into Cecilie Jepson's excited face.

"I knew it was you!" Cecilie said eagerly. "I was in the car with Lawrence, and I saw you cross the road." She seized Dorothy's hand. "How lovely to meet you again! ... I've heaps to tell you, and you must come and meet Lawrence. I was going to ring you up this morning, but we were shopping and the time passed. I'm going to be married next month."

She talked all the time, dragging Dorothy back with her to a side-turning where a car with a man standing beside it was drawn up at the kerb.

"This is Lawrence," Cecilie said proudly. "And this is Dorothy Little—you know all about one another, and—oh, I *am* so pleased to see you again."

Dorothy looked shyly at Lawrence; he was rather a thick-set young man with sandy-coloured hair, but he had very nice eyes, and there was something about him which she instinctively liked.

"We're going to be married on the eleventh because it's Lawrence's birthday," Cecilie told her excitedly. "It's only to be a quiet wedding because father isn't very well yet, or I should have asked you to be my bridesmaid, but you'll come, won't you? It's to be in London."

Dorothy said she would love to come.

"Are you going to have a proper wedding dress?" she asked. Cecilie sighed and shook her head.

"It didn't seem worth while, and Lawrence said he didn't mind anyway. We're going to Norway for our honeymoon. When shall I see you again? We're got to go back to-night, but we shall be up again next week."

She was so intent upon her own affairs that she asked no questions, and presently Lawrence said that if they stayed much longer the police would be after them, so almost before she could realize it Dorothy found herself alone again. And that is the second time in one day that I've met someone I didn't expect to meet, she thought, as she hailed a taxi because it was getting late, and gave Mr. Rachett's address.

Perhaps now there would be a third meeting, because people said that queer things always happened in threes.

And so Cecilie was to be married quite soon! ... There was a faint touch of envy in her heart as she recalled her friend's radiant face. A pity it had got to be a quiet wedding

—Cecilie would have loved a proper wedding dress, and lots of guests; still, if she was happy—and there was no doubt that she was—what did it matter?

A honeymoon in Norway, too! ... It all seemed very romantic. The cab stopped at Mr. Rachett's house, and with a sigh Dorothy opened the door, and got out.

"Mr. Rachett has rung through to say he won't be in to dinner," Sue told her as she entered the house. "He told me to say that it was a business appointment, and that you were not to wait up as he will be late."

"Oh!" Dorothy said, and somehow she felt the house was a little depressing as she went up to her own room—perhaps because of the radiant happiness she had just seen in the face of another girl.

She ate her solitary dinner without much appetite, wondering how she could pass the long evening. Then she drew a chair up to the fire, but she left the nearby magazines untouched and her thoughts were all of Cecilie and of her happiness.

Of course she would go to the wedding—and perhaps she could persuade Mr. Rachett to go with her! She would buy a new dress for the occasion—a blue one perhaps—and then without any apparent reason she was suddenly thinking of Pauline. What kind of a wedding had hers been? Very grand, no doubt, and she must have made a very beautiful bride.

Funny that Pauline had not written to her though she had promised she would. And what were Brandy and Soda doing? It made her a little sad to remember their faithful vigil outside their master's door; it only showed that there must be something good about Bertram Charteris to deserve their devotion.

A week ago now since she had left The Fortress, but it seemed longer, and now she was seeing Wilfred's face as he had looked when he said with rough emotion: "I can't pretend any longer—not with you, Little and Good—so—you know who I am talking about, don't you?"

And the "other" girl? Perhaps he had been spending his time with her this week, and that was why she had seen nothing of him! Did the other girl know about Pauline? Somehow Dorothy was sure that he would tell her, for no matter what it cost him, Wilfred would be quite honest and straightforward.

"You see, my dear—there's—somebody else."

And at the memory of those words, the jealous pain which she had tried so hard to crush, stirred again in her heart.

Somebody else! ...

Dorothy rose suddenly, afraid of her own thoughts, and taking the box of draughts from the cupboard, began to arrange them on the board with unsteady fingers.

Why did she feel so depressed, she wondered? She had been happy enough until she met Cecilie.

"It's because I'm alone," she thought, and with a touch of humour she rose and set another chair opposite to her own on the other side of the table.

But that seemed to make things even worse, for it was not Mr. Rachett's quiet figure she could visualize there, but Wilfred's.

"*Your* move, Little and Good."

She even fancied that she could hear his voice, but of course it was just imagination. Rather a hopeless job, trying to play by oneself! She rested her chin in the palm of her hand and looked down at the rows of draughtsmen with unseeing eyes Nothing was ever any good if one was alone!

Funny that Willie Guest had said that most people had too many relations—for with her it was just the other way about!

She sighed, realizing that she might perhaps have gone to the theatre with him to-night had she known that Mr. Rachett would not be home! It was not his fault, of course. Still ... the door opened.

"Pleased to see me?" Wilfred asked, but he did not smile or offer his hand, and there was a moment of silence before Dorothy said vaguely:

"Mr. Rachett won't be in till late."

"So I hear." He took the empty chair opposite to her, but he did not say—as somehow she was sure he would: "Your move, Little and Good." He just sat there, almost as if he had forgotten her presence, till at last she asked timidly:

"Shall we—play?"

He raised his eyes slowly.

"Charteris is dead," he said.

Dead! She heard the word quite distinctly, and yet it conveyed nothing to her. *Dead!* ... It was just an empty word!

And then Wilfred said, with the impatience of deep emotion:

"Well, say something—say something! Don't look at me like that. Say something!" and he pushed back his chair and rose, walked away from her in a queer, jerky way.

"I—don't know what to say."

She watched him with tragic eyes as he strode up and down the room like a lion she had once seen pacing his cage—up and down—up and down—with no way of escape, and yet—refusing to admit defeat.

It seemed an eternity until at last he stopped and stood, with his back to her, staring down into the fire.

"Well, that's that," he said.

She tried to speak, but her lips would only form one word: "Pauline?"

He laughed shortly.

"She rang this evening—an hour ago—to tell me—— He died quite suddenly—they thought he was out of danger—he died quite suddenly——" he said again, as if by repeating the words he hoped to fully understand their meaning.

Dorothy mechanically began to put the draughtsmen back in their box; there seemed nothing to be said—her mind felt curiously numbed and empty—as if it had been plunged into icy water, and yet little pictures kept appearing before her and vanishing again, as if someone was lifting and dropping a shutter with the intention of tormenting her.

Pauline, with the tears on her lovely face—Brandy and Soda outside a closed door—Wilfred carefully burying the dead leaf as if it was something of tremendous importance.

She gave herself a little shake as Wilfred spoke again.

"You know what it means, don't you, Little and Good?"

And now her brain was alive and active once more, so that she could answer steadily:

"It only means—what you will let it mean."

He turned round, with his odd, crooked smile.

"Life is such a simple thing to you, isn't it?" he said. "But if you had had my experience you would know that it's something—that even a man of my size, cannot always tackle successfully."

And then as she did not speak he asked with a touch of impatience: "What are you thinking about now?"

"About Pauline."

"She has all your sympathy, naturally," he submitted ironically. And then suddenly he came back to the chair opposite and sat down, looking at her steadily across the table.

"And what about me—and—the other girl?"

A little flicker of pain crossed her face, but she spoke quite steadily. "Does she know—about Pauline, I mean?"

"Yes, she knows."

"And what does she think you ought to do?"

"She thinks—as you do."

"You mean—that you must be quite honest?"

"Yes."

And then Dorothy asked slowly and very deliberately, though her heart felt sick with jealousy:

"And does she love you—very much, Wilfred?"

His hand, which was resting on the little table, jerked convulsively, though when he spoke his voice was quiet and even a little expressionless.

"That is what I would give my soul to know."

She had not been looking at him, but now she slowly raised her eyes until they met his, and there was a tragic silence during which she could feel the blood ebbing from her face, and then Wilfred said with infinite tenderness:

"Yes! it's you, Little and Good—I thought you understood," and then as she still could not speak, he went on quietly: "It's all right—no need to be upset. I'm not asking you for anything—for of course you don't care for me—in that way—why should you? But—you see why it's not—too easy for me to do what—I suppose you would say is the right thing." He took his pipe from his pocket, stared at it, and put it back again, and his mind was a sick weariness as he remembered Pauline's broken words on the telephone, and his own inadequate attempts to be—kind! *Kind!* . . . was that what it had come to?

He pushed back his chair with an intolerable feeling of anger, and resumed his restless pacing up and down, until at last Dorothy said sharply:

"Don't do it, Wilfred—don't *do* it—please sit down again, please!"

He flung her a quick glance.

"Sorry!" and he went back to his chair, his fingers playing a nervous tattoo in the table, and at last he broke out in an odd, jerky way:

"You see—later on, of course—she'll expect—you see—I mean—we always thought—hoped—that marriage would be possible."

She caught her breath sharply.

"And now—it will be," she said.

Wilfred turned in his chair and leaning his arms on the table, looked at her with hot eyes.

"You don't care, do you!" he taunted her. "You'd like to see me—tied up against my will—you think it serves me right, don't you? You think all men are cruel and selfish—only caring for themselves—you wouldn't believe me if I told you that for the past weeks I've gone through hell—knowing that I'm caught in a trap—a trap of my own making, if you like, but that doesn't help——" He laughed grimly as she gave a broken cry of distress. "You see, I'm not pretending now——" he said harshly, "I've done with pretence—and yet now I'm in earnest, it doesn't seem to please you. The truth is ugly, isn't it—*Ugly*!" He brought his fist crashing down on the table with uncontrollable passion, but Dorothy did not move and after a moment he said shakenly:

"I'm sorry—I beg your pardon—I haven't been drinking —if that's what you think." And out came the pipe again, and this time he made a clumsy attempt to fill and light it.

She watched him in silence for a moment and then she spoke his name: "Wilfred."

"Yes?"

"If you—really loved someone—you wouldn't want them to be dishonourable, would you? I mean—you'd always want to be proud of them and to know that—whatever they did— it was right."

"You mean—*you* would," he answered curtly. "Go on."

But it was a moment before she could steady her voice sufficiently to say simply: "You see, I love you—too—perhaps even better than you have ever loved—anyone." The faintest smile crossed her face. "I think I—loved you—even before that day—in the train—from the moment I saw your picture in Mr. Rachett's study; at any rate—I've—loved you ever since, but I thought . . . you see, you always treated me as if I were a child, and so—how could I know? And then

149

—there was—Pauline——" She stopped, only to continue steadily: "And there is still Pauline, isn't there?"

Wilfred suddenly stretched his hand to her across the table. "Give me your hand, Little and Good," he said hoarsely, and as she obeyed and his fingers closed around it: "Now say it again—say that you love me."

"I've always loved you," she said, "but I love Pauline, too—and you belong to her, if she wants you! and I know she does."

They looked at one another very steadily, and then Wilfred said: "And does that seem a sufficient reason to you to break my heart? Or don't you believe I've got a heart to break? Perhaps you don't even believe that I really love you? But I do—better than my life—and if you send me away——" He rose abruptly and taking her by the shoulders, drew her to her feet, and she stood in his grasp like the child he so often called her, quietly waiting, and he said with sudden passion: "I want you for my wife, Little and Good, if you love me——"

She broke in then, and for the first time her voice betrayed her suffering:

"If you love *me*—you will please go—*please* go!"

"And—if I never come back?" he asked. It was a moment before she could answer:

"If you never come back ... it will be—all right—and I shall ... know why!"

But she had not foreseen that happiness which is borne of self-sacrifice is a short-lived thing, although during the days which followed the truth slowly forced itself upon her.

Endless days they were, in spite of the fact that she devoted herself to her new housekeeping jobs, and never failed in her attention to Mr. Rachett.

"After all, he's all I've got now," she thought when sometimes she realized that each day merely consisted of long hours between nine o'clock when she waved to him from the front door, and half-past six when she saw him turn the corner on his way home.

There was a very real affection between the old man and the girl who had so strangely entered into his life and, although they were too shy to speak of it, they were both conscious of a sort of comfort in their companionship, and a certain pride in knowing that they belonged, and so it seemed the most natural thing in the world when sometimes Mr. Rachett spoke to her of little intimate things which had come his way in the course of business, and even—tentatively—asked her opinion, which she always gave with great care and gravity.

And then one night over the game of draughts which had become more or less of an institution, Dorothy suddenly asked whether he considered that it was right to sacrifice one's own happiness for another's. In her own mind she was sure it was right, and yet there were ever increasing moments during which she felt heartsick and hopeless, and life seemed to be a purposeless affair.

Mr. Rachett pushed his spectacles up over his forehead and looked at her consideringly for a moment before he replied, and then he said: "It would depend on circumstances; for instance, the sacrifice which a mother might make for her child would be entirely justified because she would see no alternative, or the sacrifice which a man might make for his wife—in each case it would be the stronger party protecting the weak, which is perfectly right and proper." He paused, but as she did not speak: "Why do you ask the question, Dorothy?"

"I was just—wondering," she answered. "In books—you sometimes read of one woman giving up a man she loves to another woman who loves him too—but Cecilie—she's my friend, you know—says it's only absurd quixotism."

Mr. Rachett considered the point with as much care as if he was giving advice for a handsome fee before he said:

"Such a question naturally, would depend on the relationship of the two women. If they were sisters, one could understand it—sisters with a great affection for one another shall we say!"

She shook her head. "No, they're not sisters—not in the case I was thinking about—just friends!"

Mr. Rachett said: "I see——" a little dubiously, and then after a moment: "The danger in such a sacrifice, Dorothy, is that when the first—elation I must call it for want of a better word—when the first elation has died down, the natural sequence must be a certain amount of regret and—unhappiness, don't you think?" And then as she nodded, he continued: "Moreover there is always the question of the man in the case. Am I to understand that he prefers the girl who sacrifices herself for her friend?"

She flushed a little as she met his gaze.

"That's just it," she said. "You see—he does, but—well——" She permitted herself a tiny white lie. "You see he was engaged to the other one, before he met her friend."

Mr. Rachett nodded. "That is certainly a complication," he admitted, and for all his legal shrewdness it never occurred to him that there was anything personal in the conversation. "Although in such circumstances," he added, "surely it is for the man to make his own choice."

Dorothy said: "Yes, yes, I suppose so." And then as he seemed to have forgotten all about the game, she gently touched his hand: "It's your move, Mr. Rachett."

The old man replaced his spectacles.

"A very interesting problem," he said thoughtfully, "but one which, in my opinion, should not be subjected to outside influence. I hope you agree."

"Yes," Dorothy agreed, and it was with such vague snatches of conversation and mythical questioning, that she managed to maintain her poise, but all the while it was as though she was carrying a heavy load, and one which sometimes she felt must be discarded no matter what the consequences.

Wilfred had not been to the house again and she had heard nothing of him, though once when she ventured to speak of him to Mr. Rachett he answered: "I know nothing of Wilfred's movements; he seems to find a strange pleasure in keeping his friends entirely in the dark as to his plans." But Dorothy had heard from Pauline several times—affectionate letters which tried in vain to express a suitable sorrow which she could not feel, and saying that she hoped soon to come to Town so that they could meet.

Dorothy had lunched once with Willie Guest, and although she had tried her utmost to keep the conversation away from Wilfred, Guest seemed determined to speak about him.

"That young man is making a fool of himself," he said in his blunt way. "But I suppose you know as much about it as I do, possibly more!"

"About—what?" Dorothy asked, although she guessed that he must be referring to Pauline.

"About this Mrs. Charteris—apparently it's quite an old

affair, although I only heard of it a few weeks ago. You've seen her! . ... Don't you remember? The night we three dined together!"

"I've stayed at her house, too," Dorothy reminded him.

Guest laughed. "Bless my soul! So you have! Well, then, you know that she's a widow now, more's the pity, and I suppose as soon as the conventions allow she'll be leading Wilfred, an unwilling prisoner, to the altar."

"Why—an unwilling prisoner?" she forced herself to ask.

He shrugged his shoulders.

"Well—Wilfred's not the faithful sort; he finds more excitement in chasing a woman he can't get than in having it all plain sailing—easy money!"

"Isn't that unkind?"

He looked a trifle abashed.

"Don't mean to be unkind," he apologized. "But I like old Wilfred and I'd hate to see him make a hash of things, and it'll be a hash all right if he marries the Charteris woman."

"I'm very fond of her," Dorothy said defensively.

He looked at her dubiously.

"You are, are you!" he submitted. "Oh well, we'll wish him good luck, whatever he does, eh?"

And the following week Pauline arrived in London; Mr. Rachett had just left for the office when she rang through.

"Is that you, Little and Good?"

"*Pauline!*"

"Yes—I arrived last night and I thought I must ring you. Are you free for lunch to-day?"

"Oh yes—and I'd love to see you."

"Will you come to the flat?"

"Yes—thank you; and—are you all right?"

"I'm very well! One-fifteen, then!"

It was only after she had hung up the receiver that Dorothy wondered with a sense of bewilderment why she should really be pleased at the thought of seeing Pauline again, when Wilfred ... and then with a pang—will he be there? "*No!*" she told herself firmly. "He wouldn't do that." And yet as she was whirled up in the lift to Pauline's flat her heart was beating wildly with a hope which was more than half fear, for she longed passionately to see him again.

How would he look? What would he say? It seemed impossible that he had ever said: "I love you—and I want you for my own beloved wife."

And then she was thinking—if he loves me, why does he stay away? If he loves me, doesn't he want to see me as much as I want to see him?

Quite illogical, she told herself firmly, for it was she who had asked him not to come again until—unless. ... The lift stopped and she found herself at Pauline's door.

"Is Mrs. Charteris——" she began to say, and then broke off with a little cry. "Pauline!"

"I knew it was you," Pauline explained as they kissed "And —oh I am glad to see you again! I've thought of you so often, you funny mite!" she laughed. "You don't grow any bigger," she protested.

"No, but you are more beautiful," Dorothy thought, and her lips trembled as she followed Pauline to her room.

"And what have you been doing?" Pauline asked. "Yes, please take off your hat and look as if you have come to stay." She sank down into a big chair with a quick sigh. "It seems years and years since I was in London," she said. "A lifetime since you were with us in the country! And yet I've had so much to do! Everything to settle up—lawyers to see——"

Dorothy asked an involuntary question:

"What has become of Brandy and Soda?"

Pauline looked a little surprised—she was not very fond of animals. "Oh, I gave them to our groom," she answered. "They wouldn't have been happy with anyone else, and he was always second-best—after Bertram." A little frown crossed her lovely face. "It was too tragic—the way those dogs behaved," she said with a shiver. "Just as if they—knew!"

"They did know," Dorothy answered, and then feeling it would be better to change the subject: "And will you live in London—now? Or down in the country?"

"I don't know: it's not possible to make plans yet. You see, Bertram hasn't left a will—which is most unlike him—or if he has, it can't be found. But whatever happens I shan't live in the country! I couldn't—not all the time. I may travel."

"With Wilfred," was the quick thought that leapt to Dorothy's mind, and she turned her face sharply away.

Pauline said: "Well, we'll have lunch, shall we? I've kept the afternoon quite free, so I hope you won't hurry away."

"I must be back when Mr. Rachett comes home."

The elder girl smiled.

"And how are things going?" she inquired. "I asked Wilfred but he said he didn't know. Haven't you seen him lately?"

"Only once—since we left you."

"I dined with him last night," Pauline said. "Don't sit over there with the width of the table between us—sit beside me."

And she's just the same, Dorothy thought; nobody would ever believe that she had experienced tragedy—or wasn't Bertram's death a tragedy as far as Pauline was concerned?

"Tell me what you've been doing?" Pauline invited.

Dorothy smiled. "Nothing very much! I had lunch once with Mr. Guest. Do you know him? He's a friend of Wilfred's."

"I've heard of him."

"And once I went to the pictures with Mrs. Greenley—she was Mrs. Rachett's friend, and she's quite kind."

Pauline made a little grimace.

"Damning praise!" she said lightly. "Don't you know anybody young? Your own age, I mean?"

"Only you and Cecilie—and now she's engaged I suppose I shan't see so much of her, but she's asked me to her wedding on the eleventh. I should have been a bridesmaid, but her father has been ill, and so it's to be a quiet wedding."

She was suddenly aware that Pauline was only half attending, so she added a little shyly: "And now tell me what you've been doing! I've thought about you so much."

Pauline shook her lovely head.

"I seem to have done a tremendous lot of things and yet nothing at all! It will be a relief when everything is settled and I can make definite plans. I think I shall sell The Fortress and buy a smaller place nearer London—something much smaller, so that it can be shut up when we—when I go abroad. I shall keep this flat on, of course—it's convenient and I like it."

"It's lovely," Dorothy agreed in rather a flat voice, for she had heard that inadvertent "we" and it was as if a cold hand had touched her heart.

Pauline went on: "Mother thinks it will be a mistake to sell The Fortress, but what is the use of spending a fortune in keeping it up when I shall hardly ever go there?"

"Your mother is not staying with you now?" Dorothy asked.

"No—she left The Fortress when I did. She was very sweet and I was thankful to have her, but——" Pauline laughed. "I'm one of those people who like my relations better when they are not in the house."

They went back to the lounge for coffee and when the maid who served it had departed, Pauline said a little nervously.

"There is something I want to tell you, and I am wondering whether I ought to!"

She was not looking at the girl or she would have seen the sudden pallor of her sensitive face, but Dorothy only said:

"Please tell me, if you care to."

Pauline sighed. "Of course I know it's very soon—I mean, it's not quite five weeks yet since poor Bertram died, and we should have to wait at least six months, I suppose, although——" She turned her eyes to the girl's face. "It's not as if I ever really—cared for Bertram," she said diffidently. "And after all——" She gave a faintly apologetic laugh. "I may as well tell you the truth at once. It's ... that Wilfred and I are to be married."

Dorothy was slowly stirring her coffee with an absurd little spoon that had a gargoyle head for a handle, and she fancied that it grinned at her with a sort of triumph before, at last, she could force her eyes away from it and to Pauline's face.

"I'm not surprised," she said slowly.

Pauline's eyes widened.

"Not surprised? But—however did you know?"

Dorothy smiled. "I can't explain—but—somehow I knew."

Pauline flushed self-consciously.

"We've known each other for years," she said. "And—right from the first he—I ... will you think very badly of me if I tell you that a long time ago Wilfred wanted me to leave Bertram for him? But I couldn't; you see, somehow—it didn't seem right," she added slowly.

Dorothy said nothing, but she looked again at the absurd little spoon. Yes, its gargoyle head was certainly grinning at her—mocking her perhaps because in a quixotic spirit of self-sacrifice she had sent away the man she loved.

Pauline went on dreamily:

"I know I ought not to say it—I wouldn't to anyone but you

—but I'm—happy now for the first time in my life—really, perfectly happy! Sometimes I give myself a little pinch to make sure that I'm not asleep and dreaming—to make sure that after all I am going to get what I've always wanted." And then she seemed suddenly aware of the girl's silence, for she said quickly: "You're not shocked, are you, dear?"

Shocked! ... she carefully put her coffee cup down on a side table and rose, crossing the room to where Pauline was sitting.

"I'm very glad if you're happy," she said, and she bent and kissed her. Pauline returned the kiss warmly enough, but when Dorothy would have moved away she caught her hand.

"And I tell Wilfred," she said eagerly, "that when we're married you must stay with us often—as often as you like—that we must take you abroad and give you a good time and introduce you to people—you'd like that, wouldn't you?"

"You're very kind," Dorothy said with an effort, "but perhaps Wilfred wouldn't—want me."

Pauline released her hand.

"Have you and he quarrelled?" she asked bluntly.

"Quarrelled? Why?"

Pauline gave a little sigh of vexation. "Only that he seemed almost annoyed when I made the suggestion—about taking you abroad with us, I mean. He said it was an absurd idea and that he wouldn't consider it! ... I was amazed, because I always imagined he was so fond of you!"

Dorothy managed a shaken laugh.

"We haven't quarrelled," she said rather breathlessly. "Only —I suppose it's natural that he should—want you—all to himself."

"That's all very well," Pauline said softly, "but I tell him we mustn't be selfish, and that he must remember he is your guardian, and besides—I'm very fond of you, Little and Good."

Dorothy turned sharply away, biting her lip to check the protesting words: "Don't call me that—it's Wilfred's name for me, not anyone else's—I won't have you calling me by his name."

And yet, what did it matter? She had lost him, and one pain more or less was of small account.

Pauline went on: "I told Wilfred you were lunching with

me and I asked him to look in for coffee, but you see he hasn't turned up!"

She laughed happily. "Wilfred is always so unexpected—perhaps that's why I love him. Bertram was so different—poor Bertram! One always knew exactly what he would do and say." She broke off and there was a moment's silence before she said diffidently:

"You won't tell anyone, will you, dear? Not yet, I mean! People are so conventional in their ideas and I should hate a lot of spiteful gossip."

"I shan't tell anyone," Dorothy promised, and she wondered with faint amusement who Pauline imagined she *could* tell except Mr. Rachett!

Pauline went on talking in an excited voice.

"But I mean to look after you, Dorothy, no matter what Wilfred says. I mean to see that you have the good time you have never had yet, and—if you don't mind—I should like to take you to my dressmaker—he'd turn you out perfectly."

"Is that where I went with Mrs. Greenley?" Dorothy asked, trying to appear interested. "Where I first saw you?"

Pauline nodded. "Yes—Maneau is wonderful with clothes. He looks one over and seems to know immediately just what will be the right thing! and you'd look a perfect darling if he had charge of your wardrobe."

Dorothy said that she was afraid she did not pay for dressing.

"I'm much too small," she apologized.

"Maneau would love you," Pauline declared. "Anyone a little different and he is in his element." She looked at the girl with introspective eyes. "And I know heaps of people you will love and who will love you," she said enthusiastically. "Lots of nice boys, too—and when you're married . . ."

Dorothy broke in quickly: "That's not very likely." But Pauline shook her head. "Nonsense! When they know all about you!" . . . She stopped and Dorothy said: "You mean when they know that I come into money when I'm twenty-one."

"I didn't mean that at all," Pauline protested. "You're sweet enough even if you hadn't a penny—but I shan't let you stay with Mr. Rachett—not after I've married Wilfred. It's quite the wrong environment for you. You ought to have a car and learn to drive it yourself, and you ought to be seen about more, in places that matter, and with people who matter. . . ."

Dorothy let her talk because it seemed easier than objecting, but she felt heartsick and weary and only conscious of the longing to escape and to return to Mr. Rachett's rather dreary house where at least she would be at peace.

She stayed till four o'clock because Pauline seemed to wish it, and Pauline spoke persistently of Wilfred and said that once they were married she was sure he would settle down and never want to wander again, until suddenly Dorothy felt that she could bear no more.

"I think, if you don't mind, I ought to go. Mr. Rachett likes me to be at home when he comes in, and it will take me quite half an hour to get back."

And so she escaped at last. "I shall see you again, very soon," Pauline said. "And next time I shall insist that Wilfred comes too."

"That will be nice."

"I'll send you back in the car," Pauline said, but Dorothy would not allow that. "I like the 'bus," she declared, and presently the lift carried her away from Pauline's lovely, smiling face.

And then, surprisingly, she knew she was trembling, as if she had passed through a terrifying experience, and although she was in Park Lane she took off her hat and let the fresh air blow on her forehead. The 'bus came along and she scrambled on to it with a queer sense of weakness, and then for a little while her mind seemed to go blank, as if it no longer had the power to think or to suffer, until the conductor touched her arm—

"You get off here, miss," he said.

Dorothy thanked him hurriedly and walked slowly up the road to Mr. Rachett's house. Pauline's flat was lovely, but she felt that she could never bear to see it again, and she tried loyally to stifle the knowledge that neither did she want to see Pauline any more, for surely Pauline had changed! Or did the difference lie in herself?

The first remark Mr. Rachett made over the dinner table was that Wilfred had called at the office.

"I really don't know why, Dorothy; he seemed to have no particular reason."

"And how is he?"

Mr. Rachett hesitated. "As a matter of fact, I thought he was looking tired," he admitted. "Older somehow—but of course we are all getting older! and no doubt the unsettled life he leads is a severe strain upon his constitution; still, it would be useless for me to protest or to offer advice. You must see what your influence can do, Dorothy."

"Mine!" she said, and there was a note of pathetic bitterness in her voice. "I wouldn't dare!" she hastened to add laughingly and then she deliberately changed the conversation and spoke of Cecilie's wedding.

"Will you come with me?" she asked hesitatingly. "Cecilie said she would be pleased if you would! and I don't want to go alone."

The old man looked at her dubiously.

"Will I come with you?" he echoed. "Well, it's a very long time since I went to a wedding, my dear, but—perhaps—well, if it will please you, I will certainly come, though I am not sure whether I possess a silk hat."

"It's to be a very quiet wedding," she told him. "But I shall enjoy it far more if you are there."

Mr. Rachett's eyes softened. "Thank you, my dear," he said, and he wondered whether it was imagination that she looked tired too! just as he had fancied that Wilfred had looked tired.

"So you lunched with Mrs. Charteris!" he said encouragingly.

"Yes."

"And is she quite well after all her trouble? A charming lady, very charming."

"She is very well, thank you."

There was a little silence before he asked: "And when is your friend's wedding to be?" Dorothy started and roused herself from the reverie into which she had fallen to say in an agitated voice. "Oh, not yet!" and then in hurried confusion: "Whose wedding do you mean?"

He looked puzzled. "The wedding we are to attend," he explained. She drew a quick breath and laughed.

"Oh, it's on Saturday! ... I was thinking of something else," and she rushed on to tell him gaily that only relations and close friends had been invited, and that afterwards there was to be a small and informal lunch party at an hotel close to the church. She kept the ball of conversation rolling until it was time to go to bed, and then as she bade him good night, Mr. Rachett said solicitously:

"You are looking tired, my dear!"

It took all her strength of will to keep the tears from rushing to her eyes as she declared that she was not a bit tired, how could she be, seeing that she had spent such a lazy day?

But it seemed a long, long way up the stairs to her own room, an eternity before she had shut and locked the door, and the need to pretend was over. But even then she dared not give way for she was afraid of the storm of emotion which was waiting to bear her down, so she deliberately turned on all the lights and walked across to the mirror to stare at her reflection with hard eyes.

"If you cry!" she threatened it, "if you cry, I'll never forgive you, never! ... never!" And then suddenly she wanted to laugh—just to laugh and laugh! But somehow that seemed even worse than tears, so she turned sharply away and began to pull off her clothes, trying to keep her thoughts fixed on Cecilie's wedding, and what she would wear.

"I'll buy a new hat and some white gloves, and I'll get a white carnation for Mr. Rachett's buttonhole. I hope it will be a fine day because they say happy is the bride the sun shines on—and I want her to be happy, I want her to be happy." And then her courage suddenly failed, and turning out the lights she crept into bed and drew the clothes tightly over her face so that nobody could hear her bitter sobbing....

And the sun shone its brightest on Cecilie's wedding day, and Mr. Rachett looked quite shy as Dorothy fastened the white carnation into his buttonhole and told him that he looked positively handsome.

"Then we are a handsome pair," the old man said, and he added diffidently: "That is a very pretty little hat, Dorothy."

"It's new!" she told him gaily, and she turned about for his inspection. "My gloves are new, too."

They took a taxi to the church, and Cecilie's brother, having asked in a whisper: "Bride or bridegroom?" showed them into a pew very near the front.

The organ was playing softly and Lawrence and his best men were already standing at the chancel steps looking a little selfconscious, and suddenly Dorothy thought—will Pauline expect me to go to *her* wedding?

She kept her eyes fixed on the stained glass window above the altar and tried to picture Wilfred standing at the chancel steps waiting ... or would they be married in a registrar's office? And then she knew that people were rising to their feet and that the bride had arrived.

She looked lovely, even though she had been forced to dispense with a bridal gown, and she looked radiantly happy too —and she carried a bouquet of blue love-in-a-mist.

When the service was over and Cecilie came down the aisle leaning on her husband's arm, she smiled at Dorothy, and Mr. Rachett gave a little cough to cover the sudden emotion which had arisen in his heart, as his thoughts went back more than thirty years to a day when he and the one woman he had ever loved.

"We must go now," said Dorothy.

They walked across to the hotel and everyone kissed the bride and congratulated the bridegroom, and then they sat down to lunch.

Cecilie's father made a speech and said how pleased he was to welcome a new son, and then Lawrence made a speech and got very red as he referred to "my wife" and everyone laughed and toasted the bride and bridegroom. And when lunch was over Cecilie's brother came over to where Dorothy was sitting and said a little shyly:

"We haven't met before, but I've heard a lot about you from my sister—I'm Jim."

"I've heard a lot about you, too," she answered, and she thought he was nice and she liked his smile. And then he went on to explain that they'd taken two boxes for a show that night: "Just to end up cheerfully," so he said. "And if you'll come, we shall all be delighted—and there's lots of room."

Dorothy began to say that she was afraid it was not possible, but Mr. Rachett interrupted gently:

"Of course you must go, my dear child—you will enjoy it. Of course you must go."

Jim said: "Well, that's topping," and he told her which theatre they had chosen and offered to call for her if she would allow him, and again it was Mr. Rachett who said it was an excellent idea.

"But you'll be alone!" Dorothy protested, to which he answered that as he had taken a whole afternoon off from the office he would find plenty to occupy his time.

"I'll call for you at eight," Jim said. "And we're going to have supper afterwards."

"Very nice, very nice indeed," Mr. Rachett said approvingly. And then Cecilie called to Dorothy:

"I'm going to change my dress—come with me." And together they went to a room which had been taken for the occasion.

"What are you going to wear?" Dorothy asked and Cecilie said:

"Oh, just a plain dress—blue, because it's Lawrence's favourite colour." She gave Dorothy an affectionate hug. "I'm frightfully happy," she whispered, "and some day I hope you'll be just as happy. Has Jim asked you to go to the theatre with them to-night?"

"Yes—it's very kind of him."

"You ought to like each other," Cecilie said, and presently they went downstairs together, and there were the usual good-byes and a few tears from Cecilie's mother, and a shower of confetti from Jim and the best man, and then—they had gone!

"A very pleasant afternoon, Dorothy," Mr. Rachett said as they drove away. "And a very delightful family."

When they reached home he took the white carnation from his coat and looked at it thoughtfully.

"This must be put into water," he said, and then he smiled as he added: "And I think—on my study table." He touched her shoulder caressingly. "Come and say good-bye to me before you go."

Dorothy chose the apricot coloured dress which she had worn the first time Wilfred came to dine at the Rachetts', and the little bandeau of autumn-tinted leaves round her hair, but she was not looking forward to the evening at all, and would have preferred to stay at home, still, she thought with a sigh, perhaps it's just as well to go—I shan't have so much more time to think.

"I've seen that dress before," Mr. Rachett said surprisingly when she went to his study to say good-bye; he pushed back his glasses and looked at her approvingly. "I think you are going to have a very happy evening," he told her kindly.

Jim came into the study looking very fresh and pleased and Mr. Rachett told him to take good care of Dorothy and not to allow her to get over-tired.

"Funny old codger," Jim said cheerily as he and Dorothy drove away; he looked down at her. "Hope you'll like the show," he said boyishly. "There are only eight of us going— quite a bright bunch."

She raised her eyes to his face.

"May I sit next to you?" she asked timidly, for she had never quite conquered her shyness with strangers.

"I'd love you to," he answered warmly.

They were late at the theatre, for in Piccadilly they got into a traffic jam owing to a collision, and the curtain was already up when they entered the box.

"I'll introduce you afterwards," Jim whispered as they took their seats. "Can you see all right?"

"Yes, thank you."

There were only two other people in the box with them, and Jim had placed Dorothy in a chair which faced the stage.

The play was a farce—the kind of thing which Jim adored, and he laughed uproariously at every joke, and applauded with all his might.

"Great, isn't it?" he asked her, oblivious to the fact that Dorothy had missed most of the rather broad humour, and was a little at sea with regard to the plot.

"It's one of the few successes in town," she heard the other girl say. "We were lucky to get seats."

"I booked them a month ago—as soon as Cecilie fixed her wedding day," Jim answered.

And then the curtain fell to a storm of applause and the lights went up, and Dorothy blinked her eyes and wondered whether she was very stupid not to have understood what it was all about.

Jim introduced her to the other two who were sharing the box. "This is Miss Baker—Miss Little—and Mr. Topham— Topham's a kind of cousin," he explained cheerfully. "But we try to keep the relationship dark."

Topham made a playful lunge at him and Jim ducked his head out of reach.

164

"They're such a pair of idiots," Iris Baker apologized.

Dorothy leaned her arms on the ledge of the box and looked down at the stalls. Not a vacant seat anywhere! and everyone seemed to be thoroughly pleased, for they were all laughing.

A tall man rose suddenly from the second row of the stalls and made his way towards the exit. Dorothy's eyes turned to him indifferently and then she felt her heart turn cold and her hand, resting on the padded ledge of the box, closed convulsively as he glanced casually upwards and she found herself gazing down into Wilfred's eyes.

CHAPTER NINE

Jim Jepson touched Dorothy's arm.

"Asleep?" he inquired. "I've spoken to you twice but you seemed to be miles away!" He leaned over to peer down into the stalls. "What are you looking at?"

"Nobody—nothing! I was just looking at the people. What did you ask me?"

"Whether you would like an ice! ... Iris and Topham have gone to the bar, and I expect the others have too—there are four more of our party in the next box, you know. Would you like an ice?"

"I think I should, thank you."

"Come along then."

She followed him down the narrow corridor and up a short flight of steps to the bar, which was already half filled with gaily-chattering people, but although Dorothy looked everywhere for Wilfred, he was not there.

Was he alone? But it did not seem probable. Was he with Pauline? But would she go out so soon after her husband's death? "I don't suppose it would matter," she thought vaguely, and yet, if Pauline was with Wilfred, would he have left her alone in the theatre?

Jim brought up the rest of the party and introduced them, and Dorothy smiled, but every name escaped her and she made no attempt to join in the conversation.

"A bit quiet, isn't she?" Iris Baker whispered to Jim, and he answered defensively that it was a treat to meet a girl who didn't chatter.

Dorothy barely touched the ice which Jim had struggled to the counter to get for her, and when she thought he was not looking, she put it down behind a tired-looking fern in a green pot.

And then once again she searched the crowd with longing eyes. If she could only see him, just for a minute! . . . only just touch his hand—hear his voice! It seemed a lifetime since she had assured him so confidently that if he never came back she would know why and understand, and now the memory only brought with it a feeling of bitterness and a sense of self-scorn.

Had she really ever been so sure of herself—and of him? But that was before she had seen Pauline again and had been forced to listen to her confession.

How blind people were! How blind she herself had been, for until this moment she had not realized the terrible longing she would experience at the sight of Wilfred, and the burning jealousy which was almost hatred of Pauline.

But not really hatred, she reproached herself hurriedly— not hatred at all, but just bitter envy! For Pauline was not to blame. Pauline had no idea that they both loved the same man, and besides, he had belonged to Pauline first!

"But not any more!" she told herself. "Not any more! He's mine now, even if . . ." and then suddenly the crowd parted, and she saw him.

He was standing by the counter—head and shoulders above the men around him, bending down a little to hear what someone was saying. Dorothy raised her tiny self on tip-toe to see who that someone might be, and it was Pauline!

Pauline dressed in palest silvery grey, with a grey chiffon cape draped gracefully around her shoulders and fastened with a spray of palest pink camellias.

She was talking quite animatedly, as if she had never known the meaning of sorrow, and she was looking up at Wilfred all the time, and Dorothy, watching them both with strained attention, suddenly saw her raise her hand to the lapel of his coat as though to brush away a fleck of dust.

The little intimate gesture hurt her more than all the rest,

166

and she turned her head sharply away just as Pauline, glancing idly round, saw her.

"Why—look, Wilfred!" . . . and without waiting she made her way through the crowd and caught Dorothy's hand. "Fancy seeing you!" she said gaily. "You're the very last person I expected to see! Who are you with?"

Dorothy explained with difficulty: "I'm with a party; we've been to a wedding—Cecilie's friends—but you don't know Cecilie, do you?"

"I've heard you speak of her—I'm with Wilfred . . . ah, here he is!" She looked up at Wilfred smilingly. "Isn't this a surprise?" she said, but it was Dorothy who replied:

"A very nice surprise, I think."

"Dorothy is with a wedding party," Pauline explained.

"And doesn't she look a picture? I love that dress. . . but you're rather pale! . . . perhaps it's the heat—I was just saying that there doesn't seem to be any air at all to-night."

The warning bell rang sharply through the saloon and people began to move back to their seats.

"I must go!" Dorothy said. She smiled at Jim who was hovering in the background. "Just coming!" she told him, and then with a last word to Pauline she turned away.

Pauline looked after her with a slight frown on her lovely face. "She does look pale!" she said again, and then to Wilfred: "You might have spoken to the poor little thing! You hardly said a word to her!"

"I said 'good evening'," Wilfred answered grimly, "and there seemed nothing else to say."

"I thought you were such friends," Pauline said, but he made no reply and they went back to their seats.

But now Wilfred sat with his shoulder turned to the Jepsons' box, and although just before the lights went down Pauline glanced up and smiled at Dorothy, he never once turned his head.

"That's Mrs. Charteris, isn't it?" Iris Baker whispered to Dorothy, and she answered:

"Yes, do you know her?"

"No, but I've often seen her first nights and film premieres. —I've seen lots of her photographs too! She's lovely, isn't she?"

"Yes."

"And is that the man she's going to marry?"

"I—don't know. Why?"

Iris shrugged her shoulders.

"Oh, one hears these things!" she answered, and then: "It seems a bit soon, doesn't it? How long is it since Mr. Charteris died?"

"I'm . . . not quite sure. . . ."

And then the theatre was suddenly darkened, and that ended the conversation. But when it was all over and they were waiting outside while Jim and his cousin found taxis, she saw Wilfred again, and then just for a fleeting moment their eyes met, and his were just a hard unhappiness, and hers! . . .

Pauline rang up the following morning.

"I looked for you everywhere as we left the theatre!" she said. "What happened to you? And when shall I see you again? Will you come to dinner one evening, and bring Mr. Rachett too! I'll get Wilfred to make a fourth! Do come!"

Dorothy answered hurriedly that Mr. Rachett did not like going out at night, but Pauline insisted.

"It will do him good! I'll write him a little note."

A little note which duly arrived, and which seemed to please the old man.

"Very kind of her to include me in the invitation," he said. "I think I should like to go; what do you say, Dorothy?"

"Of course, if you would like to go," she answered, but she clung to the hope that Wilfred would not be there—a vain hope as it proved to be!

"Well, this is very pleasant, very pleasant indeed," Mr. Rachett said as he looked round Pauline's lavish drawing-room. "You have wonderful taste, Mrs. Charteris."

Pauline smiled with pleasure. "Do you think so? I must show you the rest of the rooms if you would care to see them —Wilfred, give Dorothy a cocktail." And she took the old man away, proud that she had evidently made a conquest of him.

There was a short silence when they had gone until Wilfred said: "It's good to see you again, my dear!"

"Is it?" She could not meet his eyes, and because everything seemed so unbearable she said gaily: "What about the drink? I'm dying for one."

168

He moved his hand to touch hers, but she drew it sharply away. "Don't!" she said, and then at last she raised her eyes to his face. "Oh, I hoped you wouldn't come——" she whispered, and he answered:

"I couldn't help it! Do you think I wanted to come?"

She watched while he mixed things in haphazard fashion from some glass bottles and presently she asked with an effort:

"What are you making? It looks very exciting."

Wilfred laughed grimly. "I haven't the slightest idea—don't drink it if you don't like it——" but he put the glass into her hand, and watched while she sipped it and then he said humbly:

"You are looking very—sweet to-night, Little and Good——" And then Pauline and Mr. Rachett returned.

"A delightful flat, Dorothy," Mr. Rachett said affably. "A wonderful view over the Park—wonderful!"

"Let's eat, shall we, everybody?" said Pauline.

Afterwards Dorothy could only remember that Mr. Rachett had been more sociable than she had ever known him to be, and although for his sake she was glad, it added to her own unhappiness for she realized that it was entirely due to Pauline's charm and influence and that if she could so easily please an old man, it was easy to understand her fascination for Wilfred. And somehow as she watched her, it seemed hard to believe that Wilfred indeed no longer cared—for she was so gay and sweet and beautiful that by contrast she herself felt insignificant and of no account.

"I am glad to see, Wilfred," Mr. Rachett remarked jocularly, "that for the moment at any rate, you show no sign of continuing your wanderings! Have you been lecturing him on the subject, Mrs. Charteris?"

Pauline's lovely eyes flashed a glance at Wilfred.

"I should never dare to lecture him!" she said laughingly. "You may not believe it, but he's really a frightful bully! And I'm simply terrified of him."

"I cannot believe that anyone would bully *you*," the old man answered with clumsy courtesy. "What do you say, Dorothy?"

"I think Pauline is joking," she answered. "And I'm sure it's quite the other way about, and that Wilfred simply adores her! All men do!"

"You shocking little flatterer!" Pauline protested happily. "Did you hear what she said, Wilfred?"

"Yes—I heard."

"And what have *you* to say on the subject?" Mr. Rachett inquired.

Wilfred shrugged his shoulders.

"Dorothy is such a keen student of human nature, that she is probably perfectly correct in what she says," he answered.

"There!" Mr. Rachett said approvingly. "And a very nice compliment I am sure, eh, Dorothy?"

"Wilfred is always complimentary," she answered. "Didn't you know that I have the world's most perfect guardian?"

And then she was thinking painfully—did I really say a stupid thing like that? It didn't sound at all like me somehow? But she went on talking in the same flippant strain, and when Pauline referred to the wedding party at the theatre Dorothy said:

"Yes, and I made quite a conquest of Cecilie's brother! . . . He has rung me up every day since."

"No doubt his father pays the telephone bill," Wilfred joked, and Mr. Rachett asked interestedly:

"Has he *indeed* rung you every day, Dorothy?"

She laughed. "Well, perhaps not every day!" she admitted. "But quite often."

"I admire his taste," Pauline said. "And I admire his persistency. He is evidently quite sure what he wants and means to get it."

"Yes—I like that sort of man," Dorothy agreed. "I think men should always know what they want—*and* get it too! Don't you, Wilfred?"

She addressed him deliberately, and her eyes were reckless.

"If that is intended for me," he answered, "may I submit that I too, am perfectly capable of getting what I want—if I am seriously challenged?"

"I am sure you are!" she answered calmly. "But I'm not challenging you. Please may I have one of those chocolates?"

Pauline passed the little silver dish.

"What a baby you are!" she said affectionately. "Mr. Rachett, I am surprised you haven't provided a nursery for her."

"Complete with dolls' house and rocking horse!" Dorothy added gaily.

The old man looked at Dorothy with rather troubled eyes.

"I am afraid Dorothy's life with me is rather a dull affair," he said regretfully.

"I won't allow you to say that," she protested indignantly. "I'm perfectly happy, you know I am!"

He shook his head as he answered: "Very kind of you to say so, my dear, but it is a true saying that youth and crabbed age cannot live together."

"I've been telling Dorothy," Pauline interrupted, "that I hope later on, you will allow her to come abroad with us—with me, I mean," she added in slight confusion. "I am sure she would love to travel, and if you can spare her I promise to be just as perfect a chaperone as Wilfred is a guardian."

"That is a most excellent idea," Mr. Rachett agreed. "I am delighted at the suggestion. What does Dorothy say?"

"I'm not going to leave you alone," Dorothy answered. "It's very kind of Pauline—but . . . I shouldn't be happy if I knew you had no one to help you in the house."

Mr. Rachett touched her hand in a little caress.

"But some day you will leave me," he said with a smile. "I cannot always hope to keep you, my dear! . . . When Prince Charming comes along. . . ." He laughed and Pauline added gaily:

"Or this determined Jim!"

"You seem to be in a great hurry to be rid of me," Dorothy said, trying to smile.

"On the contrary," Mr. Rachett assured her. "But I imagine that Wilfred would assert his authority if I entered a kind of caveat against the possibility of your ever marrying, eh, Wilfred?"

"I don't suppose Wilfred would care one way or the other," Dorothy remarked carelessly.

Wilfred's eyes suddenly blazed.

"That is an abominable thing to say!" he said hotly. "When you know—when you know. . . ." He stopped, and Pauline said in gentle amazement:

"*Wilfred!*"

He made a quick gesture of repudiation.

"Sorry!" he said shortly.

"Don't be sorry," Dorothy answered. "You've got a perfect right to say what you think—and so have I, for that matter."

Mr. Rachett cleared his throat and picked up his wine glass. "This is very fine claret!" he said with an obvious attempt to change the conversation. "There is no finer wine than a good claret."

"It is some my husband bought," Pauline told him. "Poor Bertram was an excellent judge of wine."

Poor Bertram!—Dorothy was conscious of a little pang as she remembered the man who had in his blunt way been kind to her, and the two dogs Brandy and Soda, who had loved him and had kept their faithful watch long after he had gone.

Pauline touched her arm: "Shall we leave them?" she asked, and then as the girl rose: "Don't be too long, Wilfred. Join us for coffee."

And when the door had closed upon them she put a hand on Dorothy's arm.

"I can't understand Wilfred," she said in a troubled voice. "He seems quite irritable and nervy."

"I think he must be getting bored with town," said Dorothy. And then she quickly changed the conversation, but at the back of her mind there were only despairing thoughts and the determination that whatever happened she would never see Wilfred again. For it was but a vague happiness which was nearly all pain—to be so near to him and yet so far away—to be forced by some impulse she could not control to say things which she knew must hurt him—perhaps even more than they hurt herself.

And she had meant to be so gentle and understanding!

"What a lot of letters!" Pauline said. She picked up a little pile which were lying on the coffee tray, and sorted them through without much interest.

"I suppose you always have a lot, don't you?"

"Y-yes . . ." Pauline's voice was a little preoccupied and presently she detached one from the rest and broke open the flap. There was a moment's silence while she read the contents, and then she laughed with a sort of relief.

"Of course I knew it would be found!" she said, and then in explanation: "This is from my lawyers, to say Bertram's will has been found in a drawer at The Fortress. I always knew they would find it, and they want me to see them to-morrow." She laid the letter aside and frowned. "To-morrow is most inconvenient too! ... I have such a full day! Still, I suppose business comes first. Now! what about some coffee?"

"Please!" Dorothy watched her in silence for a moment, and then she said: "I am sorry you will be selling the house."

"You funny child! Why are you sorry?"

"It's such a lovely place."

Pauline shook her head. "It has no happy associations for me, and I am not fond of the country. The only difficulty may be to find a purchaser. Still, fortunately I am not in need of money." She suddenly raised her eyes. "Why are you so determined not to come abroad with us?" she asked.

Dorothy's colour faded. "It isn't that," she protested. "I should love to go abroad, but—I really don't want to leave Mr. Rachett. He's been very good to me, and I should feel —almost, as if I were destroying him."

"But, darling," Pauline protested. "As he says you won't always be able to stay with him! Some day you'll marry—of course you will!" she insisted as the girl shook her head. "I *want* you to marry! Some nice boy who will adore you and make you happy."

"I don't think I like—nice boys!" Dorothy answered, "and they don't like me very much, either!"

"Not even Jim?" Pauline chided her, and then she turned her head quickly as the men entered.

"You haven't been very long!" she said.

"We were anxious not to miss the company of two such charming ladies," Mr. Rachett answered with a little bow.

"That's very sweet of you," Pauline said. She patted the chair beside her. "Come and sit next to me—do you like black coffee?"

"Plenty of sugar and cream, please," the old man answered.

Wilfred had gone over to the window; it was quite dark but as the curtains were still undrawn he could see the lights of the Park and the road beneath twinkling like a thousand stars.

"Coffee, Wilfred?" Pauline called to him, and he turned.

"Thanks—no sugar, thanks."

"Would anyone care to go to a late film?" Pauline inquired. "There's an excellent Italian picture at the Curzon; do you like pictures, Dorothy?"

"I am sure she does," Mr. Rachett answered for her. "Though it may surprise you to know that I have only been to a cinema twice in my life."

"And did you like them?" Pauline asked.

Dorothy was hoping that he would say no, but he said instead that he thought they were most entertaining.

"Then we'll go," Pauline said determinedly. "There won't be any need to ring up for seats—we'll take our chance. You've got your car, haven't you, Wilfred? Or shall I 'phone for a cab?"

"I have mine," he answered.

"Then finish your coffee," Pauline said gaily, "and we'll be off."

"I hope you really want to go to a film," Pauline said to Dorothy when they had gone to her room. "I'm not dragging you there against your will, am I?"

"Oh no! And Mr. Rachett seems delighted, doesn't he?"

"I think he's such a dear," Pauline answered warmly.

So they drove away in Wilfred's car—the two men in the front seat, and when they reached the cinema, Pauline drew Wilfred aside: "Sit next to Dorothy, dear," she whispered, "and do be nice to the poor child——" and before he could answer she turned away.

And it was Pauline who manœuvred so that Dorothy sat between Wilfred and Mr. Rachett, and she herself on Mr. Rachett's right hand.

The big picture was already being shown, and she whispered to Dorothy to know whether she had a good view.

"Thank you, yes." But Dorothy sat stiffly erect, her hands folded in her lap, trying to keep as far away as possible from Wilfred for she felt that if her arm just touched his, it would be the last straw, and that the steel band which was so tightly folded round her heart, would snap and then . . .

She kept her eyes fixed steadily on the screen, but the story passed her by almost unnoticed, for what was the pain of imaginary people in comparison with her own?

"You've dropped your bag," Wilfred said in an undertone, and he bent to recover it for her, and as she moved to take it from him, under cover of the darkness he kissed her hand.

Then the burning tears rose to her eyes, and fell slowly down her cheeks, but she did not dare to wipe them away, she just sat there perfectly still, fighting hard for composure.

Now and then she heard Mr. Rachett say "dear, dear!" in a very sympathetic undertone when the screen portrayed a moment of tragedy or suspense, and a little sob broke from an elderly woman in the row in front of them.

And then the lights went up without any warning and the credit titles appeared.

"Is that—the end?" Mr. Rachett asked disappointedly, and Pauline answered:

"Yes—what a tragedy, wasn't it?" She leaned forward to look at Dorothy and saw the tears on her face. "And this poor child is quite upset!" she said. "And I really felt like crying myself."

Wilfred glanced quickly away and Dorothy fumbled for her handkerchief and dried her eyes murmuring that it was all—so sad, though she had no idea what the story had been about.

Mr. Rachett patted her hand.

"It's only a story, Dorothy," he said consolingly. "You must not take it too much to heart! But it was a fine production—a very fine production."

"If anyone feels like supper——" Pauline said, but Mr. Rachett answered with surprising firmness that it was time old men were in bed, time young ladies were in bed too, and that he had spent a thoroughly enjoyable evening.

"We'll get a taxi," he said, but Wilfred would not allow that.

"I'll drive you home," he insisted.

And when they reached the silent street Dorothy kissed Pauline and thanked her, and Wilfred followed them up the steps to the front door where Mr. Rachett was already fumbling with his key.

"I must be getting a little blind," he apologized, "because I cannot find the keyhole—and that sounds terribly bad, doesn't it?"

Wilfred said: "Allow me, sir," and took the key from him.

"I'll put on the light," Mr. Rachett said.

He entered the dark hall, and Dorothy turned to Wilfred:

"Good night," she said, and he answered softly:

"Good night, beloved."

But even those words could not comfort her, and all the time she was undressing she was tormenting herself with the thought that no doubt he had often said just the same thing to Pauline—and would perhaps say it again! For when they were married, surely his old love for her would return! . . . Who could help loving Pauline if she wanted them to love her!

At breakfast-time Mr. Rachett was full of enthusiasm about his "evening out" as he jocularly called it.

"Everything was most delightful," he said. "We must ask Mrs. Charteris and Wilfred to dine with us, eh, Dorothy?"

"I am so glad you enjoyed it," was all she said.

"And don't forget to write a little note of thanks," the old man said. "I shall do so too, of course."

"I won't forget," Dorothy promised, but she rang Pauline instead only to be told that she was out and was not expected in until the evening.

"With Wilfred," she thought at once, and then remembered that Pauline had an appointment with her lawyer.

But it was only lunch-time when Pauline herself rang through.

"Is that you, dear?"

"Yes, I rang you this morning."

"Did you? I haven't been back to the flat yet. I'm ringing from my Club—are you busy this afternoon, or can I see you?"

"I'm not busy."

"Then will you be at home? May I come round—I feel that I must talk to someone—you see . . . something rather distressing has happened, and I thought—if I could tell you . . ." She paused, as though sensing Dorothy's hesitation, and then the girl said at once, though with an effort:

"Yes, I shall be in—please come."

Something rather distressing! . . . Dorothy went up to her room and changed her dress and tidied her hair. Probably it was nothing very serious—she might even have had a little quarrel with Wilfred! . . . She looked out of the window,

176

wishing Pauline would hurry, but it was nearly an hour before she arrived.

"Sweet of you to let me come!" was her greeting. "It's queer—but when you're in serious trouble, it's surprising how few people there are to whom you can go! I've got so many friends and yet——" She paused and laughed a little self-consciously. "As a matter of fact, you're the only one who knows!"

"Who—knows?"

"Yes—I mean, about Wilfred! You see, this concerns him as well as me."

They went into Mr. Rachett's study and she shut the door. "Something—bad?" she asked hesitatingly.

Pauline nodded. "*I* think it's bad—but he doesn't know yet! And I don't know what he'll say! . . . You see—a few months ago I should have been quite sure, but now—*you've* seen how different Wilfred is, haven't you?"

"Different?"

"Not to me," Pauline explained quickly. "But he's—in a way, so unlike himself. So moody and—changeable——" She sighed. "And when I tell him about the will . . ."

"You mean—Mr. Charteris's will?"

"Yes. I told you it had been found . . . Bertram had put it away in an old desk which was never used as far as I know. I always thought, naturally, that it was with his lawyer—that's why there's been so much delay. However, we have it now—and—it's not an altogether pleasant will."

Dorothy made no comment, and presently Pauline said in a tense voice:

"Bertram leaves everything to me on the condition that I do not marry again. And if I *do* marry—all I get is a paltry five hundred a year."

There was a profound silence and then she continued almost angrily: "I think it's such a mean thing for him to have done. I am young, and why should I stay single all my life just because of Bertram's jealousy! He *was* jealous, you know! Jealous and suspicious—sometimes he made my life a perfect misery with his suspicions——" She stopped again and Dorothy said:

"He's dead——"

Pauline flushed. "I know, and I don't want to be unkind

177

about him—he was always very generous to me—but this . . . I think it's most cruel. It almost seems as though he—guessed —that if ever I was free, Wilfred and I would wish to marry."

"But—does it make any difference?" Dorothy asked.

"Difference!" Pauline laughed. "Difference! Can you imagine me with only five hundred a year! . . . it's an impossible position."

Dorothy raised her eyes to the portrait of Wilfred on the wall opposite, and presently she said: "But—hasn't Wilfred plenty of money?"

"Wilfred has about three thousand a year, I believe," Pauline answered. "He has never actually told me, but I think it is about three thousand."

"It seems a lot of money."

"A lot! . . . Do you know what Bertram left?"

The girl shook her head, and Pauline said:

"If I remain unmarried, my income will be very nearly thirty thousand a year!"

"Thirty thousand! However can anyone spend so much money?"

"*I* can!" Pauline answered, and then, almost apologetically: "You see, my dear, I've been used to luxury, and to having everything I want. If I marry a poor man, neither of us will be happy—I shouldn't be, and if I wasn't, Wilfred wouldn't be happy either. Five hundred a year is absurd. Why did Bertram do that to *me*?"

Dorothy stared at her with blank eyes.

"But *is* a man poor—with three thousand a year?" she asked at last.

"You don't understand," Pauline said again. "Everything is a matter of comparison, and three thousand a year with income tax deducted—well, it's nothing!"

"*Nothing!*" They looked at one another almost with enmity, till Dorothy asked very slowly: "Then what are you going to do?"

Pauline lowered her eyes.

"What would *you* do?" she said pointedly.

Dorothy sat down in Mr. Rachett's big chair, gripping its arms with trembling hands, and tried to think.

"I should marry him . . . of course," she said quietly, and Pauline answered:

"That's because you're so young and romantic—and un-worldly—but I'm not like that! . . . I must have plenty of clothes and money—I must go about and have a good time—love in a cottage doesn't appeal to me—you see . . . I just couldn't!"

She raised her eyes appealingly.

"I thought you'd help me," she said.

"Help you?"

"Yes . . . you see—I don't know how to tell—Wilfred."

Dorothy turned her face sharply away.

"Tell him—what?" she asked.

"That I can't marry him! . . . Oh, darling, do try to under-stand and to see things from my point of view. It's not that I don't love him—I've never loved any other man, but how long would it last if we hadn't enough money to make it possible? He would hate it as much as I should! He's always been so used to doing just as he pleases—going abroad when he wanted to—living in the way he likes best, and if he had me to keep as well, it would be—simply an unbearable existence for us both. . . ." And then she began to cry. "I think it's cruel of Bertram—after all, I always did my best for him, and now—when I thought I was going to be happy at last . . ."

"You can still be happy if you want to," Dorothy said. "But if money means more to you than anything else . . ."

"It's not that!" Pauline wept. "It's not that at all. And I'm thinking about Wilfred's happiness as well as my own! He would hate it, too, you must *know* that he would! Oh, darling! Don't be unkind! I'm unhappy enough as it is."

Dorothy kept her face averted, and there was an amazed thought in her mind that she must be talking to a stranger—someone who looked like Pauline, but was not Pauline at all! Someone who was calmly proposing to throw over the greatest happiness in the world, for the sake of thirty thousand a year! And she had believed Pauline to be so different! . . .

Pauline wept on, and Dorothy listened in cold indifference, till at last the elder girl said: "I suppose you des-despise me, don't you? In a way I think I despise myself—but I can't help the way I'm made—and it's not my fault if I have to sacrifice my happiness."

"To—sacrifice it?"

Sacrifice it! Then perhaps the word had an entirely different meaning from the one she had always imagined?

Pauline dried her eyes and carefully powdered her cheeks.

"Wilfred will never forgive me," she said hopelessly. "And if you only knew how I dread telling him——" Her voice broke on a sob and at last Dorothy turned her head.

"And I thought you were so different!" she said fiercely. "I thought you loved him so much—I thought nothing else mattered if only you could marry him! . . . and now, because of this money——" She stopped, appalled.

Pauline bit her lip.

"I'm sorry if you think badly of me," she said at last. "Somehow, I thought you would understand. I thought you would be sorry, and—help me. I *do* love Wilfred—I shall never love another man as I love him, but . . . oh, my dear, *can't* you understand that it means cutting myself off from everything I've always had—always been able to have! We should have to live in a small flat—like ordinary people—I should never be able to keep my friends—they wouldn't want me any more——" She suddenly rose and crossed to where the girl sat like a figure of stone.

"Aren't you a little sorry for me?" she asked. "Do you think it will be any pleasure for me to tell Wilfred what has happened, and to know that I am breaking his heart?"

And then Dorothy was conscious of the most terrible desire to laugh—to laugh in sheer derision or from sheer happiness —so that she had to bite her lip hard to control the desire, and until she could steady her voice sufficiently to ask:

"Why did you—tell me?"

"I—don't know!" Pauline answered, but she knew well enough—knew that she longed for Dorothy to say that she was right—to stand by her, and to rid her of the dreadful consciousness of worthlessness and littleness which was suddenly making life unbearable. Perhaps she was aghast at the discovery that Wilfred only mattered after other things, and not before them—perhaps she was despising herself even while she knew there could be no alteration.

Dorothy stood up and moved away from her and Pauline asked humbly:

"And does this—mean the end of our friendship, Little and Good?"

And then Dorothy said with a passionate impulse which she could not control: "Don't call me that—it's Wilfred's name for me," and at once she tried to laugh as she hurried on breathlessly: "I'm sorry, but . . . you see—I can't bear him to be—treated like this . . ." Pauline said:

"You're very hard, dear—perhaps—some day—you'll understand—better——" She stopped. "Perhaps I'd better go," she said, but Dorothy neither turned round nor answered, and presently she knew that she was alone.

For the rest of the day she lived in a state of confused unreality in which she could only think again and again "It can't be true! . . . I'm dreaming, and it simply can't be true." And yet her joy in the thought of Wilfred's freedom was completely marred by her disillusionment of Pauline.

She had believed her to be so different—had imagined that her love for Wilfred would come before anything in the world, and yet for the sake of money, she was quite prepared to set him free rather than to lose all that money meant to her.

Dorothy really had a great affection for Pauline which was no doubt largely influenced by her charm and beauty, but she was young enough to feel aghast at her mercenary outlook, and whole-hearted enough to believe that the world ought to be well lost for love.

"It can't be true! She can't really mean it!" she told herself a thousand times, and so strong was the conviction that she was afraid to look on the other side of the picture and to realize that she probably stood on the threshold of her longed-for happiness.

"You're looking very well this evening, Dorothy," Mr. Rachett said during dinner. "Our little outing last night evidently did you good! . . . And, by the way, have you written to thank Mrs. Charteris?"

"I rang her up," Dorothy answered. "And she came to see me this afternoon."

The old man nodded his approval.

"Very kind of her—she is a delightful woman. I wonder, by the way, whether they have found her husband's will? If you remember, you mentioned that it was missing."

"I think it's been found."

"Strange how such an important document can go astray," Mr. Rachett said. "However, if it has been found, well and good! No doubt Mrs. Charteris will be a very wealthy woman."

She looked at him. "Do *you* think that money matters so very much?" she asked. "More than anything—almost?"

"It depends upon one's point of view," he told her. "I have had some very odd experiences amongst my own clients; there was one in particular where a girl—quite a young girl —broke her engagement because her father objected to her fiancé and in his will he left a proviso that if she insisted upon marrying him, she was not to benefit."

"She didn't really love him," she said positively, and the old man smiled.

"Love is a strange emotion, Dorothy," he answered, "and although you may entirely disagree, it is one which is, unconsciously, very much influenced by other things. Then I had a case of a widow—she must have been nearly forty, I imagine, and although her married life had not been too happy, her husband left her and her two children in very comfortable circumstances after his death, on condition that she did not re-marry. And then, within a year or so, she met another man for whom she had a great affection—quite a poor man who could not afford to keep her in anything approaching affluence, but without a moment's hesitation she married him and gave up her income which she was never able to touch again, and which was automatically settled upon the children by her first marriage."

Dorothy's eyes glowed. "And was she ever sorry?" she asked.

Mr. Rachett shook his head. "Not to the best of my belief —I seldom see her now, but the last time we met I was struck by her obvious happiness and by her rejuvenation."

"How nice."

He looked at her with a tolerant smile.

"And now Youth is speaking," he said. "But some day, Dorothy, even you may think differently, for it is not very easy, when one has been used to luxury, to descend to the bread and cheese of life without some misgiving and regrets. One so often hears people talk glibly of not minding in the least if they are suddenly confronted with the proposition of living on a few pounds a week, but I find that they are

182

usually the people who have never had any experience, and so cannot appreciate the difficulties. Besides—there is an old saying that when Poverty comes in at the door, Love flies out of the window, you know."

"You can always shut the window."

"Yes, but it needs a very secure fastening—one which will not easily yield to the cold winds of enforced economy and altered circumstances."

There was a little silence she asked:

"And don't you think it's wrong of a man to make a condition like that? That his wife shall not marry again, I mean?"

Mr. Rachett hesitated before he said: "On the face of it, yes, but sometimes there are extenuating circumstances, and it does not do to judge unless one knows all the facts." And when she did not speak he went on: "You see, my dear, when one is young—as you are—one is apt to mistake so many different things for what you call love! And so often an apparently idealistic boy and girl love-affair is nothing more than a temporary attraction of which either one or both soon weary! And then the trouble starts."

"But if you have loved someone for a long, long time," she persisted earnestly. "If you have waited years to marry, and then someone leaves a will—like that—to try and make it impossible—what ought you to do then?"

Mr. Rachett pushed back his glasses and looked at her steadily.

"If the party concerned has any doubts, or hesitates in a choice for one moment," he said at last, "that is an all sufficient answer."

"Yes, I suppose so," she agreed slowly, and then a little shyly: "Mr. Rachett, do you believe in love?"

There was a short silence before he answered:

"I believe in loyalty and affection—in lasting affection, which having been tried and tested through the years, is unshakable. But one has to be my age before one can have such an experience," he submitted. "Perhaps even, one has to lose one's life-long companion, Dorothy, to understand the true worth of such companionship." He was silent for a moment before he continued. "My greatest friend—he is dead now—told me after he lost his wife, that although theirs had been a most happy and successful marriage, if ever he met her again, as he hoped to do, he would first of all apologize to her for not having given her an even greater devotion and appreciation. 'I didn't do enough for her'—were his exact words. 'I can see now that I never fully realized all that she meant to me'—A sad admission which must apply to many of us."

"Yes," she whispered.

They had finished dinner, but they sat on at the table, forgetting the time in their mutual interest, and she was thinking: "Shall I tell him about Wilfred?" But her feeling of unreality restrained her, and the inability to believe that Pauline really meant to do as she had said.

But when she was alone that night her misgivings died, and she could think only of Wilfred and of how soon Pauline would tell him and set him free. And then of how soon she would see him again and what he would say . . .

"I must buy some new clothes," she thought with childish excitement. "I must look my very best—to-morrow I must ask Mr. Rachett to give me some money so that I can buy lots of things to make myself look as nice as I possibly can."

She rested her cheek on the hand which Wilfred had kissed in the darkness of the cinema and then she fell asleep.

Next morning there was a letter, and her heart leapt as she saw it, wondering if perhaps, already, Wilfred might have written, but as she took it up she recognized Pauline's handwriting, and her excitement died.

And Pauline had written:

Dorothy dear,

I have thought so much of what you said to me this afternoon, and perhaps of all the things you thought and didn't say too! and they make me feel ashamed. I am very fond of you, almost as if you were my little sister, and I cannot bear you to think badly of me, and so I am going to try to do what you think is the right thing, and what perhaps I too know in my heart is the right thing, and so I shall not tell Wilfred anything for the present, but I shall give myself time to make quite sure and if, as I know you would like, I

184

find that he is all that matters, I shall marry him, and I promise you there will be no regrets. Come and see me soon, or write to me and say that I am forgiven.

Yours ever affectionately,
PAULINE.

The letter fell from Dorothy's hand and fluttered down to the floor, but for a long time she never moved, hardly suffered, except at the one devastating thought: "And *I* did this! ... It's all my fault!"

Then she moved, very slowly as if her limbs had suddenly grown stiff, and she got up and bathed and dressed and went down to breakfast, feeling as though she were in a dream.

But she chatted away to Mr. Rachett, helped him into his overcoat and stood at the door to watch him as far as the end of the road, before she turned back into the house with a sensation of utter blankness and futility.

Wilfred was not to know—perhaps never! And once again her mind became a confused unreality in which only one thought was quite clear—"It can't be true!" for she knew that deep down in her heart she had, after all, been quite sure that her happy ending was in sight, and now Pauline's letter was the death blow to that hope.

No need for new clothes, for there was no one in particular to care how she looked, and she was merely conscious of impatience when later on in the morning the determined Jim called to inquire bashfully if he might take her out to lunch.

She said no at first, and then hurriedly changed her mind to say yes, she would be very pleased.

"Any news from Cecilie?" she asked, and he said they had had one post card and apparently everything in the garden was beautiful.

So Dorothy and Jim lunched together, and afterwards they looked at the shops, and Jim insisted on buying her a bunch of huge shaggy chrysanthemums, and they walked through one of the big stores, and then across the Park, and finally home.

"I've enjoyed it very much," she told him, which in a way was the truth, for at least his company had taken her mind off other things. She wrote to Pauline that evening to thank her for her letter and to say she was glad, and then realizing how far from the truth it was, she tore it up and wrote another just thanking her, and saying she hoped to see her soon.

And that's not the truth either, she thought in despair, but it would have to do, and before Mr. Rachett came home she slipped out and posted it.

It was a terribly long week; sometimes she fancied that Mr. Rachett was watching her in a puzzled sort of way and then she redoubled her efforts to appear gay and carefree.

It was on the Friday evening that he said suddenly, as they were facing one another across the draught-board:

"Wilfred called at the office this morning."

"Oh! ... did he?"

"Yes."

She carefully set one of the black pieces on its square. "Your move," she said.

But Mr. Rachett only pushed his glasses up over his forehead and looked at her steadily as he said:

"Dorothy, have you any idea what is wrong with Wilfred?"

She caught her breath sharply before she answered:

"Wrong with him? Is—anything wrong?"

"That is what I should like to know," Mr. Rachett said. "You see, in spite of everything, Wilfred is the type of man it is impossible not to like—and as a matter of fact I have a very real affection for him, but just lately—he seems to have utterly changed—he is like a man with something on his conscience ... something ... of course, I may be quite mistaken."

"I think you must be," she said evenly, and then again: "It's your move, Mr. Rachett!"

The old man moved one of the pieces in vague fashion, his thoughts evidently still far away from the game, and presently he said:

"And why does he never come to see us now? It must be weeks since he was here! ... Not that I flatter myself he ever came to see me, but I certainly thought that he had quite an affection for you."

"I think he has," she said faintly, though in her heart she was crying out: "Oh, please stop talking about him! I can't bear it, I can't bear it!"

But Mr. Rachett continued: "Of course, he may be in money difficulties—it would not be the first time, although of recent years he has had quite a handsome income. But if it is that, why doesn't he tell me? I would certainly do my utmost to help him, if only for the sake of my friendship with his father."

"Didn't he—say anything?"

"Nothing! It seemed to be an altogether pointless visit, and yet all the time I had the feeling that there was something he wished to say, had indeed come with the intention of saying, but that he could not make up his mind to do so! I asked whether he thought of going abroad again, and he said yes, he supposed it would come to that in the end! 'Come to that!'—it seemed a strange expression, and then quite abruptly he said good-bye and went away. But he left me with the uncomfortable feeling that in some way I had failed him, Dorothy, as if all the time he had been asking for my help, and that I had not understood." He shook his head thoughtfully. "Poor Wilfred," he murmured. "A strange man, and yet if he had the right influence I feel there is infinite good in him which might ... why, my *dear* child, what is the matter!" for she had suddenly pushed back her chair and had covered her face with her hands.

Mr. Rachett rose and went round the table to lay his hand on her shoulder. "My dear child," he said again in deep concern, "if I have said anything to hurt you ..."

She shook her head. "No—you haven't ... it's nothing! It's only ... I'm tired, and my head aches—and ... if you don't mind, I don't think I will play any more to-night" She let her hands fall and tried to smile. "I'm all right now," she told him, "but just for a minute——"

"I shall get Dr. Fraser to see you," Mr. Rachett said firmly. "I have thought for some time past that you have not been looking at all well—I have thought——" He drew up a chair and sat down beside her. "I have decided that it is not possible for you to go on sharing my life, Dorothy," he said gently, and when she would have spoken, he silenced her with a gesture. "Please listen to me, my dear, and believe that I am only speaking for your good. The other night Mrs. Charteris very kindly suggested taking you abroad with her—well, I have decided that you shall go. For three months, perhaps! Travelling will do you all the good in the world. You need change and the society of young people and Mrs. Charteris——"

Dorothy suddenly sprang to her feet.

"*No!*" she said passionately.

The old man looked up at her in amazement.

"But—I thought you and she were such good friends," he protested blankly. "I thought. ..." Someone knocked at the door and Sue appeared.

"Mr. Clifton's here," she said.

"Well, well," Mr. Rachett said with a sigh of relief, but Dorothy remained where she was, her arms hanging limply at her sides, her face quite colourless, and she did not raise even her eyes as Wilfred came into the room.

Mr. Rachett went forward to greet him.

"This is indeed a pleasure," he said affably. "We were talking about you only a moment ago and. . ." But Wilfred broke in almost roughly:

"I want to speak to Dorothy ... alone, if you don't mind, sir."

The old man's extended hand fell limply and he turned slowly round to look at the girl, stared at her, and then without another word, he left them, closing the door firmly behind him.

But out in the hall he stopped with an air of complete bewilderment, and then he said slowly and aloud in blank astonishment:

"Bless my soul!" and then again: "Bless my *soul!* Where in the world have my eyes been! ..."

And behind that closed door Wilfred was saying brokenly:

"Little and Good! ... Little and Good! ..." as if they were the only words in the world and when very slowly she raised her eyes until they met his he held out his arms and she tumbled into them.

"It's all right—it's all right ..." she heard him say through her tearless sobbing, without understanding in the least what the words meant, until at last he picked her up bodily as if she had been a child and took her on his knee in Mr. Rachett's shabby old arm-chair so that she could hide her face against his shoulder.

And then there was a long silence until Wilfred said again: "It's all *right*, Little and Good ... do you understand?" and very gently he turned her face upwards and looked down into her eyes.

"All—right?" she echoed faintly, and their lips met in a long kiss before he answered:

"Yes. You see, I couldn't stand it any longer. ...." And then as she did not speak he went on: "I have told Pauline the truth"—he laughed grimly—"and she has told *me* the truth!"

She raised herself from his shoulder.

"She told ..."

"About Charteris's will, and what *you* said—and about the letter she had written to you." His eyes searched her face for a moment before he said: "There's a strong will in your tiny body, my sweet! ... a stronger will than there is in my lumbering great carcase, because—you see, *I* couldn't go on any longer, but you could."

"It broke my heart," she whispered with trembling lips. And then: "But when ... did you ... tell her?"

"Only an hour ago, I am afraid. I came straight to you."

Her eyes fell as she whispered: "Oh, poor Pauline!" And Wilfred answered:

"I think it is what she wanted most, what we both wanted."

"But it is still poor Pauline," she insisted sorrowfully, "because—she doesn't understand what she is losing."

"I understood what *I* was losing," he answered grimly. "And never more so than when you deliberately remarked the other night that you liked a man who knew what he wanted and who was determined to get it ... I could have killed you for that!"

"I shouldn't have minded," she said, and she turned her face away. "I think—anything would have been better than sitting there—with you—and having to pretend that—it didn't matter."

"*Did* it matter so much?" he asked.

She raised her eyes slowly to meet his, and then she put her arms round his neck pressing her cheek to his in a silent, passionate caress.

When they both came down to earth again, Wilfred said in his old nonchalant manner:

"To-morrow I shall go to the great expense of a special licence, and if you're hoping for a grand wedding you'll be disappointed, my child, because I am a very impatient man, and there has been too much time wasted already. And if you are about to say—as I can see you are—that you cannot leave Mr. Rachett, you can spare your precious breath, because the

189

old gentleman has already made plans for his own future, and they are that he will live with his widowed sister—did you know that? And that you shall be provided with a home where you will get the society of young people." His mouth went up in its attractive crooked smile. "I admit that he was probably not thinking of me as a young person—but possibly he will consider that I am a suitable substitute."

She asked breathlessly: "But when—did all this happen?"

"This afternoon. I called at his office, and we talked about you, or rather he did—you seemed to be rather on his conscience. He said that you were not looking well, and that the present arrangement could not be allowed to continue. But you're looking beautiful now, dear child."

"Because you've come back," she whispered.

He kissed the hand which was lying so happily in his. "To proceed!" he said briskly. "It was Rachett who added the last straw which broke the camel's back, by suggesting that you were unhappy, and so I went straight from his office and ... but you know the rest!"

"And what did Pauline say?" she asked slowly.

"She said," Wilfred answered, "that—if it had to be anyone else, she was glad it was to be you——" But he did not tell her it was only then that Pauline had broken down and wept.

"And you don't think you'll ever get—tired of me, do you, Wilfred? Do you think that—some day you will want to go off alone again without me?"

He frowned with pretended severity.

"Is that what you are already hoping for? Even in these early days?" he demanded. "Then once again, you will be disappointed, my beloved, because now I've got you I mean to keep you, in spite of all the determined Jims in the world! ... and if you knew the hatred there was in my soul for that young man, when you calmly said he had rung you every day since that infernal night at the theatre ..."

"I couldn't help saying it," she told him in quick remorse. "It hurt me much more than it hurt you."

"I wonder!" he said with grim retrospection, and then he spread her little fingers on his broad palm. "Do they make wedding rings for children?" he inquired interestedly.

She flushed in beautiful confusion.

"Oh, Wilfred!"

They looked at one another in perfect contentment, until he asked: "And where would you like to live? Or haven't you any ideas on the subject?"

She shook her head.

"Anywhere! I don't mind—as long as we are together."

He laughed. "It will be together all right, my beloved," and then he put her gently from his knee and stood up, stretching his arm above her head. "Not even as high as my heart!" he said with a sigh of pretended tolerance.

"But I got there all the same, didn't I?" she asked.

"You did indeed." He looked down at her. "Darling, will you be able to forget, do you think?—I mean—about the past? If I thought it would ever come between us . . ."

She put her head on one side consideringly.

"What—past?" she asked, and then before he could speak: "If I ever knew you'd had one, I've forgotten—I've got a very bad memory, I'm afraid." She caught his hand as he turned away. "What is the matter? What have I said?" she asked in alarm, and he answered:

"You're a thousand times too good for me, that's what is the matter, Little and Good—and why on earth you should ever have given me a thought——"

She laughed tremulously.

"It doesn't suit you to be humble," she told him. "I like you much better when you're ... oh, Wilfred!"—for he had suddenly caught her to his heart, and it was some time before he could say calmly:

"And now, I suppose we must break the glad news to the old boy."

She brushed back her tumbled hair.

"The *darling* old boy!" she said. "But somehow—I think he knows already."

THE END

James Clavell
TAI-PAN

Now only 10/6
704 Pages

In this turbulent, panoramic novel of the
founding of Hong Kong, James Clavell, author of
KING RAT, narrates the saga of how one
man, with majestic vision, ruthless will and
ingenious grasp of command, guides the development
of a colony destined to influence the course
of history. It is a masterful re-creation
of a momentous epoch in the history
of the British Empire.